ATROCITY

KASSIEN AND CALYPSO'S SONG: BOOK 2

C.F. RABBIOSI

Author Website: Deliciously Dark Reads

"One thing I have learned is that love, rage, and desire are all universal. From star to the very farthest star, you cannot escape it."

— KASSIEN

SONGS THAT INSPIRED THE STORY: OTHERWORLDLY

1. With or Without you — Amy Lee
2. Not Strong Enough — Apocolyptica
3. Can I Exist? — Missio
4. Deep End — Ruelle
5. The Promise — In this Moment
6. Nothing Else Matters — Metallica
7. Anything but Love — Apocolyptica
8. Wasp — Motionless in White
9. Hand of Blood — Bullet for my Valentine
10. Early Grave — The Contortionist
11. Trip the Darkness — Lacuna Coil
12. Unbreakable — Fireflight
13. Feel — Skarlet Riot
14. End of the Dream — Evanescence
15. Blacklisted Me— Reprobate Romance
16. Stay Close — Fireflight
17. We are the Fallen — Through Hell
18. The House of Shame — Lacuna Coil

A WARNING FROM THE AUTHOR

This dark romance contains violent themes, forced seduction, complete power exchange and possible triggers. So dig in if you don't scare easily, and remember you've been warned. Now please...

Enjoy deeply.

Love,
  Faith

PROLOGUE
KASSIEN

Hooks pierce through my flesh, a broken body hung by the shoulder blades and denied the mercy of death. It is the Koridon way, and I would expect nothing less of my brutal kin.

A traitor's death.

It won't be long now. Tenak dangles beside me in the prisoner's quarters, but the blood-soaked image of him fades along with the corners of my vision. I thrash my arms and legs, shoving the steel deeper, *tearing* the flesh and begging it to rip through. Darkness swirls and I fight it back, sure that oblivion will never release me this time.

I've failed her.

In the eye of my unconsciousness, Calypso struggles on the ground, beating into Brekter's chest. He will have taken her carnally by now. Maybe even this very moment he has her broken beneath him! Screams tear from my throat and seep through my dream, blending with her own cries. I gasp in precious air and the world floods back to me. I should have known Brekter would risk everything, *kill everyone* to have her.

I would.

I'm tearing my own body to pieces to get to her. The steel spikes through my muscle, scraping bone and holding blood vessels off from rupturing. Hooks hold me under the collar bone no matter how my thrashing has ripped at them; strong bones have held, aching and never ceasing. But I'm bred for pain. It's nothing to me. *Tear through me already, you damned meat holders, and I'll land on my feet, ready to fight!*

"Tenak, brividend cerncri... my friend," I say to my first in command. "I have brought this upon us." Guilt throbs beneath my breastbone, cleaving through my heart more painfully than the slow death washing over me. "I must get out of here. I must save us." The words send a sharp pain through my stomach as I remember Ariquoi bleeding upon the ground and Tenak grieving over her body before he was ripped away to hang beside me. At least she is at peace, unlike my perfect warrior, Efaelty, after shots pierced her chest. If she does still breathe, her father, Drakon, will have brought her home to recover in the west.

I hate that she was also a victim of my obsession. It was a deep, unyielding lust making me no longer myself, but I justified it, thinking that everything I did was to save our race. Calypso is a human woman but also of Koridon blood, so like her, our child would have survived the unfavorable conditions of this planet.

We thought we could escape fate when we fled our dying world, but this world we have stolen is devouring us. Little by little, our children refused to come into the world. The hundreds of bacterial organisms that humans have a natural symbiotic relationship with are toxic to our newborns.

In Calypso, I saw survival, hope, and a new reason to live. We could have united our people and built a new world where her kind would no longer be forced into hidden villages, out of the light and buried beneath the rubble of their past.

I force away thoughts of Calypso being ravaged by the enemy and remember her the way she was. She twirled when she danced and trilled when she sang, and though it was an odd way for a being to move and to sound, I couldn't take my eyes from such beauty. Was my species ever like her? I can't see us as anything but brute warriors, and anyway, singing and dancing sure as hell won't get me off this hook right now.

Tenak's chain creaks as he sways slowly beside me, his lips so pale and cracked, they say nothing to me any longer.

Numb fingers hardly move upon my signal, but I tug at the leather pants that hang from my waist. They slide down easily now from my emaciated form. My fingertips scream from poor circulation, and I focus every fiber of my being to holding onto them. I grunt as extra stores of adrenaline pour, empowering my weak limbs, and up my knee rises to allow one pant leg to come off. I hold firm with my foot as they slip down, my flesh on fire around the hooks. If my grip fails, they'll drop to the ground and it's over.

The leathers dangle, held by the tops of my toes, and I feel them slipping regardless of my desperation. The fatigued muscles in my thigh shake, and the material I had a mind to use to hoist myself off the cruel steel falls away.

1

CALYPSO

The shining half-moon sends light glittering off every leaf and puddle left by the morning rain. The forest's beauty assaults my bitter eyes as my feet drudge through the mud, still cracked and sore from yesterday. The rope around me cuts into my waist as Glenda falls once more.

The big one who lingers near sneers, and I hoist her up. "Deep breaths," I say into her ear, hoping her damaged lungs will disperse more oxygen as we're forced to move forward without rest. "Don't let them think you're weak." I push her gently, though it pains me. As horrifying as it would be for her to be mated by the monstrous enemy, it would be worse for them to play with her to death because she's of no use to them.

A memory of Glenda plays through my mind: the covers pulled up to her chin, her face pale, her body trembling. So many days came where Finn's lively expression dulled in worry and distraction made him falter during our lessons. Even now her frail body drags itself along in her ropes, her breath wheezing painfully, and there's no relief in sight. The Koridon males who have stolen us from our village watch with predatory arousal in their silver gazes as they ride upon their beasts. Will they be cruel to us as Brekter is, or will any of them prove to be more like Kassien?

Last night as Brekter laid with me in the dirt, the exhaustion of the day's events forced sleep to overtake me. But rest never found me, for I dreamed. I relived the excitement of finally being given to the prince I wanted, the despair of him casting me aside, and finally the fear of being fully bedded by the massive and deadly Koridon. Finally, fatal shots rang out in my subconscious and shook me awake, leaving me to reimagine the rest of the scene in my light slumber. Brekter's dispassionate touch re-burned into my body as he hurt me, my princely husband likely being tortured as I writhed.

My fingers drift to my belly, and a hard lump forms in the back of my throat. Brekter says I carry a child now, one that could be the savior of their people. The conditions of earth, though favorable in water and oxygen, still bears down on their species. The females are conceiving less and less, and if they do swell with seed, the child doesn't reach term and is lost from the body. Kassien realized when he saw me lying broken on the forest floor and used by another that I was special.

That I was one of them.

What will these imprisoned girls, my village mates, think of me when they find out my secret?

My mother always knew what I was, that our two species could breed, but it had to be hidden to protect me, the children born of Koridon explained away as mutations left after the war. The child growing within me flows with 75% alien blood and will exhibit superior size, strength, and senses...

But my child will not lose human values. They are bred for size and skill, but a human can be beaten down twice as hard and will still crawl to their feet. We don't give up, and we will devise a way to beat our enemy.

I just wish this could have ended with me. How could I have let Brekter follow me to the village? Hot tears sting my eyes, but there's no time to wipe them away. Glenda stumbles, and as the ground moves toward her I lunge forward to catch her. The Koridons close in with cruel countenances, and the big one who always hovers near Glenda lifts a fist at her.

"Brekter!" I scream and the giant pauses. His fist flies toward us, and I hold the small Glenda into my chest. My eyes burn into the aggressor as pain rips through my cheek, and I try like hell to conceal how much it hurts.

"Keep moving!" he bellows.

"Hit me again if you want," I yell back, "but let us rest before we all collapse!"

The huge Koridon in armor scrunches his brows and unsheathes his sword of moving metal. "Perhaps if she is too weak to walk, then she should never be bred with our superior genes." The tip of his blade divots the skin of her neck and she whimpers, fear emanating from her shivering form.

"No!" I growl and hit the strange weapon away. The skin splits on my forearm and warm liquid seeps to the ground. "Send her back home, but don't hurt her!"

Brekter jumps between us and grabs my bloody hand. "What have you done?" He bristles as my crimson mixes with the dirt on my feet

"This brute would kill Glenda! Don't let him!" I reach my fingers around his wrist and squeeze.

He shakes my grip away and pulls Finn's sister from my arms. She hits the ground, the corded rope indenting her exposed belly. The women behind us groan as they're yanked forward, though I try to hold my position. "Kraetorr, you may be the first son of this sect's commander," says Brekter, "but unless your father orders it, do not harm the breeders."

His eyes like molten quicksilver, Kraetorr looks upon Glenda with pinched features. "I do not understand how we are expected to mate such sorry beasts." His blade finds her chin, and, with its scathing promise, she scurries to her feet. His shadow eclipses her, and though I'm larger than most girls I grew up with, Glenda is positively tiny for a seventeen-year-old. The hovering monster grasps her dress material and rips it apart in his fingers. She sucks in a breath as her breasts are exposed to the cool morning air and her satin lips part, but the protest cannot be born from tortured lungs.

"Stop this," I growl and remove the coat Brekter had placed upon my shoulders yesterday. I cringe putting it on her, seeing her surprisingly mature body. The males must be stirring into a frenzy.

"Why should I stop? Everything will be done to her soon enough." Kraetorr squeezes Glenda's nipple. Her chest heaves with an accompanying whistle as he kneads her pale breast. "Perhaps I will claim this one after all."

Every nerve in my body lights on fire at the thought of this careless ogre bedding my dear Finn's younger sister. Finn became more than my friend, but he was the first one to ever make me feel as though I looked acceptable when my odd features and coloration had always made me feel so low. We were betrothed before Kassien took me to be his, but he must hate me now.

I led the monsters we had always been warned about straight to his sister and all the beloved women of my village.

I had only thought to change things for my people by marrying one of them and having his child, for all we do is hide from them and fear every moment of the day. With a Koridon prince at my side, we could have arranged marriages between our species and done things in a proper way that would benefit everyone.

"She can't be claimed at all," I say. "None of us can be."

The sword tip invades my vision, sitting an inch from my eye, its strange material blinding, and I fight the urge to jerk away.

"Not another word, half-breed, or I will do it here," says Kraetorr, "where everyone can watch her tear apart from the inside out."

Poisonous words beg to slip from my tongue, but I bite the defiant muscle and glare instead. What he could do to her with his oversized form is monstrous, and though it will be done eventually, I can't bear to watch it now.

Kraetorr bends down to Glenda and takes a handful of her hair, letting it slip through his fingers slowly. I wish she had the power of the good witch she was named for so she could drop a house on his arrogant face. He leans down and breathes in her scent, and the air around him changes. Pupils enlarge, overtaking his silvery irises, and the azure shimmer in his skin flushes with heat as he grips the girl to his chest.

"She calls to me," he says, his voice a song of bewitchment, and Glenda whimpers as he crushes her. His breathing is as sharp and pained as hers now, and I fear he has been possessed. Our human pheromones hypnotize and tantalize parts of them that have been long dormant. They have evolved in the way of size and strength, so sex is a duty to reproduce, not in any way meant for enjoyment, but a woman's scent turns their blood to liquid fire. So long without such intense feeling, it shocks their system with ecstasy so strong he may love her to *death*, slowly, painfully, leaving nothing but a pile of broken and bloody flesh.

Brekter tips his head, his face a mask of warning, and the Koridons' stallions strike the dirt with their hooves and snort.

Kraetorr wildly takes her by the neck. "My loins ache, and

though I am built for pain, she makes me hurt beyond understanding." He shudders and rips the ropes around her to shreds. I jerk with the force and plead toward Brekter. He and Kassien showed control with me, but some are incapable when intoxicated by a woman. Why won't anyone intervene? Is this clan full of nothing but rabid beasts?

2

K raetorr's thickness bulges through his leathers as he rips the remaining cloth from Glenda's body. "Wait!" she cries, hitting the ground, her weak arms flailing as she thrashes beneath him. "Don't do this!"

She has no idea the love that can be transferred from Koridon to woman. All she can imagine is the carnage they leave behind in the dirt. The girls cry out, their own fates displayed before them, their nightmares brought to life. Brekter grabs Kraetorr's shoulder and yanks him off, but the possessed fool sends him flying backwards.

"Kraetorr!" a voice booms. Drakon rides up, and dust clouds over their chaotic movements. "Not here! Compose yourself, I demand it!"

Kraetorr rips himself from Glenda, releasing a roar that frightens the birds from their roosts. I reach for her but am knocked back as the crazed Koridon attacks again. Drakon jumps down from his horse, and, together with Brekter and another, they finally subdue him.

The forest is alive with screaming and heavy breaths as

they drag him away. They yell at him in Koridon, though our language is second nature to them. I can already make out several words, such as *survival, control* and *mate*. Kassien told me they speak the language of the land in order to converse with their stolen home's inhabitants about growing in our soil, medicines for our bacteria, and other vital survival aspects.

All I'd like to know of their language is how to say: *fuck yourself dead.*

I drop next to Glenda. She sobs while grasping for the torn pieces of nightgown that hang over her chest. "Shh, it's all right, you're safe now," I whisper.

"No I'm not!" A strong voice finds its way out of the meek girl as she rips the coat from my hands. She swipes back tear-damp locks and moves back into her place at the front of the line. "You should have just let him do it!" she cries out, her frightened gaze cast toward the scuffle. "We're all dead anyway!"

I flip her around to face me. "No. We—" I almost tell her that we have a chance to survive and make a new world with our feared enemies at our side, but I forget that she isn't part Koridon like me, and not all of us will survive the pregnancy. The males are so large that I fear one growing in the belly of such a small woman will be fatal in the last couple of months.

They will choose to save the child, letting it kill the mother before taking it from her body.

"As I thought," says Glenda, despair thick in her voice. She wheezes in a pained breath and touches her chest weakly as the adrenaline surge crashes.

She chokes and blanches, and all I can think about is that we knew this day would come. Since the day we could understand, we were taught about the otherworldly monsters that came here and destroyed everything two hundred years ago. We couldn't hide forever, but while I can't promise everything will still turn out fine, I won't deny the hope welling up in the dark places of me that still remember Kassien well. My unreasonable love for their prince suddenly penetrates the last days' trauma and stabs through my aching heart. My throat swells, and I swallow back tears.

If Brekter hadn't interfered, I would have been a royal and had the chance to change the world for the best. It wouldn't be like this, with all of us in tethers, our feet bloody and the leering eyes of monsters moving us along. Most of these ladies have never even been out in the forest before.

"Glenda," I say. "I've been around these beings for a time now, and I promise you, not all of them are bad."

"Finn loves you," she says, the harshness in such soft words surprising me. "He didn't rest the entire time you were gone. He knew they were lurking out there, but he kept looking for you."

Finn was always kind, and he didn't complain when they matched us together, even though I was doomed to die early. The thought of him comforts me now, strangely.

"They seem vicious, I know," I tell her as I glance back at Scarlet, the flaxen-haired ball of fire I've called the closest friend in my entire life. She's focused on Brekter and Drakon as they continue to hold the mad Koridon back. Since being dragged out of the village boundary by one of our trusted leaders and ravaged to near death, she appears a pale shadow from that girl I knew. If Kassien hadn't scented us when he did, we would both be dead already. I raise a brow and touch Glenda's thigh. "But we as women have something special to offer them." The thrill speeds up my words. "They are capable of deep passion and give very *deep* pleasure." Something dark dances behind Scarlet's gaze. While the other women are alive with horror, she seems to glimmer with amusement.

Two more of the giants move closer to the scene in case Kraetorr breaks loose.

Glenda snaps me back to attention. "You mean to say that creature who just threatened to tear me up with his cock is capable of love?" She shakes her head. "We're nothing to them but helpless animals, so I can't believe that." Shaking her head slowly, she moves behind me. "What if they can't stop him?"

"You must believe it," I say and touch my belly. "I am loved deeply, I assure you." In that moment, Brekter locks eyes with me through Kraetorr's wind-blown hair, and a chill slithers down my spine. He and I certainly don't share love but perhaps something more dangerous, something growing beyond reason. I want it so badly to be Kassien's seed that has taken hold, but as I ripened, I received both males' essence, so I don't know whose child swells my belly. It's only been a few days, but already I feel different. "See how he's become crazed by you?" I ask Glenda, turning my head slightly toward her. She begins to pant again, and I help her to the ground. "That's power."

She breathes easier, and the smallest smile threatens to touch her lips.

"Quiet!" one of the males commands as he checks the ropes along the waists of the frightened women. His long hair, tied back in an ornate braid, gleams more aqua than cobalt like the other Koridons possess, and so brilliantly, even in the dim light of dawn. His touch lingers along Mary-Shelly's waist. She stifles a cry from his sheer proximity and jerks away, bringing a memory forth.

She used to glow with love for the boy who had been chosen for her to marry back in the village. They would exchange wistful smiles in the lunch hall, and their happiness was clearly exuded the day after their one night together. We aren't allowed to love with freedom because of the dangerous world we find ourselves in, children and the scent of arousal both forbidden, but they give us something.

How dare these creatures take a married woman!

The ones with a mate should not have been forced to go. But we were lucky to get the deal we did, as they first planned to take our men as well to use as slaves and kill the ones too old or young to be of use.

Mary-Shelly stares fearfully ahead as the Koridon male drags his fingers past the rope and touches the shadowed area of her nightdress. He must be curious about the desperation Kraetorr displayed and the yearning that crazed him. He leans down and sniffs her neck. If any one of these huge bastards loses control and breeds one of the girls, the scent of forced desire will infect the rest of them.

"Arek!" Commander Drakon yells. I study him as he rides over with regal grace, his features sharp and his hair lighter than the others. "You were all ordered to stay away from the breeders." Sneering, he stomps his beast over to the one he called Arek, who has remained fixed on Jane. "You all know the consequences of these women's spells! Do you want one? Do you wish for a child to grow within one? Then they are not to be touched for now. Don't even look at them!" He rides by and shakes his head. "Tearing them to pieces would be amusing. But pointless."

Arek removes his touch as though anvils are attached to his wrists and snaps his gaze down. A light dew grazes his muscular chest, and the space around him vibrates with frightening intensity. A little thrill pulses through my belly at the sight of such a love-struck creature. He isn't like Kraetorr—his animalistic impulses suffocate, but he buries them deeper at will. The sight of his controlled desperation twists my soul and drives me to want Kassien again so badly it hurts.

"We still have quite a journey ahead of us," says Drakon,

bounding from his horse. "I will not have a single one of them harmed. You will bed them according to mating law and will wait to be matched accordingly!"

Brekter secures Glenda's ties, and, watching his fingers move, all I can think about is the crushing weight of him—outside, inside, and the frenzied touch of his lips that had never felt another's upon them. Kissing is a *human* thing, and this warrior race has no thoughts of it... until that soft yet powerful intimacy is unleashed upon them and they're helpless to watch as their unparalleled strength drains away. But in our story, does true love's kiss conquer all?

Doubtful.

Drakon appears behind Brekter. "You are to heed this warning as well," he says to my wicked lover. "The girl you keep risking everything for has yet to prove yours." He glances at my belly, and thoughts of my mother and what she went through eat at my already shaky sanity. She was impregnated by one of them long ago when she was transferring villages and survived my birth, making me a rare find indeed. Whichever of the otherworldly beings creates life within me would see their child born of very high Koridon genetics, unlike the human women around me who would produce only a half-breed.

Brekter straightens his spine and meets Drakon's threat with a confident smirk. "Calypso is mine."

The commander lets out a humorless laugh. "Was it not Kassien of the royal family who first spilled seed inside her?"

"Yes, the same prince you left for dead." A head taller and a million miles from being intimidated, Brekter taps the weapon at his side and brandishes a smile that would shame the Cheshire cat.

"So you would attempt to steal his heir?" Drakon circles us and I prepare to push Brekter onto the commander's bizarre sword if only the chance would arise. Brekter peers at him knowingly, and it puts a dark sensation into my heart.

Drakon hisses, "What a disaster that was. My warriors driven mad by the lust in the air. My own daughter shot." He purses his lips and spins around. "I am ruler now and will say who she and her child belong to." The other Koridons nod and murder glimmers on Brekter's face.

"Does Kassien live?" I blurt out. Brekter seethes at my concern and his firm grasp lands around my wrist.

"Do not concern yourself with such things," he breathes from behind, rubbing his palm along my stomach. "I will not have you putting stress on my child."

"It's not your—" He smashes his forefinger into my lips and tips his head, a warning playing across his face.

Drakon sheathes his weapon. "Let us continue! We waste precious time." The Koridons hoist themselves upon their animals and the line of women stirs.

"Tell me, Brekter!" I take hold of his leather wrist armor as he walks away, and he takes my hand and twists me around in turn. He holds my arm in an awkward position, and sharp pain travels up my radial nerve. "Let go. You heard your commander! You can't touch me."

He slams me back-first into his chest and reaches between my thighs. As he pushes my under garments aside, his breath burns my ear. "You belong to me in every way imaginable. I will claim you when we reach our destination, and my cock will find every warm, dark place your body has to offer." He pinches the sides of my clit and rolls the tissue around it up and down, creating a trill of paralyzing pleasure. "And my tongue will find its every satisfaction upon your responsive flesh." As though he commanded it, my nipples harden to the point of pain. "There will be no rest for you." I flush as he strokes the sensitive spot between my legs within its own hood, and the hungry eyes I feel upon us only slicken his fingers. A rush of heat plays against his strokes, and my legs weaken.

At that moment where my soul turns black and welcomes any perversity that will push me over the edge of climax, he shoves me away and the rope burns a painful line around my ribcage.

The day drags on as we're led under low hanging branches and over fallen debris and boulders. Glenda bravely presses forward, stumbling easily and weakness hindering her every movement, but she doesn't give up, no matter how strained her breath becomes.

We stop to rest in a grove of Hollow's-Eve touched trees with swaying leaves of red, gold and orange. The ones that dance upon the ground bounce under my shaky hands as we sit in a circle around a fire. Hunger eats at my stomach at the smoky scent of deer and boar roasting over the flickering flames for our midday meal. Scarlet rests one leg over the other and blows the hair from her face. She still has a kind smile for me, though my existence has placed her in such danger. Again. She drapes her arm around my shoulders. "You survived their—" her brow raises suggestively, "*attacks,* didn't you?"

I nod. "After Kassien found us out there, he took me to his ship." Black-haired Alice and blond Alice both snap their heads up to hear about the venture into my own rabbit hole. The others listen attentively as well, though Sybil and Mary-Shelly both stare off with tears glistening. "It was like something we've read in books," I say, trying to put our misadventure in an intriguing light. "It was huge, sort of spherical, though some parts weren't. It's hard to explain. The walls had this mirroring ability to make it invisible, but from the inside it was translucent. You could see everything around you."

"Do you think that's where they take us now?" asks Scarlet. "To their *spaceship*?" The word sounds ridiculous, and yet it's the only way to describe the grounded vehicle the Koridons came to Earth in. Arek brings water to the horses, and I wonder why they choose to ride around on beasts of the earth instead of some high-powered gadget they must surely have with their technology. Kassien told me the energy to power even their fancy weapons is in short supply here on this planet, though, and cannot be reproduced with our elements.

I shake my head in thought. "They might be bringing us to a similar place. But we aren't headed to my husband's sector."

Sybil's mouth drops open. "Your husband?" My village mates lean in closer, except Glenda, whose hurt expression steals my next musing. Finn mattered to me, and I want to tell her that, but I can't find the words. Not here. Besides, as much as I cared about her brother, it wasn't enough to stop me from desiring Kassien to the very core.

"You married one of them?" asks Mary-Shelly. She brushes back red locks and scoots forward, the rope pulling taut.

Brekter's heated gaze settles upon me as he slices open a boar to clean for the roast. "Yes," I say quieter. "I was bedded by their prince in a ceremony in which all of their kind watched."

"Is that what will happen to us?" asks Scarlet, and the others flick their curious eyes over each of the huge males that keep us prisoner.

"Maybe," I say, but I'm worried they have no plans of honor or tradition toward their *breeders*.

"If you're bound to one of those monsters," says blond Alice, "why has another taken claim over you?"

"My true mate will come for me." I throw a glare of daggers at Brekter. "And he'll pay on his knees before my lord."

"But..." she draws her finger in circles through the dirt. "You seem to like him."

My stomach wrenches, and I hate myself for letting Brekter titillate me so easily. I'm so inexperienced, and his fingers find buttons I didn't know could be tapped, manipulated, and sprung to life. It happens so fast I can't think, and I'm deeply ashamed for my betrayal. I can't even put anything into words to counter blond Alice's observation. Luckily Sybil saves me.

"Do you know where they come from?" she asks. "And why they look like that?" Sunlight plays off the Koridons as they work, and I notice something I've never seen before: the lightest hue of blue/green in a scale pattern gleams off their skin.

"They came from a dying planet being swallowed by the sun, and had turned to the deepest parts of their oceans as the land was scorched. I imagine they took on certain characteristics of marine life over the years." Their hair feels different too, so fine that when it's loose, it seems to float on the breeze. Even now, as I really study them, they seem to tread along the bottom of a clear ocean, graceful and effortless.

Scarlet asks, "Why were you forced to lie intimately with him in front of the others? That's absolutely depraved."

And yet, being loved in front of an audience was still better than what Brekter did to me in private. "You know how our queens of old had to be bedded in front of the court to prove the marriage had been consummated?" I say, remembering enchanting stories about a time long ago and lost forever. "Well, it's like that, but also—" My hand lies across my impregnated abdomen and I cringe, remembering how I was still dripping from Kassien when Brekter shoved inside. "They traditionally have the ceremony and mate their females when she is ovulating."

"You're with child?" asks Mary-Shelly, blanched fingers digging into her bare thighs. "As we will all be?" An unexpected hopefulness lights up her smile, and shame burns my cheeks. If there is a child growing inside, who does it belong to? How could I live with myself if I had my enemy's child? Then a surge of confidence lifts my chin. It *is* Kassien's seed that held, and he's too damn stubborn to die. He'll come for me.

I won't lose myself no matter what happens in the future, or what happens tonight, when the sun goes down and Brekter moves my dress up in the dark. There's hope, not just for the freedom of our people from fear and bondage, but individually as well. I see it reflected in Sybil and Jane's expression as they watch the warrior males move about in their tasks, chiseled with such muscular perfection. No man in our village could ever look like that. Kraetorr wipes his forehead as the fire roars and black clouds billow around his massive form. I cringe, because he's larger than even Brekter, who was Kassien's leader of defense.

And how his predatory gaze scorches with Glenda's scent in his blood.

"Imagine what this could mean for us," I say, still trying to convince myself that everything could work out. "We've been forced to hide inside a small village cloaked by their technology since we were born. Married but hardly allowed to touch for fear of becoming pregnant. If we join their race, we might all be free one day."

"And what of our current husbands?" Blond Alice says as the sizzling meat is pulled from the flames. She reluctantly takes a piece offered to her. "And what about our fathers? Brothers? Are they to be enslaved now, being that they have no womanly cavities to abuse?"

They were left behind in the village when we were taken, but now that their location is known, all of our families will have to pack up and travel to the other villages immediately. Hopefully with the attention all on us, they'll make it safely. "It's a start," I say to blond Alice. She snickers as she chews. I understand her reluctance with this situation, especially having been married to Oliver only last year. "We have an opportunity here. There was no future for us as it was."

"Forced to be brood mares for monsters is a future?" She throws her meat into the dirt and stands. "I would rather die today than be touched by those horrid aliens!" Arek and the other watchful males begin moving toward us.

"Don't fight them!" I whisper loudly. "Or you will suffer."

Blond Alice flips her long locks back and stands tall. "Good. You may have a future with them, Miss *Mutation*, but we don't. We are all going to die."

I so badly want to tell them who I am, that I'm *half* horrid alien. But I can't yet. How can I admit that I'm one of them? One of the creatures that have haunted their nightmares since they were old enough to understand the truth? *No.* I shake my head at the thought. *They can't find out.*

"Stop being dramatic," says Scarlet as the males approach. "This is the best chance we have, and you're throwing it away!" Jane cradles her head, and black-haired Alice hums under her breath.

"What?" Blond Alice retorts. "You think these *things* are going to care for you? That once you have a child for them, they will just let you go?" Visions of us being ripped from our medical beds and placed in chains to be impregnated steal my breath.

"She is pretty, that one with the poison tongue," laughs one of the Koridons. They stand around us, partially-eaten meat hanging loosely from their grips and dripping blood into the dirt.

Arek closes the distance behind her, his sheer size creating the vision of a demonic creature creeping up on a helpless child. "Some of us do not wish to breed you at all!" He grasps her shoulder and flings her around. "Some of us would also rather die out than taint our perfect race with animal woman genes." A painful groan slips from blond Alice's mouth as her knees hit pebbles on the ground. He holds her face in his hand and her lips puff out from the force. "I will see that scornful tongue severed if you speak again in a way that offends me." Tears spill down her cheeks and swirl around the Koridon's fingers. "You would be truly blessed to have a mighty Koridon's seed filling your unworthy crevice!" He rips her nightgown and full breasts pop out. "And you do not need a tongue for that, do you?"

3

Blond Alice hits her back, and we fight against the conjoining ropes that burn into our skin and jerk us with her. I look to Drakon, but the yell dies on the back of my tongue as he crosses his arms and appears every bit resolved to allow his subordinate to teach her a lesson. *One we'll all feel.*

Arek snaps blond Alice's knees apart, and her shriek shakes the forest. The girls turn their heads, but there's no damn time for blushing.

"You can't allow this," I say to Drakon, my voice steady though my insides quiver. "Is this your plan for us? Is this how you wish your children to be brought into the world? By a hateful mother?" The fire in Arek's eyes tells a story of rage and desire—so much so that he would rather make her hate him, too, than take her in love.

Blond Alice grunts, trying to close her legs, and strikes into the Koridon's chest. "Get off me!" she growls. "I won't do it, I'll never let a fucking beast inside me!" A vein surfaces across her forehead, and her legs kick wildly. "Animal!" She spits in his face, and he backhands her. She staggers backward and hits the ground. Sliding her hands into the dirt, she wipes the muck down her breasts, then all over her face. "You want to stick your cock in me now?" She shoves her hands in the forest floor and smears it in her hair.

Arek studies her humorously, the sneer on his lips dissolving as she slaps more mud onto her skin. "Stop it. Stop." He takes her wrists and forces her reluctant gaze to him. "It doesn't help." She licks the dirt off her lips, and a wicked smile graces her lips.

"Enough!" Drakon says, raising a hand.

He chooses to stop this now? All right, I guess he just wanted the violence. His weapon gleams at his side, and I think the second he falls asleep I'll stab him in the face with it. I keep telling myself there's a future for us with these aliens, but while Arek and even Brekter show signs of weakness for us, Drakon is cold as nuclear winter.

The fire crackles and flickers as Arek drags hesitant fingertips down blond Alice's full lips. He touches the inside of her thigh and gazes upon the swell of her breasts, the taper of her hips. Koridon females are built for fighting, the delicateness of sexual beauty overwritten by muscle and hardness. Her hair is long and wavy, her eyes the liquid gold to their silver. Every woman is a different work of art. Arek hates the girl his gaze feasts upon as much as she hates him, but he can't stop the pounding of his heart or the softening of his mouth as he touches her. We are slaves to our feelings, and these warrior males are no exception.

The corner of Drakon's mouth lifts, and he brings his hands together with a hard clap. "Detach the girl from the others and put her on your horse, Arek. I wish to remove ourselves before we waste any more time." I quickly pluck the rest of the meat from the ground and shove it in my mouth before standing in formation. The Koridons gather around to see us back in order, and Arek does as commanded. Blond Alice's body hangs as though lifeless as he hoists her onto the seat and brings a leg over to settle himself behind her.

Mary-Shelly's frown is deeper than the rest as she watches blonde Alice's head lay back against Arek's chest.

"Are you all right, Mary-Shelly?" I ask.

She snaps from her daze with a shudder. "No. I miss my husband." She dips her head as we're pulled along, and dread fills my heart. Arek had shown her attention earlier, and I wonder if she too had entertained passionate thoughts about him throughout the morning. It isn't strange that such thoughts might intrude her mind. These males are the epitome of what women are attracted to by nature's push. It isn't just their towering forms with abounding muscle and strength; these males exude power, a dominance that exists without regard to logic. Each of them have similar coloration though their facial features vary, but I haven't met one yet whose eyes didn't sparkle with the shade of fiery passion.

The evening sun descends below the mountains and dims the vibrance of the wild growth of trees and brush around us. But with the evening comes a new beauty, one that touches the senses with a feeling of magic. It floats on the breeze and tickles my skin; it *rushes* into my lungs with every breath. We are confined to our village and don't have endurance for long treads through overgrowth, but in some ways, I'd still rather be here, amongst vicious beings from another planet, than locked up again. But I've always been different and fearless with a sense of adventure the other girls lacked. Kassien once told me my dauntless spirit is proof of my Koridon roots.

Blond Alice stirs from sleep and blinks rapidly as she

bounces against Arek's lap. He holds her firmly with one arm, and when she twists around and sees his face, her eyes squeeze shut, pure disgust splashing her face.

My foot hits a stone and I stumble, helpless as the ground flies up toward me. Pain stabs through my belly as I brace against the fall. I roll onto my back, grabbing my stomach, and grit my teeth.

"Everyone halt!" comes Brekter's voice like an echo through a barrel. He rushes over and places a hand on my shoulder. "Let me help you."

A strange sensation seizes me like nothing I've ever felt before. My pelvic region pulses with shocks of pain. "Wait, no. Something's wrong. I think the fall—"

He lifts my hands away, and I suck in through my teeth. "Get up. You are acting weak."

"I'm not weak." The lining inside my stomach still aches sharply, but I hit his hand away and stand up. His fingers outstretch toward me, and I smack them away again.

He smirks, and it's irritating how he enjoys taunting me. I don't know if I'm imagining things, but it seems like something is changing inside me already, although it hasn't been long enough for me to feel a pregnancy yet.

His arms snake around my waist, and my nose presses into his chest. His heady scent sends a thrill through my blood and his leathers tighten at the crotch, pressing against the flutters in my belly. He groans, knowing the havoc he causes within me. "I will give you your tea tonight with nutrient X2. You need it more than ever now."

"They should all begin taking it," says Drakon. "It will course through their weak genetics and prepare them properly for carrying a Koridon child." He turns his horse in a tight circle. "We rest for the night presently!"

My insides scream upon remembering the orange and

violet flower that grows from seeds brought from their planet. Since being given the nutrient I've needed all my life, I crave it, and like others who were born secretly of the otherworldly species, I would have died in my early twenties without it.

The males unload the deer and boar carcasses they had hunted throughout the day and build a fire. Our ropes are loosened as we sit around the flames and listen to the sound of nocturnal creatures scurrying and calling out under the flood of moonlight.

The meat and tea rejuvenate my spirit as we sit around the fire. All the girls have the same dead-tired stare as they chew, half in this world, half in the next. All of us strangers, floating through time and somehow thrown together. Sometimes I think some kind of higher power has set all this craziness in motion. Otherwise, if life is so rare and delicate, why do *I* get to be here now? Why has my existence been allowed through infinite space and time and gifted to me in this very short moment? It is another question I will put forth to Kassien if I ever see him again. We had such a short time together.

Oh, Kassien. A ghostly presence still lingers around my wrists from his fevered grasp and my heart still feels the constriction of his touch as well, no matter how ridiculous it must seem to everyone else. Within days of being with him, he intoxicated me with the desperation pulsing from beneath his skin, always reaching, but always starving from fear of hurting me. Tales from the old leather-bound books unearthed from the wreckage spin round and round my thoughts. I used to marvel at why ladies of England with titles and wealth would give up everything to be paupers for love, and why Romeo would drink a vial of poison to lay by Juliet's side for all eternity without it. I fantasized about such a thing to live for, to die for, and felt it grip my soul, but nothing could have prepared me for this. Love fucking hurts. Especially when one is loved by the enemy.

"My only love sprung from my only hate," says Scarlet with a laugh alive in her eyes. "I know you're thinking about your prince." Since we were children she has known my thoughts, and I love her for it. The flames flicker over her face, magnifying her defiant beauty.

My fingers dig into the dirt. "Do you believe this union between Koridon and human could be like that story?"

She leans back to bask in a magnificent sky of stars. "Where we die at the end and everyone's crying?" She nods. "Yeah."

"Yeah." I look down at my feet and listen to the murmur of Koridons talking amongst themselves, and the tearing of animal flesh with their teeth.

"Are you truly in love with their prince?" Scarlet asks.

"Yes."

"Do you think—" she nods toward one of the males who meets her attention with piercing gems. "The one that beds me will love me too?" Her first time experiencing sex was born from pain and absolute terror, so perhaps she has nothing left to fear.

"Under his desperate possessiveness you'll be unable to breathe and yet wish for it with all your heart when his crushing ceases."

"Will it hurt?" she asks, touching the inside of her thigh where an old scar surely reopens.

I refuse to let the thought of Brekter's ridiculous girth shoving inside my unwilling body shadow my expression. Their size in that area does not slide in with ease, and without proper excitement, it's excruciating. Conversely, being filled with such a male's cock in the midst of pure love is ecstasy. "It was the most amazing thing I'd ever felt, Scarlet. But after what was done to us by Alexander, I was terrified." It is a mystery how something so beautiful can be twisted into something so wretched, just as a pleasant dream can turn to bloody terror upon the sudden veil of a nightmare.

Jane nudges me with her shoulder. "I've been thinking about what you said earlier. About what giving our bodies to these beings could mean for the future of our families. I am with you."

Blond Alice tosses a piece of bone into the fire. "Fools."

"Perhaps," I say, "but you haven't seen what I have. You haven't bathed in such—"

"And I never will." She gathers a pillow of leaves and crashes onto her side.

"And so we beat on," Glenda's voice cuts through the tension. "Boats against the current, borne back ceaselessly into the past."

"*The Great Gatsby*," I say warmly, the familiar quote warming my insides. "I cannot fix on the hour, the spot, nor the words that laid the foundation," I recite with little trills of excitement dancing through my veins. "It was too long ago."

Scarlet, Mary-Shelly and Glenda say the last line with me: "*I was in the middle before I knew I had begun!*"

Jane stands up and bows playfully. "Why, that was your very own Jane Austen who said that!"

Glenda kneels before Scarlett and takes her hand. "I've loved you more than I've ever loved any woman, and I've *waited* for you longer than any other woman."

Scarlett throws the back of her hand to her forehead. "If I said I was madly in love with you I'd be lying, Rhett!" She whips her hair back in exaggerated O'Hara fashion, and we burst into laughter. The males across from us cease their conversating with identical looks of annoyance and mild fascination. They utilize our books to enhance their survival but not the silly ones meant only for entertainment, according to Brekter. But these old classics are all we had to escape our small lives, and they taught us to dream. Reciting the words from those worn pages creates a familiar space that I'm welcoming whole-heartedly right now.

"This is just like the full moon celebration, isn't it?" says black-haired Alice who sways under the stars, her arms wrapped around her chest. Her foot accidently nudges blond Alice, who lets out a loud sigh that ruffles the leaves.

"What is this you do?" Kraetorr asks, sitting with elbows rested against his thighs, a piece of meat hanging from the side of his mouth.

The moment of happiness fades, and it seems none of us knows what to say. His harsh voice is an intrusion, and I don't want to share my humanity with him.

Glenda says, "We were just pretending to be the characters we were named after, is all." She wrings her hands. "Well, except me, I was playing Rhett from *Gone with the Wind*—"

"You play games?" asks Kraetorr, his confusion almost laughable.

"Don't you?" She smiles softly and so bravely at the frightening beast that nearly ravished her blindly this morning.

Arek storms over to us and rips Glenda down to her place beside Scarlet. "Of course we do not play games! Not even our children are allowed to."

"What children?" blond Alice adds under her breath.

Another coarse voice chimes in. "Silly women." The Koridon was sure to say it in our tongue so we wouldn't miss it. "They sit on the edge of death and play make-believe as though it will help them survive." He laughs and throws a half-eaten, greasy boar leg at our feet.

"Survival is *not* all that matters!" Mary-Shelly directs her voice toward Arek. He stands a mountain over her. "Why do you even wish to survive without joy?"

"*Joy* is beating something down into submission." He leans

into her face, and an aqua-touched dark strand falls over his eyes. I purse my lips, feeling the sting of his utter beauty. "It is conquering," he hisses.

"Then I feel sorry for you," she says, her lips flush with his. They tremble slightly, and I sense Arek's impulse to tear away from her. The intimacy of the near kiss, which he has likely never known before, sends bolts of heat into his loins; I can almost taste it, desire thick in the air. I wonder if he has any knowledge of the slick warmth a woman's body creates, or if he has ever felt one buckling from the pleasure of his knot as he fills her to bursting. Their laws used to forbid coupling with humans, but that didn't stop some of them. Arek's aggression toward blond Alice during lunch today could mean either he really does think us a lower species, or he's been with one before and hates himself for it.

Drakon makes an abrupt noise, and it sobers Arek into backing away. "Would you perhaps pretend to be someone else from your books? Perhaps... Adolph Hitler?"

The girls cringe at the name, and even blond Alice, who has held her position of ignoring the scene, turns over.

"Of course not," Sybil says. "We would never take pleasure in such a dark character."

"And who have you been named for?" he asks her.

"The tortured love of Dorian Gray, sir." Sybil curtsies.

"Ah." He has no idea what she speaks of. "Hear this. You and your terrible species are no longer allowed to bask in any of your human heritage. I will not have it tainting our children." My one joy in this world, reading about faraway places and adventures that will never be... he would take that from us and forbid us to pass it on?

Blond Alice sits up. "Why do you hate us so much?"

I could give her a list but instead try to instill some understanding in her and the other girls. "Because before the war, they came to us for help." I cut Drakon's snide remark off, whatever it was going to be. "Kassien's mate, the one I was to replace, told me the truth about our past. True, the Koridons are a violent and warrior-bred race, but that isn't why they came to Earth. After defending their beloved home for three billion years, it betrayed them, becoming a hostile wasteland as their sun imploded. They were forced to reach out to the nearest life-giving planet in the Milky Way galaxy, and the shape they were left in didn't warrant a fight. Our world leaders offered them help at first, then unleashed nuclear weapons on their ships all at once."

"Which is the reason most of you died," says Drakon. "Our reactors are powered by what your scientists were just discovering and call element 115." His hands mimic a great blast. "You *dridnaks* destroyed your own planet."

"They did that! The people of the past. Not us," I remind him. "And I'm sure your hands aren't clean of blood. How many planets have your people destroyed?"

Brekter steps through a cloud of black smoke that billows in the wind. "Well, now. I think you meant to say *our*. How many planets have *our* people destroyed."

With shining eyes, I beg him not to reveal my secret genetics. Not yet. How can I be a comfort to my friends if they deem me one of the enemy?

"What is he saying?" Scarlet turns to me.

"They do not know?" Brekter laughs. He bows before me, much like Glenda did while we were reenacting *Gone with the Wind*. "Say hello, then, to Calypso: the future embodied."

"Calypso?" Glenda's brow furrows as she takes in my tall stature and strange coloration, and she already knows. In fact, it must seem obvious now.

"I don't have genetic mutations." My voice comes out strong as it reflects the pride I feel for being much more than

33

the poor outcast they thought me. "My identity was hidden from me until a few days ago."

Blond Alice sneers. "So everything she's told us has been on their behalf. She's one of them!"

"No, I was raised with *you*, I am not one of them." My gut twists on the lie. Being a part of their bloodline has opened my eyes to many things and has empowered me: the thrill of cutting myself in the dark behind the men's quarters, the pain giving me a rush, my brazenness compared to other girls... and, of course, the blue tinge of my hair, much like the cobalt shine the Koridons have. Finding this part of me has enlivened my entire being. But as Scarlet peers at me with distrust, I would do anything to just be her best friend. "Listen to me. I still love you and my mother, all of our people. And if I could go back, I'd cut my throat before accidently leading them to you."

Blond Alice plays with the rope along her belly. "It's never too late."

Scarlet's palm flies into blond Alice's cheek, and she grasps the angry skin in shock.

"Don't you ever say that again!" She stands over blond Alice and takes a fistful of her hair. "Calypso's our sister, our friend, and she's proof that we have a future!"

Brekter guides Scarlet back to her spot. "Time for sleep."

"Yes," Drakon pipes in. "Enough talk. Not at all what we took them for, anyway. Perhaps a muzzle is in order." He and the others saunter away, but Brekter, with his wicked half-smile, props himself against a boulder and pulls me into his lap.

"I wish you wouldn't do this in front of the others." Jane and Mary-Shelly lay next to blond Alice, too exhausted to care, but Scarlet and Glenda can't help their watchfulness of me. It's torture to have my torment witnessed by my closest friends. Why can't he just drag me into the forest? "I don't love you," I sneer and send a sharp elbow into his ribs.

His groan quickly bends into a laugh, and he hardens against my backside. "Mmm. Keep wiggling," he breathes, prying his way up my tattered nightdress.

"I'm going to kill you, Brekter. And it's really going to hurt. I promise you."

He takes a defiant breath and plays with the sensitive nub of my nipple. The light touch of his fingertips, followed by a sharp pinch, sends a pleasant shock straight between my legs. "Do not rest too deeply," he says. "I am always watching you and do not know if I can hold myself back tonight."

"Touch me, Brekter, and I'll tear your eyes out just as you knot me. I'll enjoy the way you cry out in pain as you're forced to climax for several minutes."

"I will be sure then to tie your hands before I shove myself deep inside. I think perhaps you will be gagged as well."

"I'm sure that's just how you like your bedmates. Ripping their skin trying to get away from you and gagging."

His arm bends at my neck, and he squeezes violently, crushing my throat. "You have no idea—" his voice is pinched, "...the love I had before. What I have lost—" I can't force the slightest bit of air in, but instead of panicking, I reach up to Brekter's face and caress softly down his cheek. His hold softens, and I twist around to jab him between the eyes. He catches my wrists and throws me off him.

I rub my sore tailbone and watch Brekter storm off. Scarlet and the others look at me in bewilderment, but I'm just as curious as they are. What in Dante's hell was he talking about? Brekter has a mate, but whatever love he speaks of... it's not about her.

4

"Calypso. Wake up!"

Scarlett's laughter echoes across my dream and sounds so strange when her voice suddenly changes. "Calypso, wake!" My eyes flutter open to find Brekter clenching my arm. He undoes the restraint around my belly.

"What are you doing?" I whisper. He shushes me by cupping his hand around my mouth.

"I found something." Hoisting me into his arms, we race through the rolling fog.

After a few minutes at his incredible speed, we stop before a dilapidated structure. I struggle out of his arms with excitement—I've never seen any buildings of old before! I wait for Brekter to lead the way, but he motions for me to go ahead. Creeping up a broken stone path, I wipe the coat of dirt from the window and peer inside. "What is this place?"

Brekter lights a torch. "One of the places your kind used to invite others to exchange goods, or whatever." I wonder how Koridon economy worked when their planet was functional. Probably some system I couldn't even begin to comprehend.

Before our world fell we were reliant on currency, but now we have to raise our own animals, grow our own fruits, vegetables and grain, or we'll starve. The Koridons had to learn how to do this too, that's why they were forced to learn our *animal language*. They couldn't have known how to grow in our soil, or in our climate.

I drag the door open through shards of glass and step into the darkness. Brekter follows, the light illuminating the dusty glass cases as it trails over them. Vines hang from the ceiling and weeds twist up through cracks in the floor, but the small shop stands untouched somehow after all these years. I grab a plastic book from the shelf and open it, but there are no pages, only a flat disc that says *Jaws*. There are at least forty of them with different titles like *Blade* and *The Little Mermaid*. I move toward another shelf and dust off a rectangular device with a glass front and puzzle for a moment before being drawn to dusty clothing on hangers. My touch brushes across one of the strange garments, and it disintegrates.

Brekter moves to my back and lifts my hair aside, his fingers trailing down the back of my neck. Tingles roll down my backbone, and I quickly move on to the next treasure in this strange shop.

"What is this place?" I ask, my eyes roaming over dusty paintings that grace the walls. With a swipe of my hand against the canvas, a lady's face appears. Black smudges under her lower lashes and a cylindrical smoking object sits loosely in pouting lips the color of spring roses. She's captivating. Why is she so sad? I take it off the wall and flip it over to find her story, but there's nothing, just a loose brown paper backing. Where are the words to this picture?

Onto my chest drops a red sparkling heart descending from a gold chain. The beauty of such a thing absorbs through my gaze and caresses my senses. "I've never seen anything like this." I touch the sparkling necklace and think about the treasures I've read about and am so thankful that this has turned the memory into something indescribable.

"This place is full of such treasures. Do you like it?"

"It's so beautiful under the fire light. I can't believe it's real." He brushes his cheek against my hair and his hand drifts past my waist. I rip the necklace off and throw it at his feet. "Get away from me."

"Why?" He steps on the beautiful jewel, and the cracking from his immense weight makes me cringe. "I thought little animals liked shiny things."

"And I thought it was beneath a superior Koridon to give such a meaningless gift." I step back as he looms over me. "I don't see how a sparkly thing helps you win a fight."

"A fight of sorts," he says, lifting me from the ground by my throat.

"Well—" I manage hoarsely, trying to break loose. "You lost." With my lungs burning, I take control of my impulsive flailing and land my heel into his crotch. He smiles as he groans and takes me to the floor, my back hitting hard.

He crawls over me and I fly up, knocking him off balance. I edge near a case of jewelry, where several guns and knives glint from their mounts on the wall. "Perhaps if you were Kassien I would have accepted the gift."

He scoffs and jams the torch into the ground between a huge crack. "You mean the one who tossed you to his second after promising to marry you?"

Heat burns through my veins as I remember Tanak trying to move his huge shaft through my opening during the ceremony while all the Koridons watched. Including Kassien and Brekter. "He thought it best," I say weakly. "He was trying to deny his heart and do what was right," I edge toward the wall of weapons, "but giving me to another wasn't what was right by *me*."

He yanks my dress down and reveals my body. I look to the side with a gulp as he drinks me in. Frozen, I can't move to reach for the dress. "Why does it have to be him?" Brekter asks.

I suck in a deep, frustrated breath in reply, still unable to meet his silver stare.

His fingers graze between my breasts and trail down to the nakedness between my legs. "You soaked me when I filled you last. I moved inside you, your body gripping me as I barely fit, and still you pulled me deeper." His breath quickens, a god-like being trembling. "Please stop fighting me," he whispers.

"I never wanted you to mate me. I begged you not to. But you did, and worse yet, you tricked me afterward into—" He inserts a finger into my warmth, and I buckle with stimulation. "And worse yet, you have imprisoned me and my village mates to do horrible things to."

He flips me around and holds me across the chest, continuing his fingering with my arms held down. "Is this so horrible?" he asks in my ear.

"Yes. You would degrade me at every turn as an animal, then fuck me like you'll die."

"Ooh, I like that word." He pulls shining fingers out then circles the bundle of nerves above, stroking me with soft nudges. He forces me to respond, even though it's a purely physical reaction and nothing to do with love.

"I'm fond of it as well." I say. "*Die* is a lovely word."

His lips find my neck and plant light kisses along the pulsing skin.

"I am mated to Kassien by *your* laws."

"If you carry my child, our laws give you to me." His mouth sinks into my shoulder, and I growl under the pressure.

"I can be given to no one."

"Don't make me force you, Calypso." He shoves me onto my hands and knees and his palm lands into my backside with a horrible *smack*. I cry out from frustration, but feel no pain from his hit. "You should be far easier to take this time. Eventually, I imagine you will open for me to slide in with ease." His fingers entangle the locks at the top of my head. "But I hope not."

I shove forward, ripping my hair to oblivion. "Damn you, Brekter! Get off me or I'll scream the forest down and bring the commander!"

His hand finds my mouth, and my neck strains backward. "Submit to me as your master, little pet, or have the breaking of your bones the last thing you ever hear. And my cock the last thing that ever makes you scream."

I jerk my head to the side, and his hand falls away from my lips. "You don't scare me," I hiss. If he were going to kill me, he would have done it back at the village instead of compromising with me as I held a knife to my belly. It goes against every defiant bone in my body, but I swallow my anger and twist around, clasping my hands in front of my chest. "Brekter, I'm another's wife. Please, *please* don't make me lie intimately with you again."

"You are mine," he growls into my face. "This body is *mine*. Now I wonder, what do I have to do to make the true parts of you mine?"

"I told you once. I asked you to be selfless, but you used it against me in the worst way imaginable. I will never be yours."

He roars and shoves my face into the ground. "Why do you think you have a choice?" He grasps my hips and yanks me against him. "I have tried not to want you. I believed that once we had all your female villagers in our possession, I wouldn't need you anymore." His crown sinks in, and bursting pressure makes me gasp. As he forces inside, inch by excruciating inch, I hate myself for growing wet for him. His pleasure-filled murmur further teases my senses. "They smell nice enough. Their bodies are soft and tantalizing enough." I squeeze my lids shut as he uses me to make his blood dance with every thrust. "But they do not still my heart. Nothing does, until my eyes fall upon you."

"That's how I feel about Kassien," I bite out through gritted teeth. His prior touch ignited my sexual responses but still his size is too much. The deeper he delves, the more I worry I won't be able to handle it. As my pulse spikes—the pain and fear overwhelming me—my hands spark with a strange sensation. Pressure builds in them, begging me to grab onto Brekter as though I could hurt him with just my touch. I steady myself on one hand and reach behind me, ready to give in to the urge...

"He hasn't tried to save you, Calypso." His fingers caress down my spine, and I plant my palms back into the floor.

"If he's alive, he will." My body responds to him against my will, moistening, blood rushing. *I'd rather be in pain.*

"But by then, I will have ruined you for him."

Rays of light break through the dusty old windows as Brekter plays with my breasts and slams his hips into my backside. I fight to stay on my hands and knees, knocking forward with such violence my neck strains. Then his movements become feverish and his breath ragged until finally he takes his last stroke. He holds me hard as his cock throbs with a knot pressing against my aching walls, and I grunt with effort to stay within my skin. When first experiencing this with Kassien, it was blissful as the ball of pulsing pressure brought me to finishing ecstasy. Sensation builds upon thoughts of him and I chase it. I remember Kassien, his fingers digging into my skin, his breath quickened, the shaking of our slick bodies as he knotted me. I quake as waves of pleasure wash over me,

41

twisting and cramping, pleasure to the point of pain. My teeth sink into my lower lip to keep from crying out.

Brekter lets out a blissful utterance and holds me tightly against him. Upon finishing, he slides out and immediately lifts me into his arms. His lips search mine and they beg for something, any small bit of hope, but all he holds against him is a corpse.

I force myself out of his arms and sniffle as I put my dress back into place. If Kassien doesn't come for me, this could be my life now. Brekter's mate. Will I be forced to accept it one day? Making children for him, taking care of them by night, working in the fields and kitchens as a slave by day?

He stares at me with wildfire, and I know exactly what shuddering thought plays through his mind. "You shook upon me," he says. "You clenched down upon my knot, and it was the most pleasurable thing I have ever felt."

"No, I—" It hits me that being aroused by my attacker was utterly depraved. What kind of woman would try to enjoy being sexually attacked?

"You do care for me." He swipes back loose hair then drags a finger down his bare chest. "You hate it, but you love me."

He doesn't understand that what I experienced was physical and in no way means I care for him. I don't fully understand what happened myself, and shame crushes my chest, horrified by the monstrous side obviously alive in me. Unable to breathe, I head out of the strange little shop and run as fast as my feet will carry me.

5

KASSIEN

My weak, dehydrated heartbeat surges with panic as the leather pants slip from my foot's shaky hold. I kick into the air, ignoring the massive weight shift that angers the hook-embedded wound. They fly upward, and though I beg my arms to lift, my hands to reach out, they only twitch uselessly in their damaged state. The leathers land over my shoulder, and I tremble with joy. "Tenak, be strong. I will save us yet."

I shift my weight to the left side, excruciating pain lighting up my right, and grit my teeth. Blood flows into my right hand as my left takes the punishment, but through harsh needle stabs prickling my flesh, my fingers move. *What are you made of?* screams through my head and I roar, fighting the immobility of the steel through my shoulder. If I could tie the legs around the chain, I could use it to hoist my weight up enough to pull one hook out and release one powerful arm. Tools in the med bay will heal me. I just have to get free...

But first, the blood must bring life back to this limb, so I wait.

Pain means nothing, and death does not frighten me. The

only thing that matters is saving Calypso from Brekter, and the others who suffer because of my dream. Dear Efaelty, she is good. I see now as I hang between the physical world and the unseen world how wrong I have been. Being infatuated with a human was easier when I could blame her for what happened to our child.

I lift my arm and sharp pain seizes me at the elbow. My arm jerks back down. Just a few more minutes and I will have the strength I need. Minutes pass like a slow eternity, and though I have pushed my little one down into the deepest recesses of my mind, he is all I can think about now.

Efaelty was big with child, though no one had seen such blessing in years. Gerakon carefully monitored her throughout the gestation, giving her plant life from the earth and meat from the free roaming animals in hope of increasing the natural flora in the child. He gave her milk from them too, and strange concoctions from the land he had made. The child was born a few weeks early, a boy, and he was *alive.* I remember holding his tiny body and never feeling more afraid in all my two hundred years. I cared for the tiny being more than myself, more than life, and saw everything I had missed throughout my lifetime in his strangely powerful and loving gaze.

The heart was ripped from my chest, never to beat without pain again when he left us. Within days he became docile, that little spark of life he'd emanated faded, and though we tried everything, I was helpless. Watching him every minute of the night, I knew every weak breath threatened to be his last. All I had wanted was just to know him. I would have done anything to see his smile, hear what his voice sounded like, and to watch him run and train.

I remember the moment I felt his essence leave. It jolted my eyes open as I lay with him in my arms. Where his beautiful, loved little life would emerge next, well, that was up to the fate of the universe. It did not comfort me, because it would take infinite time and infinite places for him to reoccur again somewhere. I would never see him again. Never hold him. Never teach him the pride of being Koridon. But worse, he would never know what he meant to me.

It was only a few years later when Calypso brought hope of getting him back. Well, not him. But maybe a piece of my heart could be returned with the birth of another.

Torture gripping me upon the sorrow of his name, I grab the leather pants. Soft in my burning hand, I throw them over the bar the chains hangs from and pull up, using it as a wrench to dislodge my body from the hooks. "Tenak! Hold on!" I roar, my arm on fire as steel squelches out of my shoulder. The leather shreds as I fight to breathe, and my numb hand slips. The pant leg pulls free and my weight smashes down entirely on the left hook, my collar bone shrieking as it digs in.

Blood pours from my open tear, and I throw the leathers up once more, my ears ringing, little dots swarming my vision. I tug on the makeshift hoist, and it falls free. A miss. Warm liquid seeps down my leg, and I force myself to focus sharply on the target above. Taking a breath, I fight to focus, pushing down the agony of tortured nerves, and toss them over. It holds. My good hand grips the legs and I hoist myself up, relieving the tremendous pressure off my shoulder. The muscle lifts off the steel, my arm shaking, weak, begging to give up. But I won't. *I will never—*

A ripping sound tears through my ears, and I'm helpless to feel myself slam back down, the leathers falling to the ground. Dread washes over me, giving way to the worst thing I have ever felt.

Defeat.

6

CALYPSO

Pink fire breaks through the mountains as the sun sets. Brekter and I reach camp, passing two Koridons coming back with fresh kills, and the girls stir near the smoldering fire. Every step jolts the achiness between my legs, and I have to focus to keep from limping. I really could have used the extra sleep robbed from me this morning for the long day ahead, but I feel very awake and strong despite everything. I resume my spot next to Glenda, who wakes and sits up.

"You all right?" she asks, pulling the debris from her light colored strands.

"Mm-hmm," I reply with a wry smile.

Kraetorr walks past, an unmistakable heat in his presence, and Glenda hugs her chest. "I want to go home so badly," she says, shivering. "I miss my mother. And Finn."

I miss my mother too, and I hate to think of the distress she must be in knowing I've been taken by our enemy. On the other hand, I'm happy Brekter negotiated for her to stay back with the rest of our people. Maybe we will all be free one day, our two races in harmony, and I will be reunited with her. It's what keeps me from cracking into tiny, insane little pieces all over the floor when Brekter pushes me to my limit. I have to believe this is all for something.

After breakfast, the Koridons push us on toward the Pacific shore. I'm a bundle of nerves, knowing the journey is coming to an end and soon my friends will be thrust into the Koridon world with relentless brutality.

The smell of pine wafts along with the breeze and reminds me of Yuletide season. Sad yet endearing memories touch upon my thoughts. We've never had much, but we still honor the ghosts of Christmas past, present and future.

For the past, we make something symbolic of what we regret, a mistake we're sorry for, and it's only for the spirit of Christmas past to know, no one else. Last year Finn crafted a doll that looked similar to Glenda and placed it under the big pine tree. He regretted spending so much time out of the home while his sister grew more and more weak. He just wanted to be with his friends and find himself, but she almost died when a nasty lung infection took her before full moon of Yuletide began. He blamed himself for not being there enough that year and hoped to aid his sister's recovery.

For the ghost of Christmas present, we honor someone of our choosing to thank them for being part of our lives. The gift could be a new coat or pair of shoes you've made, or taking on their chores so they're free to do as they wish for a day. Last year I asked Scarlet's father to go out and collect wild berries so I could make black-haired Alice a dessert from one of the old cookbooks. I had to substitute several ingredients but was able to make a sugary tart she thought was wildly fun to eat. It was called a "jelly donut," and I baked it on the bread stone.

Finally, on the third night of Yuletide we sing songs from the old time, passed down over the years, and we write to the ghost of Christmas future about our plans for the upcoming year. We vow to be better in some way so we don't end up in an early grave with no love and no happiness as Ebenezer almost did.

"*Silent night, oh what a night. All is calm, all is light,*" I sing as we trudge through the brush. "*Around young virgins, mother and child.*" Several angelic voices join in, the forest so silent as it revels in our morning song. "*Sleep in heavenly peace. Sleep in heaven with me.*"

The sound vibrates in the air and breathes life into my aching soul as we vocalize, then laugh when we mess up the words. The Koridons watch us curiously and we wait for them to ask us to shut our mouths. But step after step they let us carry on. Brekter once berated me for singing, saying I was just like a little bird with no purpose and nothing better to do than open my mouth. But my heart swells with each song, each dance and each passage we recite from our favorite books. I am not ashamed of my humanity.

We don't stop when the sun is at its highest point like we have the past few days to eat lunch, and I know it's because we arrive soon to whatever fate has planned for us.

Before long, the dirt and rock become soft under our feet and strange white birds fly overhead with their trills echoing. We are led up a hill, and the moment we crest it, a moving, vast blue phenomenon stretches across the land. It ripples and crashes along the rocks, and in this moment I know the ocean in which Moby Dick looms truly exists.

"We arrive!" shouts Drakon, cutting through my misty enthrallment. His horse's hooves kick up golden grains of sand and I shield my eyes. "Come along!"

In the distance, a gigantic house comes into view, and

several humans work to clear debris and tend the grounds. Kassien didn't have slaves where he kept me, and every dirty, emaciated man and woman takes on the face of someone from my village as we pass. Is this to be their fate when they're found? A young man smooths his blond hair back and watches us, his clothes soaked with sweat. "What colony are you from?" I ask him, distracted by his eyes that reflect the same blue-gray as the sea.

A sweet smile breaks through his tortured demeanor. "I'm Jonah, from his highness, Summer Sun's village, lady."

"The village down south?"

He nods, and I tell him where *we* have been stolen from, in the midland. Those ocean eyes like the sun reflecting off rippling waters dart toward Glenda, who trips on a rock buried in the sand. The boy drops his shovel, and though he's shaking with exhaustion he helps her up. She hugs him, eyes squeezed shut.

Kraetorr's huge shadow steps in front of the light and he puts a boot into the boy's backside, sending them both careening to the ground.

"You cursed, fucking beast!" I yell and help them up, my hands trembling with rage. I turn on him and am taken aback by his haunted expression toward Glenda as she grimaces and holds her wrist. He takes a step backward, and I raise a brow at his odd behavior.

"Back, slave!" Brekter takes my arm and shoves me along, the others jerking with the force of our conjoined ropes. "You will be brought into the human manor and settled into a room in preparation for the mating ceremony."

"Wait, you mean they are to be claimed?" Unable to focus on the horror of being properly bedded by Brekter, I'm filled with relief for the others. What I had imagined was the women strapped down in one of the giant grounded ships and mated daily until seed took hold. "Will they be shown proper honor, as I was?"

He snickers and pushes me forward when my feet slow. "You mean forced to be impregnated by an aged male when you thought it was to be your prince?"

I sigh and shake off the memory of Tenak's rough hands and the drag of his soft beard across my face. "You know exactly what I mean." This gives me hope; perhaps the women can learn to love their new husband. I hurt for the ones who have already been engaged to a man in our village, but this could be promising. We have to look to the future and realize that to protect those men we love, we must blend our species and become one race free from constant fear and confinement. "How are they to be chosen? Who will be mated together?" I ask.

He squeezes my hand. "I care not. All I am concerned with is mating you properly and before the clan."

A creeping sensation turns my stomach cold. My heart is chained to Kassien, and though his mate's family—Drakon and this bunch—refuse to see our marriage as real, I feel completely bound to him. He killed for me. He fought until he was beaten into the ground for me. He suffers from an unnatural attraction as most Koridons do to human women, but when he handles me with his gentle roughness, shaking and unsure, a different side of him is revealed. He wants what we want: a family, love, and tradition, but he's been fighting for his life for so long that love confuses him. It confounds all of them, actually.

"What about your real mate?" I ask as we near the mansion by the sea. Lorai had backed Kassien over Brekter when he and Gerakon ambushed him in the woods and stole me away. She must be horrified that he has joined Efaelty's family with the intention of taking me as his woman. And on that note, how many other angry females will be waiting for us *here*?

"She is a traitor and no longer my concern," he says. The other night, when he stormed off saying some confusing thing about having loved deeply or whatnot before, he didn't give me the impression that Lorai is who he was speaking of.

"*She's* the traitor?" I ask, confounded by his logic. "You have broken your laws and betrayed your prince! *You* are the traitor! You all are." I look pointedly at Drakon, who already rides off with several of the others as a huge metal gate looms before us.

He takes me by the back of the neck and sniffs close to my face. "We arrive now." The note of calm in his tone confuses me, completely mismatched from his wild expression. "I look forward to spending much time with you in the coming days."

The black iron gate opens and we're ushered up stone stairs to a stunning house that has somehow withstood the war and two-hundred years of wear. Brekter and Arek open the big double doors and haul us by our ropes through the threshold.

"Welcome," a husky feminine voice says. Inside the lavish room, a female Koridon steps out of the shadows. "I am called Vaerynn and have been tasked with your care." Her features are sharp, and though she stands only a bit taller than myself, her body ripples with profound strength. "See them to the bathing chambers," she commands.

Led through a corridor by the three Koridons, we come to a large room with shiny rock floors, and in the middle stands a large, square tub. Our ropes are released and we're ordered to strip as several older slaves bring in buckets of steaming water.

"Undress!" Vaerynn says again, and Brekter glances at Kraetorr with a flash of anger. "Why do you give pause? Do you believe these males will be unable to control themselves upon seeing your naked bodies?" She takes hold of Sybil's collar and rips her nightshirt down. "Do you think you are so beautiful, so sexually superior that we all will bow before you?"

She twists her nipple, forcing a cry from her lips and bringing her to her knees by the forceful pull of her breast.

I quickly slip the dress down my body and straighten my spine. Vaerynn shoves Sybil, who quickly grabs for her reddened areola, and stands in front of me. She takes a strand of my ice blue hair and rips it from my head, but I continue to hold her eyes without flinching. "And you're the half-breed," she says with a smirk. "The reason this insanity is taking place."

"Not my choice," I say. "Nor was it my mother's when she was raped by one of your kind."

A slap sears across my cheek and I clack my teeth to readjust my jaw.

"If your mother was set upon by a Koridon, she has received a gift unworthy of her." The female's lips tighten as she studies me.

I think of a girl who had received such a gift. When the hunters brought her back to the village, she was brutally mishandled in a fit of lust by a Koridon. Bleeding, bruised, and with broken bones, the male had deformed the appearance of her body. "I've seen such a gift first hand," I say. "It's a gift of death, I suppose. You're right. Who wouldn't want that?" I feel my eyes glaze over at the thought of a similar fate for all of us here.

Vaerynn searches me a moment. "I had heard fabled tale about half-breeds existing, but I could not have known how incredibly strange you appear. I can't believe this is what our future is to look like." She turns from me toward Brekter, and as her words sink in, they sting. I've felt different my whole life, ugly and defective, but I know who I am now. I'm strong and beautiful.

"The prince assured me he was besotted with my appearance, ma'am," I say.

"I have heard you may already be holding his offspring." She stands back and crosses her arms. "Is this true?"

Brekter cuts in. "Her belly was ripe for wanting of seed. And she had it. Quite a lot of it."

"You?" she sneers. "I heard that your betrayal of the prince was for the sake of Efaelty, who was being thrown aside for the human. But now I see why you have convinced her father to turn from our old ways and begin affairs with these animals."

"It was not for her," he says. "I only took her so she would lead me to that pathetic village."

Anger glows red in my core, and I snuff out the urge to attack him. No easy task. I realize my fists are balled and my every muscle rigid before forcing myself to breathe again. He was able to trick me because I was exhausted and scared. I'd chosen to have faith in his word as though it were Kassien who spoke it. A fatal mistake.

"Well, until the day her pregnancy is confirmed," says Vaerynn, "and the child within accounted for, she will be treated as the rest. And if she is not carrying a child, she may very well be mated to someone else."

"She is mine," Brekter says too quickly, and Vaerynn marvels at his change in demeanor.

"So we are to be given a husband?" asks Scarlet, whose pale skin shows in my peripheral. Everyone had removed their gowns during the heated discussion, and the degradation makes my bareness prickle with goosebumps. *Little animal...* I hear Brekter's scathing nickname settle along my blushing form.

"You will all be kept in a large room guarded at the door," Vaerynn says, running her fingers down blond Alice's cheek. "You will be taught how to behave in our world and trained to serve our needs." She notes Arek's burning gaze upon blond Alice. "Of course, your main function will be to produce a

Koridon child, but until that day, you will be little more than a slave."

Blond Alice's face pinches in anger. "I will kill myself before letting one of you impregnate me." She blinks up at Arek with fire flickering in her irises.

"You will be tied down and used by every male in this compound until you are raw and insane with exhaustion!" Vaerynn sends a fist into her side and she doubles over, gasping.

The others stir and whimper, all the tales of these monsters striking up their fear once more. We had never been allowed outside the safety of our village barrier, never allowed to be a sexual people for fear of a Koridon male being nearby to scent it.

Vaerynn takes blond Alice's face in her hand and forces her head back against the wall. "Say one more hideous word and you will not even be allowed to bathe. I will have Arek remove you to your bed where your legs will be spread apart and each limb locked tightly down." Vaerynn's touch wonders between her legs. "Has this ever felt a tiny little man's *krivit* inside it? I hope not. It will make the bedding by a Koridon even more excruciating. I look forward to watching you break."

"You're going to watch?" blond Alice asks. Growing up, I never realized how fearless she was. Angry yes, rude to me, without a doubt. Stubbornness will only get her hurt here, but I secretly hope she never breaks.

"I will oversee all of it."

"Will there be a proper ceremony?" I ask.

"Enough questions," she snaps. "Wash your horrid bodies." She points toward the tub. "Then we shall begin."

7

Soapy water slides down my arms as I scrub off the caked dirt from my skin. The bathing chamber is like nothing I've ever seen before with its silvery walls and pillars. I entertain ideas of princesses bathing here, with the ladies-in-waiting lathering up their long, golden hair as they contemplate what prince to marry.

Brekter, Arek and Vaerynn speak to each other in their language from the corner as we bathe. I catch several words they use and try to piece it together, but a strange tingling sensation brings me to distraction. I look up to see the girls staring at me with expectation.

"Tell me what will happen to us," says Mary-Shelly, crossing shining arms over her chest.

"I don't know any more than you do," I say, happy for the cover of bubbles. We were always taught modesty by our parents, and no matter how I try to break from my instilled beliefs, I still feel hopelessly awkward for the others. It's not as much *my* nakedness as it is seeing my village mates this way.

"Yes you do," accuses blond Alice. "You know exactly what

will happen to us if they force themselves inside our small bodies." Long locks stream down her chest as she sits against the side unmoving.

They deserve to know what being mated will feel like, and understanding what to expect might make it easier. "I have lain with two of them for a total of three times." Mouths drop just as my defenses had to say this. I can't believe I've been with Brekter more than Kassien at this point. It's like I really do belong to him now.

"You were forced by two different ones?" asks Scarlett, wading her fingers through the pearlescent water.

"No. Just one of them." A few of the girls steal a look at Brekter, and the others fight to avert their attention. "At first, the prince tried to preserve me until the ceremony. But each time we were alone together he would lose his resolve a bit more. You see, the Koridons aren't like us in passion. They, along with their females, are purely bred to be warriors. It was a survival necessity. They mate only for reproduction as their women do not secrete... um... love hormones? I guess you'd say."

They study Vaerynn and her hard appearance. We know from our books of science how we secrete pheromones and how chemicals possess our minds and bodies in glorious ways. Sybil asks darkly, "They don't feel love then?"

"No, they do! They most certainly do. For some reason, human women possess them and have reactivated those feelings of lust and love that have long been repressed. And it's so much all at once that it drives them mad. That's why we have seen women torn apart by them. They're just so much bigger, so much stronger."

"But that could happen to us," says Glenda. "You survived, but that's because you're one of them."

"But I've been weak my whole life, desperately lacking in a

nutrient I need from their planet. And that was my plight when Kassien mounted me." I am stronger now that I've been supplied with it every day and won't die early as previously thought.

"How did you survive then?" asks black-haired Alice.

"I was afraid, so every time the prince came close to fully bedding me, I found a way to get out of it. But once we were presented in front of the others in true ceremony, I seized upon my inner strength and the love already blossoming between us, and I trusted him to control himself and be gentle."

Blond Alice scoffs. "We're dead."

"They have to love you?" Scarlett asks. "Is that the key? They have to love you or else their base needs will destroy you?" I am taken off-guard by what she has concluded from my story. Could it be true that love is stronger than lust and can be the reason behind their sporadic control? Icy chills race down my legs as I think of Brekter and his hands upon me, his tongue thrusting through my slit. I feel the tactile memory of his knot as he climaxed, pulsing and stroking me to the strongest sensations I've ever experienced.

"I don't think so," I reply. "They're very intelligent beings and can control themselves once set to task."

The girls begin to breathe easier, but I know what else they wish me to tell. The silence between us screams the question.

"They're—" I grimace, trying to find the right way to talk about their sexual anatomy. "They're very large, obviously. Now, I don't have much experience by way of our own males, but these ones have rod-shaped... um... *cocks* as thick as eggplants." It shouldn't be a complete surprise that their sexes reflect their size. They're giants, and what hangs between their legs is as such. "The tip is larger still, but as he works it inside you gently, your body will expand, be stimulated, and accept it."

Jane catches herself staring at Arek's crotch area, and her cheeks flush.

Mary-Shelly has been married for some years and spoke to me once of the marriage bed pains, saying they'd become very pleasurable after a few times. She shrugs. "A man's penis rubs nicely inside. I can't imagine something of that size though. That just isn't natural."

My first time, hurting and broken in the dirt by one of my own kind, reminds me that all I've ever been used for is pleasure by bigger, stronger males. "I don't have much to compare it by, but when done right—" A thrill stabs through my belly, remembering Kassien's rough desperation and his scent like seductive aggression. Then Brekter's memory cuts through, turning Kassien and me to ash. "It's amazing," I say shakily. "When done right, it's beyond words."

They reflect in silence as they finish scrubbing the forest dirt from their hair and nails. Am I horrible for enjoying the love of a giant otherworldly male? Am I depraved after all? I burn with shame for what I said as I watch Glenda, her small pale fingers shaking with effort, and wonder if I should add a warning. What if I've told them they'll enjoy sex with a Koridon only to be shocked when their bodies begin to bruise and their bones begin to crack? They could still be torn to shreds, and I tell them it's *enjoyable*? *Oh God.*

We're supplied with strange feeling slip-on dresses that tie in crisscrosses over the chest. Vaerynn, with her strong silence, takes us to a room high up on the fourth floor. Barred windows let in sunlight from every angle, and another graces the ceiling, showing the magnificent sun overhead. Small beds that don't seem to belong to such a magnificent room line along the walls.

Vaerynn says, "This will be your sleeping quarters until you're properly mated. You will be watched at all times by myself or one of the males."

I raise a hand. "Are there not any other females here?" The thought of Brekter or any of the males that we've gotten to know watching us while we sleep makes my skin crawl.

She clenches her teeth. "The others were not chosen to be in this position." She spits *chosen* as though it were verbal poison.

"It isn't safe to allow any Koridon male to be in this room with us alone," I say.

"You misunderstand your place, human," she says. "You are the absolute property of these males, a piece of *meat* until you have proven your worth and produced a superior Koridon offspring."

"What if we... can't?" asks Mary-Shelly, lightly touching her stomach. Through careful practice, she has not become pregnant during the one time per month allowed to sleep with her husband. Resources are too scarce and space too cramped to allow everyone pregnancies, not to mention the dangerous world we'd be bringing the most fragile of beings into. But it still happens, obviously. Men and women find ways to be together against all odds. Mary-Shelly's chin juts forward slightly, and her face gleams with yearning. I'd never given much thought to having children during the days in the village. I never expected to live long enough.

"Then you will serve in another way," Vaerynn says darkly. "But today an exam will be performed on each of you to assess your fertility and the probability of your success."

I look at Scarlett with curiosity. Could there be other factors involved with our compatibility?

"The examinations will be uncomfortable, but you will endure them as a Koridon would: with strength and composure." Vaerynn signals toward the beds. "Our children will not be born of weak mothers."

"We aren't weak," says blond Alice, clasping her hands behind her back.

Vaerynn's leg sweeps her knees and she hits the ground. Stifling a groan, blond Alice forces back a grimace and stands to her feet, tall. Tipping her head, her unwavering expression reads, *See?*

Vaerynn cracks a smile, and it's odd touching her stern features. "Find your beds. The *havistonn* will be in shortly to perform your examinations."

The softness of the bed caresses my side, and my body sings with restful relief. But my eyes refuse to close as they drink in the magic of the sparkling blue water that disappears into the misty sky.

The others find a bed and have a seat or lie down, but Glenda places her fingers against the window and gazes past her reflection at the foamy waves. The ones left at the village, including my mother, will probably have moved on to the south. I imagine Mother taking heavy steps away from our home with the peach and white pack we made together over her shoulder. She would be guiding the animals along and holding a cage of chickens upon the rocky trail.

As I lie on the soft mattress, I lift my hand in front of my face, turning it back and forth. The strange sensation that arose in them during Brekter's rough handling is something that hasn't surfaced for a long time. *But I have felt it before.* Once when I was younger, I had been cornered out in the vegetable fields by a group of older boys. One of them took me by a strand of loose hair which was always kept back. He taunted, "Weird Caly, why do you look like that?" My heart was pounding as another boy poked me in the shoulder. "You're a weird girl!" he said and shoved me. The kids laughed as I hit the ground, but it didn't hurt. They knew exactly why my hair was an icy blue and my eyes a glowing cerulean, and I couldn't believe they would be so cruel to someone who was cursed with such a short life. The children chanted their ugly words and their feet landed into my sides and back. Though I wanted to cry, I didn't, but instead I *embraced* the pain. Each blow sent a jolt through me and welled up in my core. Every nerve seemed to soak up the hits and form a ball of energy. My eyes focused with deadly sharpness and the kids around me moved in slow motion. I burst up, and a loud pop broke through the air like it had ripped open. The boy, Tommy, who acted as the main aggressor, grabbed my wrist but immediately let it go again with a sharp breath. The color leached from his face and blackened, tearful eyes darted around wildly.

Momma tore across the land after us and all the kids scattered, Tommy not so quickly. The sight of her disarmed me, and what was left of the heavy swirling deep in my flesh dissipated. She took me into her embrace and stroked my messy locks. "Are you all right?" she asked and rocked me gently. I was all right. In fact, I was vibrating. "They just don't understand." She leaned into my ear. "They don't know it, but you are amazing. You are more special than them, me, and everyone we know."

Different didn't feel amazing or special, and I wanted so badly to blend in with the rest of my people. The kids who hurt me that day were punished so severely it never happened again, and with time, the pain of their attack and the strange sensations that overtook me faded away.

"He arrives." Vaerynn's voice cuts through my sleepy state. "Sit on your beds and quietly await your turn." She turns slowly and says, "You are not to scream at any time. No matter what."

Before full realization can sink in, the door swings open and a young male steps inside wearing a strange mask. A familiar sense of knowing strikes me, though his hair is cut short and his features are obscured by the mask. "Gerakon?" slips out, and he looks at me with deceitful pools of lightest silver. "You betray Kassien again?" I eagerly shimmy to the edge of the bed on my knees. "Is he alive?"

Vaerynn grunts in warning, but Gerakon raises a hand and lays a bag on the table in the center. "I only stand with what I believe, right or wrong." He lays out a series of metal tools that make my blood flow cold. "We miss crucial opportunities by trying to preserve your race." He palms a silver object and presses a button, activating it to open with moving claw projections. "I cannot stand back and watch my race suffer any longer. Hang yours if we must."

"This is our home, and we have been taken against our will," says Glenda. "I don't give a damn about *your* race."

"Ah," he says simply. "Then we understand each other after all."

"No." Glenda sits up and pounds a fist into the mattress. "You are breaking more than your own laws by hurting us. You break the *universe's*."

Vaerynn stands behind Mary-Shelly and holds her down by the shoulders. She shakes her head slightly, fear seeping from her pores as she fights the urge to struggle.

Gerakon taps the inside of her legs, and as they reluctantly fall open, a short sob exits her throat. Glenda and Sybil look away, but I have to know what happens. He positions the tool at her opening and pauses. But only for a second.

"Gerakon." I stand up, and Vaerynn stiffens. "Something we do at home before receiving treatment for something is telling the person exactly what's going to happen."

"Sit down, girl," says the bristling female, her fingers digging into Mary-Shelly's shoulders. My friend grits her teeth from the pressure.

"I will, but she won't be as scared if you explain everything she will experience." I sit back down as instructed and hope Gerakon has some amount of compassion within him. He played a part in beating Kassien down when I first arrived to their part of the world, a place that seems so far away now. But he was forgiven by the prince, and they had joined forces to accept me.

Vaerynn smacks the wall, and the windows rattle. "Close your mouth or see it sewn shut. If you become a problem, I will take back my kindness of having Brekter and Kratorr stand *outside* the door during this intimate procedure."

Gerakon clears his throat. "This is a device that will be inserted within your vulvar cavity and expanded. Its claws will pierce your tissues and take samples of blood, flesh, and hormone levels."

I gasp inwardly. Perhaps he had the right idea about getting it over with without much talk.

"It's uncomfortable, painful." His eyes flick up and lock onto Scarlet's, who takes him in right back. "But—" he tears his gaze away from my beautiful best friend and prepares the tool once more toward Mary-Shelly's quivering flesh. "You will survive it." He pushes it in, and she groans deeply, her back arching. I look away and bite my lip as her scream rises.

The seconds tick by, and Mary-Shelly's cries become desperate. That tool isn't meant for humans, but all I can do is hope the procedure ends soon, because they're going to do this whether we fight them or not.

"Please," Mary-Shelly pleads, her pale legs shaking. Strange sounds chirp from the tool as though receiving information, and Gerakon pushes a sequence of buttons on the handle.

"How necessary is this?" asks Sybil, her voice an octave too high. "Can't we just try to have a baby for you? Why isn't that good enough—"

Blond Alice jumps out of bed and flings herself against the window. She bounces off the bars and flies backward. Vaerynn screams for the backup that waits on the other side of the door.

"Stay perfectly still!" Gerakon cries out as he gathers readings from the device that begins beeping severely. Mary-Shelly cries quietly, her face squeezed in pain, but she doesn't move amidst the chaos. Brekter storms inside, followed by Kraetorr, the big brute. "I do not understand why this is hurting the woman so much," says the Koridon scientist. "Something is wrong."

I'm already kneeling over Alice before fully absorbing what Gerakon said. I brush golden strands from the angry flush of her face and reveal a lump forming on her forehead. "Please," I say, holding her hand, "please don't fight them! *Love* them. *Win* them. You have the power in this moment to change the lives of everyone you love." She shudders out a soft cry. "And you will love, too," I say. "More than you ever thought capable."

"But I love Tiberius already!"

"You—" Surely she meant her husband, Oliver, and not the Hollow's-Eve time leader of our village? Her determined expression undoes my confusion. "I didn't mean the love of a man." I move away from her unintended reveal. "You will have a child, Alice."

Vaerynn picks up blond Alice by her throat and flattens her onto the bed. "This one is obviously weak in the head," she says. "You might want to record this incident in her evaluation."

Gerakon removes the device from Mary-Shelly and inserts it into a cylindrical tube while Kraetorr and Brekter remove her clothing.

"I asked you to do this with dignity. With strength," says Vaerynn. "I knew it was too much to ask of you weak animals."

She shoots Brekter a look that says, *Why are we doing this again?*

The males watch us as Mary-Shelly's stomach is examined, her waist is measured and her breasts are prodded and pulled at. Gerakon swipes his fingers through the air and orange symbols light up where he touches. "How often do you have blood discharge from your womb?" he asks.

Mary-Shelly shrugs with streaks lining her face. "Do you mean my menstrual?"

He blinks pointedly and touches her lower abdomen. "From here, how often do you bleed?"

"Usually every month. Unless, well, sometimes it ceases." She crosses her arms over her chest and turns her head toward the window. "We sometimes find ourselves with very little food and starving. It doesn't come during those times."

"Do you have any maladies? Any abnormalities throughout life?"

"I feel fine. Always have."

"Have you conceived before?" he asks.

A sob racks through her shoulders in reply.

"She doesn't have any children," says Glenda hesitantly. "None of us do."

"That doesn't mean she has never conceived before." He pulls her up to face him. "Has your belly ever held a child?"

Her mouth opens in a silent cry and she shakes her head. "They took it from me."

"Who?" Gerakon squints and tips his head.

"We aren't allowed to have children. Back where I come from."

"Are you saying that you have had a life ripped from your womb prematurely?"

She closes her eyes and swallows hard, slumping as though the life once taken from her has been stolen once again.

"Hmm," he sits back and peers at Vaerynn. "There may be damage to her body. This may complicate future pregnancies."

"What do you mean?" She sits up, her small, pale breasts mottled from the cold. "They said I would be unscathed afterward, but it hurt. Oh, it hurt so badly!"

"Lie down," says Gerakon. "I am sorry to scare you. Worry not about this until the tests yield the results." He rearranges the glowing symbols in the air before him. "Her date is three days from now."

Vaerynn tosses Mary-Shelly's dress at her. "Next. This one here." The female motions toward Glenda, who flings herself back and bunches the blanket in her fingers.

"You can stick that thing inside me, but I'll tell you right now that I have always been sick. I won't survive being bred. Maybe not even by a man, let alone your species."

Gerakon searches her small, frail body. "What sickness do you suffer from?"

"My lungs flare up and I can barely force air inside. And when Yule Tide season comes I often fall sick with infection for weeks."

"What does she speak of?" asks Kraetorr, those haunting eyes swallowing Glenda.

"Their flesh is subject to foreign invaders," says Gerakon, "as well as genetic defects such as *asthma*, as it is called."

Vaerynn rips Glenda's head back by her hair to lay her down. "And this is what you would turn us into. Weak, daily tortured beings."

"We get sick, yes," Scarlet says. "But I still want to be here. I want to live even if it means I won't be happy all the time. It's worth it."

"We will continue with the test, *havistonn*," the Koridon female says.

"She is very small." Gerakon holds the device loosely, as

though it has transformed into a venomous creature that may bite at any time. "There may be a question of whether she can carry a Koridon child or not as it is."

"*Dividond bakkis*," she hisses. "We have our orders."

Kraetorr backs against the wall, his chest moving up and down rapidly. He wipes beads of sweat from his forehead and opens his mouth, but nothing comes out.

"Perhaps the males who aren't *havistonns* with masks should remove themsel—" I put my hand over my mouth as Vaerynn spreads Glenda's knees and Gerakon shoves the alien device into her depths. Her pained gasp pierces the air. He activates the claws and she bites her lip to stifle the sob bubbling up in her throat. Her breath sucks in and out, wheezing, rasping...

8

K raetorr braces himself against the wall.

Vaerynn snaps her head up and eyes him curiously, but Gerakon pays no attention, studying the symbols appearing in the air as Glenda's readings populate.

"Stop the test—" Vaerynn manages, but it's too late. Kraetorr takes Gerakon by the back of the head and slams him down. A beast possessed, his knuckles blanch, squeezing the young doctor's throat. Vaerynn shouts and shoves him away and his body falls, but he's back up in an instant, locked on Gerakon for blood. Brekter holds him while Gerakon scrambles up, but the attacking Koridon breaks away and strikes him again and he flies down next to Scarlet.

Her big emerald gems fill with determination as she edges in front of Gerakon, an arm held out protectively in front of him.

What is she doing? She stands, a ten-year-old opposing Aslan the lion!

The big beast huffs wildly, and as he reaches for Scarlet I imagine claws preparing to rip her face off. But he stops, the madness flickering out. His breath settles, and his mighty form backs away, giving Vaerynn and Brekter the opportunity to seize him.

"I lost myself!" he roars, his entire body rigid. "What is happening to me?" They drag him out of the room as he yells with pure torment.

Larger than the others and built with iron rippling from beneath his skin, he seemed to grow even larger somehow with the instinct to protect her. What if she really is given to him as a mate? I turn away with intrusive thoughts of her thin form beneath him, a powerful thrust ripping her in two, the snapping of bones within his fevered grip...

Gerakon stands with bewilderment splashing his face at a frozen in shock Scarlet. "What has happened?" he asks her, his mask on the floor.

She turns around slowly, not a ripple of fear tainting her spirit. "I—" Gerakon towers above her, but she lifts her chin to meet his gaze. Her mouth squeezes shut, and she shakes her head. "I wanted to stop him." Her words sound weak compared to her unwavering presence, and the space between them sparks. Gerakon sniffs the air, and his breath quickens. He moves toward her and she flinches, severing their near-contact, but the intensity between them thickens the air.

Vaerynn storms back in, long hair flowing around her shoulders, and stops dead in front of them. "*Havistonn*, you must continue. I tire of this, finish quickly."

He shakes his head as though waking from a dream and puts his mask back in place. "This is madness. These women are not what I thought—"

"You agreed to this. You wanted this," she says, closing the space between them. "Do what you have sworn. Enough of the small one. You will now study—" She nods past him toward Scarlet. "*Her*."

Brekter steps inside. "No more males should be allowed inside this room during examinations."

"And what of you?" Vaerynn asks. "How will you control yourself when Calypso's turn comes?"

Stormy eyes flick up at her wickedly. *Because he's already had me today.* The spell has been lifted just enough to cut through the fog and return his senses. Though with him, it never feels like desperation or instinctual possession. Just rage.

Gerakon picks up the fallen device. "I will not continue until speaking with the leader about what has happened here."

"It's fine," says Scarlet. She scoots back on the bed and pulls a sheet over her waist. "Just do it. I'd rather the nightmare be over." Gerakon approaches, his eyes moving over her form as though seeing for the first time.

After a brief hesitation, he bends between her legs and taps her thigh. "O-open. Please." She immediately spreads them for him. Placing the device under the sheet, he penetrates her and beads of sweat form at his hairline. With a tensed jaw, Scarlet's bare feet dig into the bed.

"So, you're their doctor or something in this society?" she asks, straining to sound normal.

"I am more of a geneticist, as you would call it. It is the reason I have come here," his gaze flicks to me. "Because I could no longer stand by as my people died."

"My people die all the time too." She grimaces, but unlike the others, not a single tear slips down her cheek. "You have taken much."

Gerakon grunts his disapproval. "We only wish to live."

"So that's why we're here. Your last chance."

Vaerynn tugs strands of her light hair, jerking her head to the side. "You do not understand anything, animal. Do not speak again." She shoves her cheek aside, then circles the room. "Make no mistake, we are using your inferior bodies as test subjects, and most of you will likely die. But it is an honor you will accept with grace."

"An honor?" I say, and she spins around. "You are larger, more densely muscled beings, but what does that matter here? You wish to survive. Have families. Well, we only have weaker bodies because our minds are incredible." We love, laugh, and find joy in everything, a perfect balance, and I'm baffled at how this female is nothing like us. She can't see us at all.

"Useless and unbearably unevolved," she says.

Scarlet's readings come to life in dazzling symbols that populate in an unseen database of some kind. "They have a beauty about them though," Gerakon says, closing out the moving symbols and removing the tool. He brushes his fingers along her leg and follows the racing goosebumps down to her ankle. "She provokes a tactile sensation in my fingertips. A softness that seems to stroke my nerve endings." Vaerynn breaks him from his trance with a disgusted groan, and he steps back quickly. "Her date of ripening will arrive in fifteen days," he says, turning away.

"Look at you," says Vaerynn, again focusing on me. "You are what we have to endure to stay alive. Our beloved children will have to look like *you*. Our only hope is to breed most of the human out eventually."

I scoff. "But, you'd have to breed them the second they became fertile. One half-Koridon bred to a full Koridon, then continue the cycle! *We* may not survive this, let alone very young ladies."

"A chance we're willing to take," she retorts. Never having had a child of her own, she must have no perception of the love a mother is capable of. If they take our children away young to be mated and possibly obliterated, we will never stop fighting. There will never be peace.

"This isn't the way." I stand up and touch my belly. "The

only way all of us will find happiness is to coexist. Love and cherish each other." I note the indignation in her crooked frown and sigh. "You don't understand those words, do you?"

"Understood but forgotten by superior minds."

"You understand it, all right. That's more than a dog would. But then to ignore its power... well, that's worse than a dog."

She bolts toward me and I wait for the impact. Instead, she cracks a grin an inch from my own. "You will learn. When that prince of yours comes to find you bedded by his enemy, there will be blood. And you will be reduced to the incubator you are meant to be."

"Is he alive?" That is all I care about. The way she smirks, I fear she only taunts me.

"Gerakon," she says without moving an inch. "Let us find out what is going on in this one's belly." She shoves me, and my back hits the bed.

"This procedure will not benefit her if she is carrying." Gerakon holds the spiked metal tool to the side. "It may even hurt the process."

She puts her hands on her hips. "Let us see if her chemistry and anatomy are truly worthy of being the savior of our people."

Brekter steps forward, tilting his head in ambivalence.

"For her," says Gerakon, "we shall see what lies inside." He takes a different tool from the table, and fear spikes through my chest. He raises the strange device over my belly. "Lift your gown."

A cobalt liquid, thick like metal, floats out toward my cringing flesh. It forms a thin, sharp object, then the tip buries in below my belly button. I fight to stay still, the pressure boring in, my knuckles white, gripping the bed. A sound rings out and a holographic image projects from the device. In vivid color, it displays the whooshing of blood through tiny vessels, through living tissue, and though it's a strange sight, somehow I know it's my womb. He clicks a few buttons and a tiny mass appears in the air and spins.

"There. A child *is* forming." He touches buttons in sequence again and the mass changes, growing bigger and taking form. "Using advanced DNA development, you can see how the machine is predicting its next sequence of growth." The image spins slowly, a small, undifferentiated mass, then develops into a fully formed, perfect baby. Its fist opens and shuts in the fluid, and the chest vibrates with a small hiccup. Mary-Shelly puts her hand to her mouth, and me... I go numb.

"If my theory is correct, the child will be ready to deliver safely between eight and ten months," Gerakon says as the holographic growth from bundle of cells to child begins again. "It is male."

My heart drops, the numbness transforming into fire. A male has never been born by a human before. Koridon women have steel bodies that won't burst from the inside out, but will my half-breed body be able to endure it? Brekter moves to my side. "Whose is it?" I ask.

"That will take longer." Gerakon clears his throat and makes the floating image vanish. More readings come in with strange tinkling sounds, data I can't begin to understand. "I will study the results." He removes the needle and puts the machine away.

I was secretly holding out hope that there was no pregnancy. *Free* from the unknown of conceiving this child. Brekter knew it. And he *knows* it's his, too. I'm ashamed because it's ungrateful, but I mourn my youth, feeling my energy seep into the growing baby to give it new life that drains my own. This could kill me even though I'm half-Koridon. What parts are human? How does it work? Did I inherit a strong enough womb to encase the unnaturally strong being?

Do I have an efficient enough circulatory system to support it, or will my heart give out? Just when I thought dying young was behind me.

"How much do your males usually weigh at birth?" I ask.

"Twelve pounds. Minimum." Gerakon places a hand on my knee, the gesture touching from such a cold male. "I will do all I can to help you through this."

"Scarlet," I whisper in the dark. Moonlight glitters down from the glass ceiling and floods over us, such beauty transforming the horror of our situation.

Her head lolls toward me.

"Are you all right?"

She lifts a hand, just to have it yanked back down by her shackles. "Great."

"Why did you jump in front of that monster today?" Kraetorr's snarling face reanimates across my memory, reminding me that he could have ripped right through her to get to Gerakon.

She lets out a shuddery breath. "I don't know. It's as though my body moved without me. I don't know."

"He stopped dead," I say. "You calmed him when no one else could."

Being thrown together is like oil bursting upon the fire, an explosive combination not easily contained as it burns through everything. How will we ever live together without being in constant danger? Gerakon wore a mask to prevent possession by our pheromones, the drug that dances through a male's blood, and Brekter takes his aggressive attraction out on me as he pleases. I don't know what's going to happen to all of us, but having children in such an environment is psychotic.

Scarlet's silent for a few moments. "When Alexander and his men hurt us in the woods that night, I think that was the day I died." The leaders of our village were supposed to be trustworthy, but he dragged us out of our beds and flayed our innocence open before the night. She's changed since that happened, giving me this feeling with every move, every word, that at any moment she'll burst out of her pale skin. The lively girl who laughed easily as long as it was something mischievous had gone, her spirit vanished.

"You didn't die, though," I say. "You just have to find a reason to live again."

"I know," she says with a note of laughter lighting up her darkness. "And that reason is why I found myself standing against the scariest creature I've ever come in contact with. What in the name of hell did I really plan to do?"

"Oh, my friend. You're bonding to Gerakon. That's wonderful." Everyone's a mess, our chemistries mixing and bubbling over, but this is the beginning of everything. We are.

"If it's him who wants to mate me, I can take whatever comes. But how can I have such hope that he can be mine? We have no control over anything here."

"Because he felt it too. It was obvious by the way he looked at you. The way he touched you. And you heard all that about how he was *swooning over the feel of your skin*. Having only heard terrifying stories growing up about the monstrous enemy out in the forest, it's confusing, right? Your heart wrenching for the enemy's touch?"

"You're a fool," says blond Alice. "They're going to rip us to pieces. By their cocks or by their horrible spawn. We're nothing but experimental monkeys to them, and we're going to die."

"Alice, go back to sleep," I say. "Stop scaring them."

"They should know the truth!"

"And what of *your* truth today?" asks Jane, her mousy voice *too* sweet. She moves to fold her hands in front of her stomach like she usually does, but her chains remind her to stay still. "Do you really sleep with old Tiberius?"

"Of course not. I hit my head really hard." Blond Alice closes her eyes. "I was out of my mind, now goodnight."

Ehh, love is such a skewed subject in our villages. It wouldn't surprise me at all if fatherless Alice did fall in love with an older man. What is love, anyway, but something we greatly need from the opposite sex only to be denied by our own laws to protect us?

"The truth of the matter is that we aren't sure of anything yet," says Scarlet. "But we're writing history."

"They look like Vikings," says Sybil. "Don't they remind you of the history books? The long braided hair and eyes that reflect a love for only blood and violence?"

"Except Vikings weren't eight feet tall," says black-haired Alice with a nervous chuckle.

"You don't know," Sybil replies. "We hardly know anything."

"How do you think they're pairing us?" asks Glenda, her voice shaky. After what Kraetorr did today, it's a wonder if it helped or hurt his chances of having her. I wouldn't be surprised if they did mate the two, his enormous strength mixed with her slight frame and weakness. If she did survive a pregnancy, it would still result in a genetically superior child. In size, anyway.

"Well, if it's based on their preference—" Blond Alice snickers, and I know she'll slit her own throat before she lets Arek have her.

I have no idea how it will be decided. For Scarlet, I hope the Koridon male chooses, but for Glenda, I hope they don't.

"Kassien is a prince, so he could claim me by his own decree. But look what happened anyway." Brekter lurks somewhere close by, I can feel it, and the thought of having his child inside makes my stomach wretch. I will surely be cast aside by Kassien then. I suppose he's good at that anyway. I wonder if he'll take a new bride then. maybe blond Alice? She's a beauty, why wouldn't he want her?

Being forced to wed Brekter is my worst nightmare, I don't know what I'll do, but I won't run away. I'd rather endure his massive cock up my slit and his ugly words than ever abandon my child. My mother didn't abandon me, and I'm sure she could have, sure the village leaders would even have encouraged it. Maybe they wanted to leave me out in the forest to be eaten by wild dogs.

Light cracks across the room, and I squint toward the hulking shadowed male. My pulse jumps in fear of Brekter coming to me now, here with my friends. If he slipped my dress up and forced me to mate, I suppose I'd have to keep quiet and not fight as to keep from scaring the others.

Clever bastard.

9

The figure walks across the room, the door shutting quietly behind him, and I can feel the girls' tension thicken. As my fear rises, it gives way to *fury*, and I realize blond Alice is completely right. I've been fighting it, so swept up in my mixed feelings for Kassien and his people. We don't owe this race anything. In fact, it's a travesty that they've taken us against our will to be sex slaves. What right do they have? Brekter says there's no time to romance us, that they will do what they have to do in their last hour.

Well, so will I.

Kassien's as mad as the rest of them, but at least he understood that some peace needed to exist between us. As I lie here, chained to the bed and Brekter's presence looming ever closer to take what he wants of me, I'm angry at the prince as well. We wouldn't be here if he'd just left me alone to die that night. They'd be safe. I'm done trying to be an example to these girls. They deserve better than being told they have no worth except as brood mares. I pull at the shackle violently until it carves in, bruises trickling under my skin.

Someone in the room whimpers.

"No. Stop!" Blond Alice shifts in the sheets, a pained cry pulling from her throat.

"You are the one chosen for me," comes the unknown voice, and in the dark, my imagination strikes up. It could be Arek, though he seems to hate her as much she hates him. But then, maybe hate excites him.

"I'll never belong to anyone," she bites out, and her free hand shoves against his mass. "Get away! *No—*" Her desperate moan makes me cringe, a sound of the most blood-curdling defeat.

He grunts and her bed shakes, two forms thrashing, and the girls' screams ring out all around me. Where the hell is Vaerynn? She should be watching over us!

Blond Alice tearfully begs, and the room is alive with panic, but we're helpless. We can do nothing to save her. She braces with unnatural pain, and I remember Brekter's claws into my wrist, the unnatural pressure in an unwilling body. "Whatever Koridon shit you are, get away from Alice or I'll have Kassien execute you!"

The room grows silent and blond Alice takes a sharp breath. "You have no power, half-breed bitch," the Koridon says, and I'm thrilled he's so easily distracted. A cruel laugh shatters the silence.

"I'm a queen being held against her will, and when he comes for me, you're first to die, *Koridon bitch*. Well," I smile into the darkness, "after Brekter."

The male bursts off Alice and his snarling breath blasts against my face. "Perhaps then, it would be fair if I get a turn on you too, before I die."

"Who are you?" I ask, sure he isn't Arek.

"My name is Kjartonn. Learn it well."

"Who in Dante's hell is that?" I ask, trying to fit a name with one of the males I've seen here.

He touches my hair and prods at my face. "I am the commander's oldest son, so you see, I am a prince too."

No, he's not. "What do you want with Alice?"

"Her face. Her cunt. She is pleasing upon the eyes, and the most beautiful woman is mine to claim."

"You dare bed her before the ceremony?"

"What makes you think I will honor a human woman with our sacred traditions?" he growls. "You aren't of our kind. We think maybe we will all take turns upon you. One monstrous cock after another knotting you until you can no longer fight. No longer *move*." His largeness presses into me as he speaks with excitement.

I jerk my head up and bash it into his nose. He hardly flinches, but I'm quite happy anyway, embracing the sharp pain in my forehead. "Wild animals do the same to their own. They sink their claws into the female's back and mate her as she roars. You aren't worthy of us higher beings."

Claws dig into my neck, sharp pain cutting off my voice, caught in the lion's paw. His tongue twists with curses as I choke, but through my tears I grin. He won't kill me, not with the consequence he would face by ending the first child conceived in years.

He releases my throat and runs his fingers down my lips. "You know what I would like to do to her? Your pretty blond friend?" He takes a deep breath, and his hand moves into his pants. "First I will mount you, and then the rest, one by one. It will make my tissues *swell* with desire, my knot growing bigger and bigger for the next." He works his cock in his palm. "Then I will put it in *her*, my betrothed mate, forcing the largest knot possible into her tight walls that milk me while she screams."

The chain breaks as my fist flies and connects into his jaw.

My knuckles crack upon impact. He rips my bed clothes up, then my drawers down. "Yes, fight me."

A light flares up in the room, and Kjartonn flies to the ground.

Vaerynn lands another foot, this time into his crotch, and he bellows. "These girls are not to be touched."

He scrambles up, holding himself in pain. "My father will hear of this."

"Yes," Vaerynn says, circling him with the torch. "You were abusing these humans, ones that may be vital to our existence, and he will need to know what you have done."

Kjartonn peers toward us, hate splashed across his face. "Edjen pretentis—"

"So they can understand," Vaerynn cuts him off, and I'm surprised at her consideration.

"I did not plan to hurt them," he says quickly. "But they fill my nostrils, their scents haunting the breeze..."

"Each one is to be matched and placed with a high-ranking male. Your body must not desecrate theirs in time for the ceremony."

"One of them is already mine. I will work her in if I please." Kjartonn touches blond Alice through the sheet, and I can feel her fear multiply.

"No, you will not." Vaerynn pulls him backward until he's on the other side of the door. "Commander Drakon has not given the final word, and until he has, she is not yours."

"Until her bedding ceremony then," he says, hitting the door open. "I will be saving it up for her, how about that? What a show it will be."

10

KASSIEN

"Tanak, *entevego levedend...* my friend." My words are a rasping sound that hurt every fiber of my being to make. "We are lost. Forgive me." He was good. He fought by my side for Calypso and was kind to her even when being forced to mate her in front of his wife.

Everything has turned black, and I know wherever my DNA reoccurs, or when, all the ones beloved to me *here* will be lost forever. Because there are no parallel universes. Just universes and randomness.

I float through the darkness, my consciousness nothing more than far off dreaming, and I muse at the feeling of death, the feeling of my essence drifting. It wouldn't feel the -400 degree blackness of space, or have the need to suck in choking oxygen deprivation. It's that chaotic dream state: the soul's consciousness, experienced when the brain shuts off in sleep, and now this is all that is left of me. I will not feel the joys of the flesh again for centuries. Longer, probably. I will not remember my lost child. My friends. My Calypso.

Muffled voices pull at my transcendent thoughts and bring them to the surface. I wake, and big eyes come into focus. "Calypso?" I mutter.

The dream figure pulls away. "It's him."

My limbs feel like a thousand pounds as I reach for her, and pain seizes my movement.

"Don't move. You're still on the brink of death, but I've cleaned your wounds and stitched them." The voice is unfamiliar to my awakening ears, and I blink several times to identify my savior. "I'm not Caly," she says. "I'm her mother." She places a cup to my dry lips. "Persephone."

My lady's mother. Here, saving my big, nearly invincible ass from death's icy grip. Of course it would be Calypso's mother. I'm thankful to her, but there's no time for niceties. "Get the healing tool, it should be in the hospital bay." The stitches pull as I force myself up and the lady easily pushes me back down. "Woman, I am warning you—"

"There's nothing here," she says, "but," she signals to someone behind her, "go see if you can find this tool he speaks of." The scuffling of feet draws my blurry gaze to the door, where another unknown figures stands.

"It is silver, with a handle and cylindrical end." I cough, my lungs shredding. "Tenak, my second," I choke. "Where is he?"

She dabs my head with a wet cloth. "Where's my daughter?"

Her words stab me deep. I love Calypso in many ways, but one of which is as someone precious whom I want with all my soul to protect. "I will get her. I swear to you."

"You will? In this state?" She presses sharp fingertips into the hook wound beneath my collar bone and I push into it, ignoring the fire in my lungs with every inhale. This time, I sit up quite successfully and she brings her hand to her lips. "Nothing will stop me from getting to her. Pain is nothing. I thrive on it," I growl, close to her creamy complexion.

A slight smile breeches her lips. "Good. She told me you love her, is that true?

"She made it back to the village?" I have the urge to embrace this woman with auburn streaks and chocolate eyes the same exotic shape of my Calypso's. My *wife's*.

"Someone tricked her," says Persephone. "She led them straight to us, but not before she told me where you had been keeping her."

Brekter. I jump to my feet and ball my fists, pulsing with pure aggression. "The slow death I promise him will scream through the ages."

She wrings out a bloody rag in the basin. "They would have taken all of us to enslave or worse, but Calypso negotiated using the life within her belly."

"She holds my child?" A wave of emotion strikes at my core where even the prospect of death and the torture of steel hooks could never touch.

"She believes it."

A young man enters the room and shakes his head. "There's nothing like what he described here." Tall, with bronzed skin over a well-developed form, I wonder what Calypso means to him. Dusk's haunting last rays of light bleed through the transparent walls of the ship, and I try to understand how many days I have been asleep. A nervy shiver racks through me, and my legs weaken.

"Here." Persephone catches my dizzy lean and helps me back to the cot. You have a fever, an infection." She forces a foul-tasting liquid onto my tongue. "This will help."

"Of course I do. Look at this primitive medical care." The tiny tissue healers of our technology have replaced need for medicinal liquids or disease agents, because the cellular bots rebuild the damaged tissue immediately. No time for infection to develop.

"And without these crude stitches and bacteria-fighting funguses grown by my people with immense care, you wouldn't make it another day." She sloshes the rag over my forehead, sending cold water into my eyes. "By the Queen of Heart's axe, are all of these bastards like this?"

"Who is this Queen of Hearts?" I ask, spitting out foul-tasting water and wondering just how many hearts she has cut out to be given such a name. "Is that one of your leaders? I would like to speak with her immediately."

"It's me," Persephone says with a snicker, "and I'm quick to give death sentences at the most minor of offenses."

"Very unwise to tease a desperate being three times your size."

"Hmm. Perhaps," she says, and her shining tongue darts along her bottom lip. "But one such as you would never hurt the mother of whom he loves."

"Never," I agree. I am shined down upon to have her come to me at my last breath and save me. I really should learn to control my temper.

The young man speaks. "What's being done to them, Koridon?"

"Them?" I ask. "They took more than Calypso?"

"Several of the women from the village have been taken." A tremor disturbs the deep steadiness of Persephone's voice.

I turn my head toward the trees that blow softly in the wind through the transparent walls around us. "They are going to force them to be bred and produce offspring."

"Like what you did to Calypso," says the young man.

The exhilarating touch of her kisses upon my skin materialize, and a rush through my veins sends a nasty throb through my head. Yet, I would never trade this feeling. "Yes. But she understood and wanted me to have her so we could build something anew between our people."

"But my sister is ill. She couldn't possibly handle what they're doing to her!" His resonance hits a woeful nerve in me.

"Finn," says Persephone, "Kassien is their prince." She turns her large eyes upon me, and they're so familiar I can see Calypso calling to me through them. "He will get them back. A prince has loyalties, *ways* about him, to conquer."

"Is that what your books say?" The way her shoulders slump makes me regret shaking her hope. "Of course I have countless arsenal at my disposal. I will send word to my rulers and they will come back to see our laws restored. But it will take time."

"Some of them don't have time," says the one Persephone called Finn. "You will have to do better."

"Get Tanak, my second. We will act immediately."

The confusion between them sets my stomach to twisting, and I already know what Persephone will say as she leans in. "I'm sorry, but if you mean the Koridon that hung beside you... He's dead. Had been for days when we pulled you down."

I think of the darkness I'd lived in for days upon days and tried to sort through the different memories in order to find when I lost him. I was delirious. For the life of me, I cannot figure it out. I drag myself out of bed, and they jump back.

"That isn't advisable," the mother says, but I just laugh at her—on the inside, as even the slightest chuckle would jar my torn flesh, and worse, hurt my soul.

"Get back, woman. Advise yourself... not to anger me." I limp toward the front of the ship to the dusty control panel and switch on communications. A simple code is shot into the universe, straight to the divine sovereigns, asking them to come immediately. It is time they returned to the planet they abandoned and deal with their children.

I am so tired of the dark, blurry nothing that overtakes me without my permission. Yet it is all I see for days more until light finally peeks through the eternal midnight.

"Awake," a voice in my language echoes, and finally, with it treading the surface like a dream, I do. I blink hard in disbelief at the pale, beautiful image of the distant relative who sits before me.

Sitting up, I immediately question how long I've been out. With the sovereign here, it could have been years. "Eladia, *drist*—"

She touches my head, and instant calm washes over me. Then Persephone appears behind her, and my soul splits in half with panic again.

"You passed out at the front of the ship after ripping your stitches open," Calypso's mother says. I touch the perfect skin on my chest and look at the lady sovereign.

"You healed me," I say, still pawing at the place where the wound had slashed to the bone. "How are you here? It must have been merely *days* since I called you." The nanomedic tool sits on her lap, and though a dull ache still lingers, it's nothing compared to the primitive stitching and poor medication the humans used on me. I am grateful, it saved my life, but I probably would have died eventually. It would have taken longer, though, and a few days is all I would have needed to drag my half-dead carcass across the world and save her before crashing face-first into the ground.

Eladia nods. "We were summoned weeks ago, your time. By whom, we do not know." Rigidly straight-backed and motionless, it's apparent how different she not only *appears* compared to a human woman, but also the power that emanates from her being.

"Perhaps it was one of my clan, when I chose to take a human for my mate." I don't acknowledge her horror at my revelation and don't plan to discuss any of my decisions in detail. "Eladia, we are not thriving here. While you have traveled to distant worlds, ours has been dying. As leader here, I have resorted to continuing our lines with the people of Earth."

She crosses her arms over the metallic blue robe she wears, long fingers out straight. " This is forbidden, to crossbreed with a different species. There are reasons for this, Kassien. We still have been unsuccessful in finding a developed water planet that we can survive on. There are things in these places you would not believe. *Lethal* predators, even for us, ice ages, scorching by the sun, setting fire to every living thing on the planet every two years... *oh,* the dangers are uncountable. *Unthinkable.*"

Even when a planet is biologically friendly, beings that have no adaptation there—those who haven't grown and changed with the environment—find themselves constantly fighting. "I need your help to undo what I have done. Innocents now suffer for my choice. The rulers in the west have enslaved women, forced themselves upon them—"

She stands abruptly and turns her back. "A travesty against the natural order of the universe. You have set things in motion that can never be undone."

Unable to understand our tongue, Persephone and Finn stare daggers at me. Instead of letting them pierce my heart with anger, I silently send this promise to them: *I will die to save her. I would die to save them all.*

"As you know..." Eladia takes from inside her garb a silver

cylinder and a blasting weapon with a chamber of moving dark matter. My spirit catches fire at the sight of such fearsome power. And the cylindrical weapon—well, its chillingly destructive abilities—sends a wave of excitement down my spine.

"I had to come here alone in the accelerated particle transport to get here quickly. But I brought these." She hands them to me, and with a flick of my wrist, I engage the dark matter blaster's firing mechanisms. With a cosmic buzzing, a beam of silvery light aims at the wall behind her. Finn and Persephone duck, but my divine sovereign only smiles. "I trust you can handle the situation with these?"

I stare into the cylinder's gleaming splendor. "Oh yes. These will do nicely."

11

As the sun rises, I blink away strange noises that echo in my dreams. As I fully wake, the sounds don't cease. I sit up in bed, the animalistic grunts and whines jolting my nerves, and peer toward blond Alice's bed. The room stands quiet. I press my ear to the wall and hear two hushed voices as the terrible sounds continue. What the hell do they have planned for us today?

Within minutes, Vaerynn ushers us out of bed, her jaw set more on edge than yesterday. Without looking at us directly, she demands we dress in leather garments that criss-cross over our breasts and matching shorts that tie closed in the front. They're similar to what I'd seen other Koridon females dress in when I was with Kassien. "Where are we going?" I ask, noting Glenda's small form as she cinches the long strings at her waist to the extreme.

"*Trimanus zer varnot,*" she replies with a smirk.

"So helpful." I shove past her. I might as well take on whatever waits down there first, before it eats my friends.

Descending the stairs, I don't see anything formidable but

instead smell an array of scents that make my stomach jump for joy. In the dining hall, a shiny rectangular table steams with plates of food, and I stop in the doorway, unsure of what the catch is. "Sit and eat," Vaerynn says loudly into my ear as she moves past me.

Digging in, as I've heard it called, doesn't begin to describe how we assault our breakfast this morning. I don't know what this all is, but it tastes how I'd imagine breakfast with Marie Antoinette would. Breads, butter, meats so salty and sweet, vegetables that should never taste so good...

Gerakon appears and slips Glenda a bowl of something green, telling her it will strengthen her lungs. With a full belly, I sip on purple X2 tea until it's gone, and then we move out to the land, my bones feeling strong, my blood rushing.

Blond Alice's feet sink into the white sand as she limps with purple discoloration newly blooming upon her arms. I don't know how far Kjartonn got in her last night, and several times I've wanted to say something about it, but I can't bring myself to. I already know how it feels to be forced by a real-life monster, and honestly, I don't want to relive it.

Treading across a wooden trail ascending across the sand, we follow Vaerynn along a snaking river that leads to the ocean, and a tall tree line looms in the distance. The smell of pine and redwood drifts through the air, making me think of home during the cold season. Human slaves in torn clothes pass us as we make our way to the shore, their baskets and cages full of small brown creatures with claws. Their weathered faces and thin bodies remind me of the people back home, the wear of relentless years upon them.

"Today, you begin training," Vaerynn says, the salty breeze blowing her hair back. "You are all thin and weak, but to be Koridon, you must emanate strength. You must have strong bodies to deliver strong children." She points to the great water.

"We will start by fighting the cold, unforgiving sea waters." She steps into the frothy water and spins around, diving backward. Her body glides effortlessly beneath the surface until she disappears. Kassien took me to the lake once, but like me, none of the girls can swim. Finally, Vaerynn reappears, water shining down her olive skin as she moves with the grace of a sea goddess.

"The cold will pierce your skin at first, but as you fight the waves, it will numb. You must feel it wash underneath you and use it to propel yourself along the surface." As she swims, I watch her arms float out beside her like a butterfly, and her feet kick furiously. "You will get tired," she says, "but you will not stop lest the deadly undertow pull you down. Go out into the deep until you hear me call you back. Then and only then may you swim back to shore." She then repeats it in Koridon as part of our learning to be one of them.

"Vaerynn, wait." I speak without thinking and touch my belly, a need to protect my unborn child a new and surprising feeling. "What if—"

She puts a hand up to stop me. "You sometimes forget that you have Koridon in you. You will survive a rough swim, and you will be expected to face every challenge the others are in order to strengthen and condition your body to both carry and deliver a large and unnaturally strong being. However," she gazes past me and I turn around to find Brekter at my back, "the child will never be compromised. Should you fail, one of us will save you." Her unforgiving expression warns me of far worse consequences than death if I do.

I take Scarlet's hand. "Don't fight the training. If nothing else, building our strength will help us fight them."

She passes on the message to black-haired Alice, and we all stand hand in hand, empowered, our unique life forces flowing from one another.

The water is liquid ice against my feet, but the memory of floating euphoria from my swim with Kassien drives me forward and I run. The waves lap over my waist, and I suck in a breath.

"Go now, all of you!" cries Vaerynn. "Give your bodies to the sea!"

I wade out until I can no longer touch the murky bottom and kick my legs to stay afloat. "Swim!" Vaerynn's voice echoes and I move farther out, watching out for Glenda. Waves knock me about, and, breathing hard, putridly salty water creeps past my lips.

"You are all stronger than you can imagine!" Vaerynn's voice drifts from the shore. "It will hurt, but you will push past the pain! Survive!"

Turning around to float on my back, I toss my head around to check for the others. Heads pop up through the water, moans infusing the air. "Go out farther!" Vaerynn yells. "Come back before I say, and I will swim you out even farther and leave you for the sharks!"

"Help," comes a weak voice to my left. Jane's head bobs under, the water washing over, and I reach out to bring her back up. "I can't do this, I'm going to drown," she chokes into my face as I hold her up by the hair at the nape of her neck.

"No, look." I float how Kassien taught me, and after struggling and thrashing, she finally steadies upon her back. Each inhale levels me in the cool air, each exhale drags me down a bit too far, but my limbs rest, my lungs relax.

A rough pull on my ankle drags me under and water floods my throat. As I fight the bruising grip, everything's black, the world cold, and my lungs scream. Finally, the grip loosens and I break the surface with a gasp. Vaerynn floats effortlessly beside me. "No resting. You will swim. You will swim for your life, or I will take it from you."

"Die slowly," I fight to say, coughing out salt water violently. "Or you kill me quick."

"Yes! Now move."

She hits me in the side, and for some reason a laugh inappropriately bursts out. "Hold on, I'm thinking."

Time moves by in slow motion, minute after agonizing minute of yearning for dry land and soft sand to collapse onto. Both Jane and Glenda are dragged back up from a watery death over and over, at the brink of failure time and again, and I'm sure someone is meant to die today. The sun hangs in the middle of the sky by the time Vaerynn stops preventing us from dragging our useless bodies back onto the shore, and Vaerynn throws the two weaker girls out beside the rest of us. We've all made it back alive. I put my fingers near Glenda's mouth to check for breath. Yes. All of us made it out of there somehow.

As Vaerynn chased us around the ocean, I hated her, and planned to conceal a kitchen knife somewhere next time to pull out and paint the water red with her sliced open flesh. But I also longed for her strength. A part of me wants to train hard and see what I'm capable of, to discover what parts of me are Koridon. As I replace the nutrient X2 from the purple flower tea, I could become the thing I was always meant to be. I want that part of me so badly. I'm a hybrid, so what am I, really? Could there be a synergistic effect between the two different sets of genes mingling and sparking within that I'm not aware of?

Beside me, Scarlet's cheek presses into the wet sand and she smiles through ragged breaths.

A slave lays a blanket on the sand and sets down a basket. At first, I believe it to be a man, shaved head peeling, red from the sun and fingers cracked as they serve us each a plate of food, but it's a woman. She's probably too old to breed or deemed to be barren. I can't wrap my head around having slaves, and the books I read containing such poor souls always seemed like pure fiction to me. I could never be so selfish or lazy to do this to another person. Vaerynn stands motionless over us, not eating, not resting, a goddess-like silhouette with her back to the sun. *Unless they really pissed me off*, I revise, becoming quite entertained by thoughts of that Koridon bitch bowing to me.

"What is this?" Mary-Shelly asks, holding up a piece of white meat with red skin. "It smells sort of like the fish our men bring back from the river but—"

"I don't care," I say and bite into mine. "I'm starving."

The others eat too, their eyes rolling back, juices splashing the sand. Blond Alice picks at hers, staring past her lunch into nothingness.

My muscles screaming, I sit next to her. I have to say something about last night, even if it hurts me, because this is bigger than me. "It doesn't hurt as much if you accept it."

"Get away from me," she says, tossing the white meat into the dirt. "I will never accept it. I would rather let him tear me to shreds than open my legs willingly. To any of them." She scoots away from me.

"Maybe the mean one won't be chosen for you after all," says Glenda.

"Right, maybe *you'll* get him instead," blond Alice says back to her.

Last night, when Kjartonn visited us, my anger and desperation boiled to the surface. Exhausted and fearing the life growing inside me, I couldn't sleep for hours. Upon morning's arrival, I thought hope would find me again, that I'd be able to imagine a world where they coexist beside us. But I *don't* feel hopeful right now. I only feel hate. Kassien saved me from death but then took me from my home and forced me to wed him. I fell for my captor, but now that the harsh day bathes me in its light, he is still just that: the enemy. Isn't he? I'm so confused about how I'm supposed to feel, one emotion stomping me into the ground and the next elevating me above the clouds.

I just want to sleep.

"I thought we could make the best of this," I say heatedly toward blond Alice. "They're going to force us. These beings will do exactly as they have said, so I thought we could find a way to deal with it." Black clouds move in and shade falls over the land.

"I see no other choice either," says Scarlet.

"There isn't," I say, "but don't betray yourself."

Blond Alice lifts her chin.

"Don't let them change you. We are magnificent, and we will show them." If we're ever going to find peace for our race, we cannot be weak. We have to prove ourselves their equals. They're brutes, and we're only a shadow of the great race we descended from, but that's enough.

Brekter and Arek tread through the sand on each side of a cage, and a low growl permeates its cover as something scrambles around within. The girls look to me and aren't comforted when I turn white, the familiar whining and snarling from this morning finally explained.

"Now you will prove yourself worthy enough to hold within you the life of a Koridon child." Vaerynn laughs cruelly. "Survival of the fittest, I believe your own books teach. A concept I fully agree with."

"What's in the cage?" I ask Brekter.

He stares straight ahead.

"You will run into the forest and be pursued by this transformed animal." she says. "Kill it, before it kills you."

"Without weapons?" asks Scarlet.

"Out in the forest you will find everything you need."

Vaerynn lifts the cover, and the snarling resumes. The feet look human but gnarled and discolored as they shift and claw up the bottom.

Glenda pales and takes a step back. "You can't do this," she says, her breath quickening. "Why would you risk killing us when you need us?"

"Why did you protect us from that beast last night, just to throw us to our deaths today?" I add.

Vaerynn pats the cage top. "I would rather you were dead than be impregnated and bring a weak child into the world. She tips her face up toward the sky. "You don't understand what it is like out there."

"Fuck you!" I yell at them. "You have no right to do this to us!" I slam my weight full-force into the cage, and the Koridons lose their footing and drop it. I come face to face with the gruesome creature as I land on all fours. I shake my head slowly at it, and Vaerynn throws me backward.

"What are you trying to do, stupid human?" she asks, and the truth is, I have no idea. I spring back up and tackle her, bringing rock-hard fists into her face.

"Caly!" shouts Brekter, and steely fingers dig into my shoulders and drag me off Vaerynn.

"Run, all of you!" cries Arek as Vaerynn gets back to her feet. "Meet your destiny!" The click of a key turning in a lock jerks my senses back and sends me tearing across the land. I'm faster than the others and am determined to find something sharp or blunt to hurt that thing. Small rocks and a few twigs litter the ground, so I continue on into the trees.

Light footfalls approach, and behind them a steady *bu-bump, bu-bump,* and then the animal leaps. Brown needles scatter the ground as the snow white creature with a blood-splattered coat jumps onto Glenda's back. She screams and hits the ground, its hideous teeth locking into her shoulder. The other girls continue running, and with gooseflesh riddling my back, I flip around searching for something, *anything* I can put up a fight with. I grab a huge stick next to a fallen tree and strike the monster in the head. It turns on me, big as a horse, and stalks forward, pain in every movement, its vocalizations twisting into frightening sounds. It's mad with suffering, and it will be my pleasure to end it.

Glenda whimpers, and with a damaged arm, tries to crawl. The creature sniffs toward her blood. "No!" I scream, and its head snaps toward me. Hauntingly human looking, it stares at me through the mangled face of a wolf.

"Whoever's in there, listen to me. I *will* kill you!" Thunder cracks overhead, and the thing jumps, hair on end. Its eyes roll around and its tortured cries ring out as it leaps.

12

B lood-stained fangs sink into my leg and I cry out, one hand beating into its skull and the other searching for the fallen stick. It growls as it devours. Brekter leaps next to me, sweat gleaming from his forehead, and reaches toward the creature. Vaerynn appears and hits his rescuing hand away. She shakes her head vehemently, demanding him to wait, but his eyes are as wild as the beast's.

I take hold of the stick and drive it through the creature's eye. Black blood gushes, and it jerks backward with an eerily human cry beneath the animal howl. It shakes its head violently back and forth, slinging blood in my face, and I wield the sharp stick once more, aiming right for the other eye. He looks right at me, and my weapon stops dead. A pang of dread shoots through my belly because I've seen those ocean eyes before. The servant Jonah appears in the forefront of my mind, helping an exhausted Glenda up from the ground. They had embraced each other, a human connection he so desperately needed. The briefest interlude, yet he will forever be endured to me. Teeth snap wildly at my face and I turn my head, his strength breaking through my hold. Brekter shoves Vaerynn away, preparing to take Jonah's head off. *Shove the stick through his neck!* I will myself to prove my worth. *End this!*

Blond Alice appears, a sharp rock braced above her head. "Wait!" I cry before I can stop myself. The poor creature shakes with pain and confusion. Blond Alice pauses and I shake my head, so torn I can't breathe. He's a boy, *one of us*, and I could sense his deeply seeded kindness the moment we met. How could they do this to him? One precious life of so few, and this is how it must end? Tragedy. Heartbreak. Damn them. His teeth drip bloody saliva and his back arches, spine popping and his body bulking abruptly, growing bigger before our eyes.

Dr. Jekyll transforms into the worst form of Mr. Hyde and twists his head toward the fallen Glenda. But there is no compassion for her this time as she lays hurt upon the ground.

Blond Alice smashes the rock into his head, and a hideous *crack* echoes through the trees. The creature spins around and stumbles toward her and she hits it again and again with blood and insanity splashing her soft features. I quickly move to help, but she doesn't stop, not even after the creature stops twitching.

The others shamble slowly back to us and we stand in a circle around the beaten and bloodied monster.

"Glenda!" I fall to her side and move red-stained hair from her face. "We need help!" My screams crack the forest open. Slash marks tear across her ribs, blood dripping into the dirt, and her chest moves erratically.

"Take her," says Vaerynn from behind, and Brekter snatches Glenda into his arms.

"She's going to die," blond Alice says casually. She lies on her side next to the dead creature, her hands cupped under her head.

I remember the instrument Kassien used to heal me after being wounded deeply by the men in the forest. "No, she won't." The tissues are healed by tiny enhanced particles so the bleeding stops. She'll hurt like the dickens, but she'll live.

Vaerynn studies the dead creature, and I realize his body's shrinking. She stands and shakes her head. "The two that stood to fight our creation, you will come with me. The others, with Arek."

"Wait, why? What's going to happen to them?" I ask.

"They must pay for their weakness with blood." Arek and Brekter round them up with the speed of lightning and take them away, and all I can do is watch as they abscond to another hellish event. But this time, I can do nothing.

I swallow hard and ask, "What about Glenda?"

She turns her cruel quicksilver eyes on me. "Come. We still have a long night ahead."

The passing storm casts an eerie glow on the mansion as we walk back. Blond Alice still glows with a spark of madness, and Vaerynn glows with something else. She's a mix of what their people hold in highest regard and doesn't lack for innate cruelness either. Like all the females, she walks how I would imagine a panther does in the Jungle Book: graceful, predatory, preternaturally.

My muscles cry almost as loudly as my heart as we move toward an event that will be of true Koridon fashion, I'm sure, as Vaerynn loves the job she's been bestowed with: *Torture the lower beings into a form that's more appealing to a warrior race.*

"What I do to you, what I make you do," says Vaerynn, "know that it is to make you better. To make you worthy, though you might find it barbaric." Vaerynn stares at the rising full moon as she speaks, mystified by it.

"Did you have a moon and a sun, where you're from?" I ask.

She squints and waves a flying insect away. "Wandering the depths of space for so many years has made me appreciate this atmosphere with its soft warmth—" she breathes in deeply, "clear waters and bright celestials." She lowers her head, and though she doesn't say it, I sense her sadness for all the hope that was presented on this planet, then taken away. I can understand her situation, but I will never forgive how they've chosen to treat the native people here. I sigh, remembering how they'd come to us for help so many years ago, and a war broke out to eliminate them instead. Now look at us—we are all so truly damaged.

Inside the great double doors, the banquet hall is lit with candles, sending dancing flickers across the room. The stairs wind endlessly up to the sunroom, every step a conscious effort, and once there, I am left to wash the blood from my skin.

The banquet table sits full of fresh vegetables and meats, but as the steam swirls about Commander Drakon and his brood of beasts, my stomach turns. I sit beside blond Alice and look up to find Brekter across from me.

"We are pleased to be joined in dinner tonight with our two brightest stars in the sky," says Drakon and brings a chalice to his lips. Several females sit beside me, Efaelty included, her injuries no longer apparent after she was shot at my mating ceremony to her husband. She must despise me, but all I want to do is embrace her. She was kind to me even though it must have killed her, knowing why Kassien needed to do it. Like the other females, she's tall, sleek bodied and wrapped in black silk, her sharp supernatural features so beautiful it's almost haunting.

"You two have already shown yourselves to be of superior quality," Drakon continues, but his attention quickly averts as a servant woman places a plate in front of him. Her gold-flecked brown eyes are nothing like Jonah's, but the terror and pain flashing behind the dead servant's tears are all I can imagine. Strange how young and virile she seems compared to the women I've seen working here. There's an aura of confidence and contentment around her, and a slight smile on her pretty lips. Not a mark on her. She meets Drakon's gaze as she sets another plate down and something sizzles in the air between them. He sinks his teeth into a golden turkey leg and the rest of his heathen lot follow suit.

"What is it you prefer amongst your people as a show of appreciation?" Drakon asks through half-eaten meat clinging to his many sharp canines. He sets the leg down and brings his hands together. "This?" He claps and encourages the others to do the same.

"The word *superior* is subjective, its power only opinion," I say, the applause stopping dead. I meet Drakon's emotionless stare, his expression as hard as his rock-like exterior.

He sits still as death, and though it hurts, I don't turn away. "So you are not superior then?" he asks, his tongue swiping over his lips. "Is that your meaning?"

"No. I'm saying that *you* aren't." I don't know what's come over me—perhaps nearly dying, my friends suffering, just... *everything*, and I don't care anymore!

Brekter raises a brow at me, a warning I ignore and allow a defiant grin to kiss my lips.

After a tense focus, Drakon takes a chunk of red meat and shoves it into his mouth. He chews and spits out a bone, which clatters off my plate. "Small human," he says, "I could crush your skull to pieces in my bare hand. Do not ever speak as though—"

"Great! Do it then, so you can die out along with the rest of your race!" I jump up and take joy in the way Arek's chair flies backward as he gets up so quickly. Kraetorr and the two males beside him freeze with nearly identical expressions of confusion splashing their faces.

"Sit down, little *bitch*," Drakon says.

I kick the chair backward, sending a loud crash echoing through the banquet hall. Scarlet and Glenda touch upon my heart, their laughter, their singing that could bring me from the blackness of despair to the light of day no matter how misty the morning. "Those ladies you refer to as being lesser beings carry with them all the beauty of this world you love so much." I look at Vaerynn and my words shut her up as poison words manifest at the tip of her tongue. "Did you know that each one of us can sew clothing, cook an array of foods you've never imagined, breed livestock, care for and medically treat their ailments? We all know what soil to plant seeds and how to fertilize it when it won't grow any longer. We sing, we dance, we perform out of our old leather-bound books at such lengths the entire village is engulfed in laughter and excitement!" Tears spill down my cheeks, and I tremble. "What can you do?"

Drakon wipes his mouth and crouches, his palms against the table top. "Let us see it then." He signals to Kjartonn, whom I've somehow forgotten about amidst all the chaos. Now that candlelight illuminates him, I see the scar that digs through his forehead and down the right side of his face, making the damaged eye look grotesque. I can almost smell his breath again against my face. "Go get the small one," Drakon commands his first born, then sits back and runs a hand through his long, black locks. "Let us all see how she *dances.*"

My heart drops. "You do this out of cruelness, not to really see, so you won't. It's exactly as I've said." Brekter lifts my chair and sets me down beside him. I dig into his arm and his skin splits, warm red painting my nails in response to his little power play.

He bites my ear and whispers, "Stop resisting the

commander, you foolish child. I do not know if I can save you."

"Making us feel helpless, that is your great power I suppose," I push Brekter's face away. It's as though everything I say is the most meaningless thing ever spoken in the world. What I find so much beauty in is disregarded as the grayest of skies, and lost on the hopelessly blind anyhow.

Kjartonn enters, dragging Glenda by the hair, her body unclothed, and I silently *dare* Kraetorr to do nothing while they torture the girl he has fixated on. Her face pales with unresolved blood loss and new terror, the slash marks across her chest closed but still an angry pink. She whimpers as she's dragged to her bruised feet.

"What a perfectly bestial thing to do," I growl and smack my plate into Kraetorr's. He jumps, panic welling in places he once thought himself heartless and soulless as Glenda falls again. "Let *me* dance or Alice, if you truly wish to see what I speak of!" Blond Alice's sparkling blues flash with warning, but she is beautiful and could enchant them if she chose to, not poor Glenda, who can barely stand.

Drakon tells Kjartonn, "Bring her close." Glenda's pushed forward and Drakon kneads her breast and breathes in the scent of her neck. "Your dear friend tells us you are quite the superior girl," He touches the nakedness between her legs, and her body shakes furiously, "and that you can show us things we have never experienced before."

She lifts her chin and finds me where I sit, and though inside I'm screaming, I give her a confident, wicked smile. With everything I am, I silently beg her to realize her worth as a woman. *They can strip you bare, they can frighten and torture you, but you are so much more than they ever could expect...*

Her weak legs give and she hits the floor.

"Sing! Dance!" cries Drakon. "Show us what a superior creature you are!" Laughter bursts through the room.

"See the stone set in your eyes..." Glenda's soft voice drifts into the air and my breath catches. "See the thorn twist in your side. I will wait for you..." She pulls herself up to her feet. "Sleight of hand and twist of fate, on a bed of nails she makes me wait. And I wait, without you." Satin pink lips part and from them, a storm holding all the pent-up emotion of a thousand lamenting souls comes forth. "With or without you, with or without you I—I can't live, with or *without* you..." Shattering beauty comes to life in the atmosphere around us, her magic realized, and Drakon's emotionless demeanor wavers.

Everyone in the room becomes motionless, connected to an intangible joy tingling in their spirit, though I doubt the Koridons understand what they're feeling at all. The servant girl with the gold-flecked irises wipes tears away, probably having first heard this well-known passed-down song by her father. Gerakon's stoic expression doesn't change, but he watches her in such a way that it would surely hurt him were his attention forced away.

Drakon touches his throat and the perfect composure he displays falters in the clenching of his jaw and his subtle, quick blink. "Impressive, young one," Drakon says, his teeth on edge. Glenda holds her head high, and I want to hear more of her enchanting, powerful voice more than any sound in the world. But the commander tells her, "No more, please. You may take your seat alongside us."

Kraetorr says, "She will sit by me." He takes her hand and she obeys him, walking beside the great beast. He pulls her chair out and adds a gracious amount of food to her plate. A tremble in her reach but with a straight posture and light hair cascading over smudged charcoal eyes, she's a vision of inner strength. She's everything we are, and now they see it. Kraetorr whispers in her ear and she smiles.

A Koridon female comes in and sits beside Drakon, her long raven hair fading to a lighter blue and fine lines drawing out at the sides of her lips. He squeezes her hand and they talk quietly amongst themselves. An intensity overwhelms the servant at the sight of them, and she frowns, backing into the corner. I'm too tired and hungry to think much about the strange relationship between her and Drakon. I'll revisit this later in case there's a way to use her against that dreadful fuck. But not now. Finally, I take a bite of my dinner. The familiarity of chicken and mashed potatoes taste like *winning*, and I allow myself to savor every flavor. I fill my plate again, abruptly leaning over the others if I must, and enjoy the hell out of seconds too.

I ignore Brekter and everyone else, only glancing occasionally up at Glenda, noting the intimate nuances between them. I'm curious about them but also fearful; what an odd match. What a dangerous match. What a glimmer of hope.

Once the table's cleared and conversation has died down, I look forward to bed and the beautiful numbness of sleep. Tomorrow may be filled with new horrors, but no one can take tonight from me. I stand and brazenly offer Brekter my arm to use him to escort me to bed, in case anyone tries to stop me.

"Sit. Back. Down." Drakon's voice stabs me from behind the moment my foot hits the first step up to my room.

Brekter smiles at me knowingly and bows deeply, pointing me back toward the banquet hall. "But I do wish I could take you up on your offer." It takes every ounce of self-control not to punch his face in as I begrudgingly make my way back. I'm greeted by the lady Koridon's malicious grin at Brekter's side.

"We still have a matter to attend to," the commander says, cuing Arek and Brekter to rush out.

"What are they going to do?" I ask Vaerynn.

"The others have to be taught a lesson," she replies.

"But you told them to run from it! That poor boy you turned into a tortured monster!" Gerakon clasps his hands together and rests his forehead against them. Of course he was the one to genetically alter the human. He spliced him together with a wolf and maybe something else. Hideous.

"And now they will know better." Vaerynn stands and places her palms onto the cluttered table. "You never run, you fight. You are no longer human and afraid, you are Koridon!"

A scuffling sounds down the hall, and the girls are shoved inside the room. Scarlet growls at them and walks strongly forward, while Mary-Shelly and Sybil are white ghosts and approach timidly.

Two slaves come forward with a large black pot, and upon opening the lid, a loud sizzle releases steam. Arek and Brekter shove iron rods into the glowing orange pot.

Drakon points his finger at them. "For the crime of cowardice, you will be branded upon your backs this night. Now come, kneel before me and do not suffer yourself the indignity of having to be held down."

Tears shine down Jane's face and her eyes dart around the room. Black-haired Alice shakes her head and moves backward, confused and panting frantically.

"You would scar the mothers who are sacrificing all to save you?" I squeeze my nails into my palms to keep my hands from shaking, fiery gaze forward but at nobody. "And what are we to say when the youngling asks about the horrifying marks riddling their mothers' backs?"

Drakon's mate nods her head at Arek and he pulls his red-hot brand from the embers. Kjartonn rushes forward and holds Jane down, ripping the shirt up her back while Brekter secures Scarlet's wrist and brings her to her knees. The thought of burning fire upon quivering flesh knocks me out of my chair.

"Brekter, don't you do this!" The voice that spills from my lips is unrecognizable as I circle him. The other Koridons ready themselves to subdue me. "If you hurt her or any of them, I'll never stop fighting you! I will never give you what you've always wanted!" I visualize his desperate breaths as he claws into my hips, the agony in his careful thrusts, the loud pumping of his heart that doesn't calm for an hour after. He watches it play out behind my eyes. I know what I ask of him in front of his superiors, but if he'd just stand up for us, perhaps Gerakon would as well, or even Kraetorr.

He moves the steaming brand over her pale skin, and with absolute defiance of my pleas, drives it into my friend's shoulder. Scarlet's agonized wail poisons the air and I attack Brekter. He shoves Scarlet aside and lifts me by my throat. "Shall I do you next?" Little squeaks move out of my constricted neck and I kick at him, the struggling only worsening the strangulation. "Yes, my brand would look stunning upon your back."

Scarlet whimpers, holding her knees to her chest, and

Brekter releases me. Sweet air enlivens my lungs and I scramble over to take Scarlet's hand. "Never it is then," I say to the demon holding his fiery torture tool. "I'll never love you, and when it is found to be Kassien's child growing inside me, you'll never be allowed to touch me again. I can't wait for the day!"

He smiles and spears his nasty weapon with clinging flesh back into the glowing orange. "Gerakon has not told you?"

"Told me what?" I brace myself for what already begins to sink in.

"Gerakon, why don't you tell my betrothed of the happy findings?"

I move my head back and forth as the fresh new air coating my lungs turns to acid. "Please, *please* no."

Gerakon stands and clears his throat, an uncomfortable moment he's hesitant to continue with. He still feels guilty for abandoning his prince and now *this*. "The child within your belly has a heredity marker factor of 8654 towards Brekter's line."

"So, that means—" I say weakly. The moment Kassien mated me during the open ceremony, his cock knotted and stuck tight as he emptied his seed inside and my womb tingled with new life. It was a moment chosen for highest chance of conception, and I *knew* Brekter was too late when he bathed me in his seed only an hour later.

But I was wrong. I wanted so much for it to be Kassien's, and now I've been utterly ruined by Brekter.

"So prepare yourself, my future mate. You will be mine after all." He takes a handful of Sybil's hair and yanks her to her knees. "No matter how many of your humans I mar." She cries piteously as burned flesh infuses the air.

Careful not to hurt Scarlet, I stroke her hair and cradle her in my arms. Screams ring out, a symphony of human suffering as Jane and black-haired Alice's skin also sears with their mark.

Anger and sadness thrash around my soul and I sink lower and lower into hopelessness. "Why are they doing this?" Scarlet whispers. "Do we mean so little?"

Arek removes his iron rod from the flame and asks Mary-Shelly to kneel. I cringe, thinking of the pleasure he will take in hurting her, his distaste for us no secret. She immediately obeys and removes the shirt from her back. The Koridons sit around the table so still it's unnatural, and blond Alice and Glenda appear as small, trembling children among them. Arek pauses a moment and the branding tool's bright orange fades. He lifts Mary-Shelly's chin. "You are stronger than you can imagine. You will survive this." The hint of gentleness in his voice disarms me, and I wonder if I've blacked out and lie dreaming on the floor.

"I'm not afraid," says Mary-Shelly, bowing her head in respect. Arek runs his fingers along her back, brushing red hair aside. Holding the back of her neck, he aims the sizzling brand over her. Her flesh smokes as he presses it in and she buckles, but Arek pulls the fiery weapon away without a delivery of monstrous strength behind it.

She breathes heavily and places a hand on his chest, shuddering sobs escaping her throat. He drops to one knee and she wraps her arms around him. He stares straight ahead, a visage of uncertainty and more than a little discomfort.

Drakon claps his hands, a mocking of our applause, and a snake-like smile creeps upon his mouth. The torture is over, and nothing else matters. Not even the sharp pain in my heart at Gerakon's revelation that any chance I had to be Kassien's princess is over. Not that it matters anyway. Kassien is either dead or has abandoned me. He was never worthy of my love.

"We are almost finished," says the commander, placing an arm around his mate's shoulders. "But there is still one more to suffer the burning."

Glenda tenses and slams back in her seat.

"You can't be serious," says blond Alice. Brekter and Arek move to her back. Snarling, Kraetorr throws himself in front of her, crouching like a hungry lion before them.

"She will not be hurt tonight. Or ever. She is my *Drakarra*."

"Third born!" cries Drakon. "That word is banned and you know why! It is nothing but shit and lies. Now step aside, I have spoken!"

Kraetorr snatches a knife from the table and the blade glints toward his father. "Mark her then." He flips the weapon skillfully in the air then kicks it soaring into the wall behind Brekter. "And we will see who lives through it." Bulging, unnatural muscle ripples down his back, one after the other, then along his spine and spreads out to his limbs and torso, making him appear to *double* in size. *Just like Mr. Hyde*, I gasp. I've never seen a Koridon do this before, not even when I was torn from Kassien's grip and abducted by Brekter. Drakon studies his son curiously, and I search for any signs that this is a normal occurrence, but he gives away nothing. Gerakon rises and draws close to the dangerous scene, no doubt medically fascinated. Kraetorr was huge before, but now—

Glenda's fingers reach up to touch his heaving back.

"No," he growls as her lips part. "You will not say you will allow it, because *I* will not."

Drakon raises a hand. "Gerakon, what do you make of this?"

The student of science shakes his head. "Best we end the night."

Brekter and Vaerynn escort us up the long, winding staircase. "Did you see that?" I ask them. "How is it possible?"

"Something has changed Kraetorr's chemistry," says Vaerynn. "You women are doing unnatural things to them."

"But why just him? Many were threatened tonight, and even I've been—" I swallow the knot in my throat, thinking about the blood spray during the mating ceremony, the desperation as Kassien tore his own skin to get free from the device that held him suspended in air. He couldn't get to me, and though it happened so quickly, I don't remember any increase in size. If my heart could shrivel any more it would, just more proof that Kassien and I aren't what I thought.

Gerakon tends the women's burns and Vaerynn checks the chains on the beds. Brekter steps in front of me and I lose my balance, falling onto the bed. He immediately lands on top of me, his weight crushing, and brings his lips to mine. "How do you feel now that you know there is no escaping me?" His kiss burns. "You are mine now, even you cannot deny me any longer."

Jane gasps as her wound is lathered in a cream and covered. They're not offering to heal them with their little machines this time.

"Get off me," I sneer. "There may be no child after all." I threaten him, forcing him to remember the moment suspended in time where I held a knife to my belly to negotiate my villager's lives. But I don't mean it. I would never harm a helpless being growing inside my body. It may be a part of him, but it's still a part of me as well.

He slams me against the pillow, and small white feathers fly about our faces. "Threaten my child again, and I will have you locked to the bed for all moments of the day." He slaps my thigh then grips the stinging tissue. "I might prefer you that way, unable to fight me."

I snap my teeth into his neck and coppery sweetness floods my tongue. He locks eyes with me and pulls back slowly, purposefully, his flesh tearing. His groan is laced with pleasure. "No, I was wrong. I like the fight in you." He pulls me by the throat from the bed and addresses Vaerynn. "I would have a word with my mate in private." I manage a quick shake of my head.

Vaerynn snaps a chain on my ankle. "I will not allow it. Let her sleep; she has had a hard day. For the child's health, let her sleep." He lets go and backs away, his smirk lighting up the intentions behind his eyes.

"What did that mean, when Kraetorr called Glenda his *Drakarra*?"

Vaerynn shrugs a shoulder. "It is an old fabled tale. When our race became slight, technology our only strength, we began breeding for strength, and sexual pleasure was also suppressed in our lines."

"You were all small once?" I marvel.

She doesn't answer. "Breeding was only for reproduction because passion gave way to poor choices such as following the heart, *you* might say. But it has been said that a few deviated from this path, centuries of suppression coming back with a vengeance, and a Koridon male would find himself overwhelmed by his heart. He called his soul mate *Drakarra*."

"Obviously fiction," I say, quirking a brow.

"Obviously." She throws a sheet over me. "Now sleep."

Drakarra. Such a word invokes that exact thought: *soul mate.* It's an interesting concept, but I hope there isn't just one true love for everyone. Because that would mean—

Barely tasting the numb peace of drifting off, my ankle restraint snaps open, and I jump awake. A shadowy head moves into my straining vision and teeth bite the nightdress off my thighs. I kick at the intruder, but he grabs my ankle and throws my legs apart, clanking the restraint around my wrist against the bed frame. I pull and struggle as a long tongue plays up my slit, and I cringe.

"I'm going to scream, Brekter."

He laughs quietly and continues his soft, wet assault along my sweet spot. "I want you perfectly pliable to take my shaft inside you tonight. I love when you drip so wet I slide in despite the pressure of your tight walls." My body becomes rigid, fighting off the sensation of his tonguing, but he knows how to work me physically. Desire spikes through my lower belly and I become slick despite my disgust. He must have a lot of secrets, his skillfulness with my body too lucky. Perhaps some of those that have been found in the woods broken and bloody have been part of his work.

Whimpers and tears fill the room upon hearing us, exhaustion, pain and fright so palpable, I have to get out of here. "Take me to another room," I say and twist my pelvis to throw his perfect lashing of my clit off balance. "I can't do this in here. With all of *them*." They need to sleep now, not watch me succumb to the man that hurt them. I shudder as I run my fingers down his face and pull him to my lips. "I want to do something to you." It kills me to think about the intimate things I'd done to Kassien to ease his sexual pain while we awaited my ovulation and mating ceremony, but if it gets me out of this room where my friends will be horrified, I can do it. And maybe there's something out in the mansion to discover. If I could find a way to run, or something to pick my locks with while unattended at night—

"Your suffering is a pleasure for me," he says. "I like your friends to watch us, hear us. It engorges my cock."

I lick a trail up his neck and he gives in to a tremble that makes his skin scent something delicious. "I want to lick you from your sack to your tip. Take me somewhere."

"Yes." He straddles me and holds himself at the base, his

ridged shaft touching my lips. "Do it. Lick me over and over, I want to feel your warm tongue." He forces my face into it by the back of my neck, and I turn my head.

"Damn you, Brekter, not like this."

"Open your mouth!" he says too loudly. "Open your mouth." I keep my lips pursed as he slides his massive cock along my face. He slaps it into my cheek, and I force back a groan.

I sink my teeth into the side, the spongey steel hurting my jaw, and he pulls it away, smacking my face again. "Yes," he breathes. "More."

I lick over the angry spot I bit, and small drops of pearly liquid seep from his tip. "Take me out of here so you can ravage me like an animal."

He groans his frustration and unlocks the restraint. "Cause any trouble, and I will beat you down. Understand?"

I nod, and he rushes me out. In front of the staircase he kisses me and I stifle my sadness. Wriggling out if his arms I say, "Let's get this over with." He yanks me down by my icy blue locks and shoves my face into him. The scent of his sack drifts into my nose and mouth, filling my blood with strange excitement. "You know I don't want this," I say, fighting my own urges to submit to a demon.

"You could take this cock down your throat without teeth, I think." The head hits my closed mouth, and he forces it hard.

I make a disgusted sound and force my head away. "Your people don't indulge in sex, they don't do it for pleasure. Why do you? Why do you enjoy all the licking, and getting me to climax? Why do you get excited by forcing me beneath you?"

"You are well aware of what your scent does to me. I breathe you in with advanced receptors and my entire body is set aflame. My entire being shifts." He pulls the nightdress off and throws me onto my back. "And I like owning you. Your body is so responsive, not like a Koridon female's. You quiver and lock around me, your skin flushes, your breasts even beg to be stimulated by my tongue. Never ask me to stop myself from wanting you because control does not exist."

"I don't want to like what you do to me." I toss my head to the side and bite my lip.

The head of his cock meets the aching need between my legs, and the pressure soothes a sigh out of me. He breaks through slowly, pushing, stretching, bliss...

Deeper.

"You belong to me," he says, "and I will abuse this body meant for pleasure until there is nothing left of you."

Nothing left of *you*, he said. Not of *it*. It's not my body he will break, but everything that I am. And these Koridons know nothing of love and respect so they'll let him. There are no laws protecting me, or any of us.

He penetrates deeper into my slit and his other hand plays with the suppleness of my breast before drawing the nipple into his mouth. His tongue shoots a current of blissful heat from the sensitive spot all the way down between my legs, where he slides in and out mercilessly, so large I need to scream and wrench my hips into him at the same time. "You pretend to want love," he whispers, "but you lie. What you want is to be rutted mercilessly, not out of love but desperation."

"You lie as well," I say through gritted teeth. The erogenous spots on my nipples peak, the cool air kissing the wetness he left. "You say you want to destroy me, but you don't. You want me to love you."

"But you promise you never will." The hall's dark with only a candle flickering in a sconce on the wall, but I still see the shadow that crosses his face. He pushes me hard into the floor as he rips away and I cover up. I'm sure now that he's hiding something. And he never sounds sad, except when he's trying to trick me into trusting him, but right now, he's comparing me to someone. He moves his back against the wall and rests an arm around his knees. "I was young when I came here. It was just after the war poisons had cleared and I was barely grown. In a new place and fighting to survive a world that was not made for me."

"But that was—" The war, the end of the peak of my civilization, was over two hundred years ago. "How old are you?"

He bows his head. "Did Kassien keep that from you?"

I assumed they were all in their twenties and thirties with their smooth skin and lustrous hair. Tenak appears older and so does Drakon, but how much older are they really? Kassien had an intense demeanor and has wisdom far beyond my years, but I thought that was due to his warrior nature and the differences in our race.

"I am one hundred and fifty-one."

I would be shocked, but I just had sex with a huge alien from another planet. So, I'm not even going to waste my time. "You know my people would consider our relationship an illegal perversion," I say.

"Makes it more scorching I think," he says with a quieted chuckle and wipes his brow. A noise downstairs makes me jump but he just shakes his head. "Servants. I am the only Koridon here, supposed to be watching over you. The others prefer the ship."

So Vaerynn knew Brekter would have me tonight no matter what. Perhaps she can feel better about it if she's not here. Of course, it doesn't matter anymore. I feel like the more Brekter wears me down, the more I lose my humanity. Maybe my depraved side will win and I'll one day love opening my legs for him. Inch by inch, blood for blood. Soul for soul.

"You were trying to tell me something earlier. I wish you'd

continue." *Tell me your secrets, mad one. Maybe it will be your undoing.*

His heated gaze flicks up. "So many years have passed since *her*. But she still haunts me, and I have never allowed myself to feel that way again."

"You loved someone once?" I ask.

He pauses a moment, lost in thought. "There was warring in the area, and we were called to eradicate the uprising. My blood splashed the snow, and I was so cold."

14

BREKTER

Canada, 4 years after the world ended

He groaned as he reached toward the metal bear trap that bit like a shark into his calf.

He'd heard the men hiding somewhere out there in the trees and scented *something else* too. It was that scent that drew him away from his war party and into the bare-limbed forest where the trees touched the sky. He pulled the metal jaws open, snapping them in half before throwing them into a tree where pieces exploded everywhere. *Clever trap for a Koridon,* he thought, planning a very slow death for the humans when he found them.

Blood poured onto the sparkling snow, melting it away, and the cold clung to him with every sinking step. He wrapped leather around the gaping wounds but his foot dragged most annoyingly from the damage. The sun, whose rays should be warm, were a only a taunting lie, and began to dip behind the mountains.

His cry for help echoed through the trees, freezing night clinging to his skin, but no one came, all of them pushed out by the sudden drop of temperature. Blood loss and chill slowing his step, he held onto a tree's thick trunk. *Cold like this is unnatural,* he thought, knowing his strong body was weak against such wintery climate. It was this moment that he realized that this could be the end.

Snow crunched underfoot and he snapped his head around to search the darkness. His pupils dilated, drawing in the faint moonlight. What came into focus was a large, fur-covered animal. He was in no shape to take on whatever that trap was intended for, but that would never stop him.

He drew his weapon and held it at the level of his head, but that's when he froze. Letting his arm drift down, he was disarmed by a soft face inside the fur: full lips, large brown eyes and a scent that made him shake his head with dizziness. Or perhaps that was just the blood loss. He fell easily upon receiving the blow to his head.

The next hours were black, even when he tried opening his eyes, so he kept them closed and enjoyed the warmth that wrapped around him.

"Can you hear me?" A strange voice broke through his fevered dreaming, and he had no idea what she was saying in her human language.

He groaned and looked upon the enchanting fur-covered creature who had saved him. She was blurry, but those nearly-black irises were the clearest thing he'd seen in years. "*Drakonis, trev duraden?*" he asked, peering around at the stone walls that flickered with fire light. He tried to sit up, but his arms pulled tight, caught by the chains around his wrists. "Let me go," he continued to speak, though she couldn't understand, and yet she seemed to, by the slight smile that pulled at her lips.

"You're my prisoner," she said, and her fingers trailed along his bare chest, a ring gleaming, all the way down to the exposed thatch of sparse hair down low. Her electrifying touch brought that scent already thick in the air to life in his senses and he yanked at the chains like a wild man. "My father put those chains in the rock," she spoke. "You won't get free. They were meant for you." She pulled a blade on him and touched the tip to his chest. "I shouldn't have saved you." The steel cut into him and he snarled. "But I didn't really save you, did I?" She leaned down and dragged her tongue along the beading line of shining crimson between his pectorals and he shuddered, the blood rushing to his cock, the aching in his wounds and entire body lost to the sensation. Were all humans mad like this? He'd never done anything but kill them, even the dirty thin females, but not one of them ever looked like her. Or put an intoxicating pleasure inside his blood, making all rational thoughts nonexistent. *Aven draga* he cursed. *Little animal.* That was what she was. He hated her.

"Mmmm," she breathed. "I've been alone here for so long, so forgive me if all I want to do is explore you. I mean, you're nothing but a killer. A destroyer. Practically an animal really. I've been thinking about what I want to do to you for the last twenty-four hours while you slept. So why shouldn't I torture you to entertain myself?" She stood up, and the blanket around her shoulders slipped to the ground. "I was never much for normal when there was real society around anyway. But being a crazy bitch made me survive you fucks. So here we are. And I'm so bored..."

"*Ivital gorgen implicet*," he threatened, making her laugh. She bent down and pulled the furs off his waist.Her glimmering gaze made his blood rush, and he became sensitively aware of his muscular form, feeling attractive as he laid helpless before her. He thought for a moment he was in an alternate universe, one where Koridons and humans weren't fighting. Maybe there was nothing out there in fact, just this cave, just this fantasy.

Madness.

"Oh my," the woman said, running a finger down the inside of his shaft. "That's, um—" She stifled a laugh then slid her palm down him again, this time taking a handful of his sack. He pulsed harder, never having experienced such a rush of desire, his mating ceremony still years off, and anyway, his females had never done *this* to him. With just her touch, he wanted to rip the chains from the walls and fill her to bursting, craved to feel her deeply and rub himself inside her darkest places. He could hear her screams as he possessed her, and it drove his cock harder.

"Well, that's interesting." The girl recoiled to stoke the fire and shook her head as though warding something off. "Your anatomy is similar to ours, but not quite the same." She brought a cup to his lips. "Drink."

"I am an enemy you do not want to keep here. I will find my way out and kill you, *aven draga*," he said, inviting his anger to kill the arousal tormenting his groin.

She squinted at his nonsensical speech. "I'm sure you're telling me how much you'd like it if I hopped on your giant dick, but the answer's no, *pig*."

Brekter scoffed at her obvious defiance of his orders.

"Drink. Let's start there. *Drink.* Say it." She pulled the liquid away.

He sighed heavily. "Drink." There, he'd learned her word and was rewarded with water sliding down his parched throat. He thought about spitting it in her face, that would be fun, but no, he would need his strength to kill her.

"I've been here for months, hiding out since you fuckers killed my family," she said, moving to stoke the fire. Without the furs, he could see her tall, slender form perfectly. Dark hair swayed as she walked, and he turned his head, but his desire was still obvious. *Why would the mad little animal take my clothes off anyway?* he wondered, hating himself for the way his body reacted to her. She was an enemy, a lower being, and the state she was keeping him in, tied and naked, enraged him further.

"The sky was red for so long," she said. "We lived in the mountains here, so only a few died from the poisonous air and the rest of us moved up farther to escape it." She squeezed the strands of his long hair, and her fingertips slid down the tips. "And all of this was because of you." She took a deep breath and laid on the ground beside me. "Oh, I didn't agree with what they did to your people. *At first.*"

"What are you planning to do to me?" he asked, yanking a chained arm toward her in a fist.

"But then you came after us." She leaned on her elbow toward him, not even flinching at his threat. "And *we* didn't drop those bombs on your ships, you know! It was our goddamned world leaders, and we all suffered the nuclear fallout too!" She punched him in the shoulder with a grunt then laid down again. "Everything's a disaster."

"Disaster?" Brekter repeated, feeling close to the word somehow. He wanted to understand her, knowing communicating with the dumb beast would increase his odds at getting out of there. "Disaster, *ovswargot.*" He taught her his word.

An unattractive snore came sawing out of her, and he snorted with disgust. Searching the room, he looked for sharp things, blunt things, and surveyed everything there was to see. He quietly pulled on the chains, nearly grunting with the force.

Every muscle taxed, but the rock restraints held. For the time being.

He had no choice but to let her sleep next to him, close enough that her arm touched his side at times and her sweet smell drifted across his skin, sending his heart racing. She was torture. She was pain. And he was fascinated with her.

The next day, she forced him to learn more of her language and he started enjoying the way she laughed, even if her joy was being produced by the awkward way he said her damn words. It was loud and obnoxious, making a strange tickle bubble up in his belly. She would dance around the cave and point to strange things upon the walls called *paintings*, and feed him something from her black cooking device called *stew*. Uncomfortable and hating to urinate in her *bed pan*, he dreaded the other bodily function being necessary. He thought it silly, for it was nothing but a natural process by which all creatures world to world must do. He had to get out of there, but as he worked the chains from the wall, his strength failed him. He needed more nutrients than the girl was supplying, and different ones not known to this planet.

Still, he couldn't help but enjoy his captor, because no matter how miserable his state was, her voice and the sparkle in her eyes when he caught her looking upon him was better than a thousand nights of comfort. For years, his life traveling through space was cold and black until he arrived on Earth, just to find the world almost uninhabitable. While he loved to fight and kill, it wasn't nearly as much fun while starving and suffering atmospheric ailments.

He was learning from the woman as well though, and realized if he could understand the human language it might give his people advantages over many things in this world. And being that every day since he'd arrived on Earth had been nothing but pain from trying to survive in an environment just slightly below hostile, there was much she could teach him.

Afternoon came and the girl arrived back from her hunt holding a limp, gray animal. She tossed it in the corner and grabbed the bed pan. She took hold of his cock and gave it aim. "Go ahead."

It twitched in her hand and little shocks traveled throughout his body from her touch. Her soft fingers brushed along his shaft, and his breath quickened. He truly couldn't have relieved his bladder if he wanted to.

"I'm sorry." She let go suddenly and took a key from her pocket. "I'll probably regret this," she turned the key in one of his shackles and freed his arm, setting the pan within reach, "but I'm tired of having to help you piss." It ached as he made soft twisting motions, and the freedom made his other wrist's discomfort glare.

"Brekter," he said, pointing into his chest. "Vek swarv, Brekter."

She nodded and said, "I'm Maria." Secretly he would still call her aven draga, because she didn't look like a *Maria* at all. She grabbed her kill by its long ears. "This is a rabbit. They hide in burrows, but if you find their hole, you can reach deep and grab them out." She split the skin on its back and ripped it violently downward, revealing tender, pink skin. *That was rather attractive*, he thought, and the animal she called a *rabbit* tasted very nice.

The weeks went by, and though Brekter was kept prisoner, he still feasted physically upon his avan draga: her black locks and equally as onyx eyes, her shapely frame and the delicious glimpses of her ass and other sensual areas exposed to him as she dressed. And the way she smelled when she noticed him watching her was oxygen. He caught on to her language quickly and sucked up everything she said. *To use against her and all her people.*

One night she lay next to him in the small cave with her long hair sprawled out around her, and he was able to piece together what she was saying: "I've been waiting here months for them." She twirled the ring on her finger round and round. "I've been waiting for my husband. But in my heart I know he's dead." Her arm snaked over Brekter's chest. His free arm moved to his side, preparing to coil her up like a serpent squeezing prey. She must have known he could do it, break her in two in an instant, so why was she holding him? It caused him to freeze and his conflicted thoughts bashed together.

She sniffled and wiped a tear from her cheek. "I haven't seen anyone in all this time and having you here—"

His powerful arm snatched her around the waist, and he yanked her body on top of his. He would simply crush her to death against him right after he had secured the key tucked away in her torn-up jeans.

She grunted under the pressure, her lungs squeezing beneath his massive bicep, and he prepared to search her pockets once she passed out. Then he would kill her. Finally, it would be over and he could get back to his... and then the thought became heavy... *normal life.*

Maria forced her head up, showing the deep purpling of her face, and her lips searched for his. He was drawn to them, an unexplainable feeling, and lifted up to meet their softness. Again and again, she planted soft kisses on his hungry mouth and his strength failed.

She burst out of his arms. With frenzied breaths she stumbled backward and held the wall for balance. Brekter's harsh breathing rivaled her own and his eyes pleaded with her, promising things his beguiling mouth never could.

"Please," he said rawly in her language.

She took a trembling step forward, and, with a tear tracking down her cheek, she jumped on top of him. His mouth moved upon hers and a spine-shattering connection entangled them as though he could feel what she did, and she felt everything that he did. Her kiss drove him to desperately seek for pleasure between her legs, everything about their encounter taboo and mouthwatering. Shaking, she ripped her pants off and dripped upon his cock, warm honey and silk sliding against the underside of him, stroking fire through his every nerve. Her body, though tall and well-built, was so small compared to his gigantic form, and she slipped upward on his shaft to press his crown into her slit. He felt her hot and wet, inviting...

But he hesitated.

Thoughts swirled through his mind, the deep bruising under the shackle that held his wrist, the powerlessness of being locked in the cave, but also the usefulness of his avan draga and his addiction to her. He was giving up his freedom for sex. Had he completely lost his mind? Ambivalence tore through him, and she sensed it.

"Please?" she begged. "Make me feel something." She used her weight to guide her hips over his shaft, but even with her fighting to move down over his oversized cock, he moved in only slightly. A rush of ecstasy possessed his blood, and the urge to spear through her mercilessly overtook him.

In a red mist, he clutched her in the crook of his elbow. "Out. Now. Let me!" he said clearly, her cheek shoved into his shoulder. She struggled, kicking her feet and putting her fists into him.

"Never, you *fuck!*" came her muffled yell. "I'll never let you have the key. Kill me!"

Brekter winced at the thought but held her against him and dug in her pockets. It wasn't there. "I would never lie next to you with your freedom so close," she growled. "It's outside under a rock." Her voice was cold and unfeeling. "I knew it. You bastards can't feel anything. You're capable of only rage and violence."

"You know how I look at you," Brekter said in his broken English. "You think I do not want you?" He shoved her away, knowing he couldn't hurt her anyhow. He couldn't utter the truth that if he hadn't turned his passion into rage, he would have destroyed her. A dark presence twisted in his being, begging him to tear her to pieces as he took every ounce of pleasure from her.

He vowed never to get that close to her again.

"I do see how you look at me. And I feel *you* too." She bit her lip and it took everything in her to keep from reaching out to him again. "I never thought I could love the enemy, but I do."

"No. I will never." He turned over and closed his eyes, his temples throbbing and his insides disintegrating. It was ridiculous, he had never even mated one of his own before, and doing so with a human animal made his blood curdle. *And scream.* And the way he had wanted to ravage her... she'd never survive it.

His avan draga had lost the spark that made her laughter so contagious and her speech engaging, though he often couldn't understand a word of it. She didn't look at him or speak to him, and all he could do was soak in her beauty, having nothing else of her. And she was so unbelievably beautiful in all her denial of him.

Another cold night fell and the embers of the fire faintly glimmered. She slept with her back to him, and once again, he fell asleep to deeply needing her against him.

A strange noise woke him from his desperate dreams, and his adrenaline spiked. Maria was still sleeping soundly on her furs, but he was on high alert from the strange clawing and thumping against the cave wall. He sniffed the air and a foul smell of salty aggression permeated his nostrils. "Maria!" he shouted and yanked at his unrelenting chain. She sat up straight and horror washed over her tired countenance as a huge figure stepped into the cave.

A giant black animal with dripping fangs stood over her, patches of hair missing from its body and a strange mangled deformity twisting its face. "Oh my god, a bear!" she screamed, and he rattled his chained arm at her. He'd never seen such a creature, yet he knew there was something unnatural about it. She lunged for her knife and the monster attacked.

Her screams filled Brekter's ears, and he leaped up with such force the chain tore out of the wall, creating a downpour of broken stone. He threw the still-connected chain over the beast's throat and ripped it off Maria. She crawled away, ruby drops hitting the floor, and cowered in the corner as the bear roared its threatening song. Brekter's fist landed into its skull and it thrashed, sending him flying into the wall.

The bear stalked toward him, larger even than the giant Koridon that crouched, saliva dripping. Maria snuck up behind the beast and shoved her blade through the middle of its back, striking at the heart. It cried out then twisted around, deep, wheezing breaths blasting from its mouth. With snapping jaws, it lunged at the small woman, and with her arms shielding her, she disappeared beneath him.

Brekter, moving like lightning, gripped its giant head, and with a terrible *crack,* snapped the neck bones. The bear collapsed.

"Maria?" Brekter hit his knees beside her. Slight

movements tremored through the bear's body and Maria startled.

Brekter touched her head. "It dies. Do not worry."

Maria stood, and with her legs shaking, she motioned toward the entrance. "Go on then. Get lost."

Brekter spotted his boots in the corner. "Of course I will." He had ripped free, finally, after so long. After so many tries. But only when Maria was in danger did he find the true strength to do it. He put his boots on and walked out, dragging the beast behind him.

The night was dark with only a sliver of moon, but not nearly as cold as it had been when he first arrived in the north. That mutated bear's teeth still felt fresh on his arm as he stared off toward the south, trying to spot the direction his clan would likely be now. Freedom rushed through his veins, yet his feet stuck into the snowy earth, held by some ethereal force. What life could he expect if he stayed? They would be found, and she would be dragged from his arms to be enslaved or killed. Maybe worse. But as he imagined being anywhere but with her...

Brekter stepped back inside the cave to find Maria on her knees. His shadow crossed the floor and she jumped. A flicker of pure relief touched her onyx jewels and she stood, breathing hard. Bloodied material fell from her chest, revealing claw marks, and he rushed to her. "This is bad," he said, touching the wound, but she grabbed his hand and held it to her cheek.

"It's nothing."

He lifted her to his mouth. They lingered there a moment and she brushed her lips over his. "Don't leave." She kissed him, and her fingertips traced down his rippled abdomen. His spine melted at her touch.

"When I think of being with you," he spoke against her lips, "I lose my mind. I think if I mate you, I will kill you." She was everything he hated and feared, a creature with a planet, a creature who belonged somewhere.

"I'm dead already," she whispered. "I have no one in the world. I would rather die against your chest than here alone. Or with another one of those fucking bears. She rubbed her cheek against his. "And yes, I would die to feel your love." The love of a Koridon, which she had to know existed somehow.

He would protect her, he would kill for her, but that didn't mean he had to possess her body to do those things. He loved her and would push away the physical need for her. "I still—"

She devoured his mouth with her kiss, cutting off words she didn't want to hear, and wrapped her legs around his waist. He fell to his back with her on top of him. She crawled down his body and worked him out of his clothes. Her tongue laved over his crown, and she stroked him with both hands twisting in opposite directions. Jolts of excitement and bliss traveled up into his chest, and his heart captured it all and swelled. She straddled him backward and tongued his sack, gently nipping at it while he had full view of her glistening sex.

He touched her there, softly at first, drowning in her intensely arousing scent, and her velvety folds drew his finger in. She pushed backward and moaned as it penetrated her, then rocked back and forth, working his mouth-wet cock in her hands. One finger filled her, and the way she bucked with pleasure made him rush and swell. She pulled off him suddenly and, pressing her palms into his shoulders, held her hips over his.

"No," Brekter whispered as she moved his heavy shaft up to her slit. "This is—" he searched for the right word in her language, but she finished for him.

"Bad. Wrong. Taboo." Her hips dipped and he breached her opening, her slick warmth gripping around his head. He was lost then and wanted all of her, his breathing out of control, his sight drenched in red. Her pussy clenched down as she moaned, taking his tremendous girth inch by inch and he thought he would die if he couldn't bury inside her to the hilt. Wet and opening to him, she slid down, easing his pain then lighting him up with complete ecstasy. He stayed still, terrified he would lose control, but his spirit writhed and screamed beneath her.

Each time she moved, no matter how slight, waves of pure desire, of pure sex, rushed through his giant, muscular body, and sex chemicals poured into his blood, intoxicating his brain. She bent over and kissed him as though she wanted to kiss him forever, then flicked her tongue along his neck, and he did the same to her. They spent an hour with him inside her but barely moving their hips, just worshipping each other.

He watched her breasts move as she sat up and forced herself over his tremendous size, up and down as she milked him. It took every bit of his strength not to throw her against the wall and rail her savagely from behind, but she was too precious to hurt, and that forced him to stay calm. Soon, pressure built in his sack and he gripped the ground as his climax began. A large knot grew in his shaft and Maria's eyes widened. "Fuck!" she screamed and sat stuck to him, unable to move. "Ohhhh—" His warm essence pumped into her, and the knot pulsed against her sweet spot, bringing her to full-body chills as deep waves of pleasure washed over.

Laying together afterward and floating between worlds, hours passed. He stroked her head, deep in thought, and neither of them could sleep, or even speak.

Every day they laid naked together, exploring each other and learning each other's ways. She taught him to get between her legs and lick her sensitive bundle of nerves while using his fingers to penetrate her. It made her very pliable for him to mount her, and she was tough, able to take his powerful thrusts as long as he was careful. But he was becoming more and more violent as the new sexuality matured in him. Bruises mottled her arms and thighs, she was often sore and bled, ut she never cursed at him or complained. She only spoke to him softly and reminded him that he must calm himself and be gentler. She was incredible, and in his heart he knew he would never leave her. Not even when the Koridons found them one day and tried to take her for slavery. That would be the day they died, but until then, he was frozen in every moment with her.

One evening as they lay together on top of the bear's fur they had fought only a month earlier, a voice jarred them from their happy state. A man with a graying beard entered the cave and held a gun toward Brekter.

"Dad!" cried Maria, holding a blanket in front of her.

"Get back!" the aged man said to her, and Brekter stood, his monstrous form hiding Maria behind him. "I'm gonna kill this son of a bitch."

"No. Don't hurt him!" she said. Taking his hand, she slid out from behind him.

Her dad puzzled at her bruises and cocked his weapon. "It's okay, honey. He's got you in some kind of hostage state but—"

Brekter moved so quickly he was a blur and snapped the weapon away. The father put his hands up and two more men rushed in behind him.

Maria touched his back, and he lowered the weapon. "This is my family," she said. "My brother and—" taking a deep breath, she thumbed the gold ring on her finger. "And my husband."

"We got stuck behind the pass during the blizzard," said her father. "There was no way to get back to you until the weather changed."

"I thought you were dead!" Maria hugged him and brought

her brother and husband into it as well. Brekter felt his world slip away as he watched them, and fury set him aflame at the sight of her *husband*. She never spoke of him, and that worried him, because maybe she still loved him and couldn't speak of him out of guilt or pain. He would have to kill him.

"Are you all right?" her husband asked, deep worry marring his pleasant face.

She nodded and hugged him again. "I'm fine, Adrien. Are you?"

He looked at the massive Koridon's naked body and the state of Maria's. "What has he done to you? Did he make you—"

"No," she said, taking his thickly corded arm. She was flooded with confusion and guilt, Adrien having been her world before she had lost him that winter. Even before the alien ships were bombed, leading to core reactor meltdowns that ended the whole world, he had been the strong, jealous type. An alpha in his own right. And now he stood there betrayed and hurt, knowing that not just another man, but the *enemy* and a being from another world, had been with her intimately. She knew her husband hoped she had been forced, but she wouldn't lie. She loved Brekter, entranced by his otherworldly heritage and their strange relationship.

But she still loved Adrien.

15

CALYPSO

The dying light of the mounted candles flicker across Brekter's face as he tells me about his first love. Crouched in the corner, he appears different to me, the cruel, confident guard pulled down, and though I don't feel anything for him, I'm fascinated by his story. "What did she do?" I ask, imagining as her husband and family return through the winter pass once spring began.

"In that moment, I wanted to kill them all and take her choices away." He jumps up to walk away, but I take his hand with both of mine.

"Tell me."

His eyes dart around and his back hits the wall. "She chose him." He shakes his head, trying to find the words. "I had a choice too, standing out in the dark, between two worlds, and I chose her. I chose death as long as I had her."

I sigh, remembering all the times he called me little animal, how nasty it sounded, but now I know the power behind the name.

"I never touched another woman after that. I was mated to

Lorai eventually but was driven mad by the memories every time a woman was near. Their scents danced through my blood and sent fire through my veins." He grips me painfully and I edge back, feeling the danger seep from his pores. "My mate did not feel like Maria. She was cold and passionless. I could not stand her."

"But you broke your vow with me," I say. He had seen in me an opportunity to gain power over Kassien and seized his moment.

"You aren't exactly human, are you?" He trembles as he smooths the tresses from my face. I could stand it no longer. The pain of desire, the jealousy every time he touched you—"

"You took me from Kassien to have a child with me. You knew we would be the most powerful couple in your society."

"That never mattered!" He pulls me into his arms. "I did not want the child for power," he shakes his head slowly, "or even for the survival of my race."

He lays me back again and rests his head on my chest as I stare at the ceiling. A child grows just like he wished, and I wonder if this is my only choice now. Should I accept him, knowing Kassien may never come for me, and because a whole world relies on our successful union? His story helped me understand some of his bitterness toward us, but his cruelty is still unforgiveable. But he's a completely different species than I am, rough and unharnessed, making it hard to hold all of it against him. Anger cringes my bones; I don't want to be with Brekter, but what could it mean for my people?

"Brekter, if I'm to make a life with you, there will be demands." I swallow the knot in my throat and let my fingers drift through his dark hair. "I will need you to be at my side for the rights of humans." If he truly wants to get into my heart, he'll do this for me.

His arms tighten and something sorrowful bleeds into me.

"I am sorry for making you hate me. I only sabotage myself in doing so. I cannot tell you why I have done these things to you."

Maria walked away from him, the first being he had ever loved. He was forever destroyed that day and uses me to release the rage. "Make it right with me, and I will accept you."

He lifts his chin and his lips find mine, something he's never initiated before. I let his desperate kiss penetrate my defenses and try to care for him, try to feel the good in him.

A female voice drifts up the stairwell, and we sit up. "You like the new girls, I see..." she says, and before Brekter can stop me, I dash down the stairs.

"No!" he begs me to stop.

Brekter nearly careens into me from behind as I hide behind a bookshelf. I bring a finger to my lips as he shakes his head in warning at me. Creeping through the parlor, a male voice echoes. "Never would I touch another woman like I touch you." It sounds like Drakon, but all I can see, hiding behind the furniture, is shadows. A strong hand yanks her clothing off and he lifts her off the ground, her legs wrapped around his back. Her voice is soft and her body so small; this isn't the mate seen at his side during dinner.

"Ohhhh," she utters, her head whipping back as he moves inside her with long, careful strokes.

"You are the only one I will ever touch," says Drakon, and he pulls her face into his. "You are mine."

"And what about your old, dusty mate, Trepedda?" the girl asks.

Drakon squeezes her until a whimper squeaks from her throat. "She is nothing compared to you. Do not even speak her name again as though on the same level."

"Then why haven't you taken me as your queen?" Palms into the wall, she pushes and Drakon stumbles back. He catches her as she falls and roughly holds her against him.

"Perhaps soon you will throw me into the House of Pain with the other tortured humans. Is that what you'll do?"

I look at Brekter with confusion, but he doesn't acknowledge me. What place is she talking about?

"Never." He leans toward her lips but she tips her head back. "Damn you," he breathes, his eyes lingering hungrily upon her neck. "How can you say that *now*?"

"Because now more than ever I see how little I mean to you."

He slaps his hand into the wall beside her. "Our time will come."

He tries claiming his kiss once more, but she's stone to the touch. "Until then, put me down. I'm going to bed." She wiggles out of his hold.

"No, not until I have spilled inside you." The shadows struggle as Drakon overpowers her easily. I see the young servant in my mind's eye, her strange presence as she placed my plate down, the look on Drakon's face that was so obviously desire now.

"You will stop," she yells, "or I'll wake everyone in this house."

His hand lands over her face. "Do it then. Scream, foolish child, there's no one here that can stop me" She hits him in the chest as he holds her down and struggles with her in the dark. Her cries muffle into his hand. She flails, her sobs filling the room, and Drakon jumps away from her with a roar. "Come here." He holds a hand out to her, and after catching her breath, she takes it. "I have never been told no before by a woman. Forgive me, *drakkara*." He rocks her as she shakes.

"No more sex," says Andromeda. "Marry *me*, and have my body and heart as one forever. Or enjoy me carnally no more."

"Cruel girl." He tosses her aside. "Get to bed as you so wish." She moves toward him and he gently pushes her back, but she keeps coming until she's worked her arms around him. Their lips meet. Brekter pulls me away, but as I strain my neck for one last look, the female shadow dashes away.

"Your leader is in love with a human," I say once we reach the top of the stairs. *She's* the reason he went along with Brekter's plan to break their laws and make women available for breeding.

"No. I think he only enjoys her to mate with." Brekter stands in front of the large window overlooking the coast and I move behind him, entranced by the black clouds that stream across the moon.

"If he wanted to mate her, he would have," I say.

No, it was her *heart* he wanted.

The next day I loathe waking, having stayed up half the night with my betrothed, but up Vaerynn rushes me and into the bath.

"What's it going to be today?" I ask, running sweet-smelling soap through my hair. "More being hunted by werewolves followed by pointless cruel brandings?"

"No," replies Vaerynn. "Worse. Today is your—oh, how do you say it? Marriage day?"

I slip under the water and stay there until my lungs burn. A tempting thought to drown myself rises up along with a little wicked glee, but soon bubbles burst from my mouth. I come up, spewing soapy bath water. "Already? Why?"

"You are pregnant with a Koridon child. Best to give you to the father by law now and get it out of the way. Mary-Shelly's will be tomorrow, her most ripe day of the month." She pats my abdomen and I nearly bite her.

"I'm still not sure I want this."

"When has it ever mattered what a female wants?" She splashes me, and I wipe stinging water from my eyes. "Our mating ceremonies are dry, mechanical acts of sacrifice. We do what we must and endure for the good of our race."

My head screeches with torment, like teeth grinding, gnawing at rock, at the thought of accepting Brekter into my body in front of an audience. "I already endured the demeaning public ceremony with Kassien. I won't do it again. I can't. I can't let Brekter, the one who forces himself upon me, now do it for an audience of my enemies."

"You will do what is Koridon. Now and forever. You must be mated by the male who has claimed you in front of the pack. They must see his possession of you and respect it. It is not a stimulating event for us. It is duty."

"It isn't anymore! What *we* experience with them is purely stimulating. And all of you that watch will feel it like never before because you will be awakened!" Doesn't she understand that doing this in front of all the males could be dangerous? Granted, they can show control, but why risk it?

Vaerynn steps back, her mouth open, a glimmer of recognition biting at her. Maybe she *has* felt what I speak of, and I wonder what she's hiding. "You will prepare yourself for the night ceremony." she recovers her solemnity quickly. "Prepare your little gash to be used for all to see by the one you hate."

I squeeze my lids shut and ball my fists, trying desperately not to hold her under the water until her cruel mouth shuts forever. It's hard to believe she and I share the title of female.

I won't do it. I'll find Brekter and convince him that while I might have to be mated to him, it's wrong to make me bare my naked body before his brethren.

They lock me up in one of the rooms on the third floor to rest and await the moment they come for me tonight. I imagine what my village friends are enduring today and wish I could talk to Scarlet. Nervousness twists my stomach as the minutes tick by too quickly, and my cries to bring Brekter to me go unanswered. Slaves bring up food and tea full of nutrient X2, but I can hardly touch it. *Please.* I try to focus as the liquid quakes in my shaky hands. *I need to drink this to be strong. I need this to survive tonight.* My fingertips tingle as I struggle to breathe, my chest heavy with panic. *Kassien,* my everything screams out to the universe. *I'm begging you, come now...*

I sob, and tears burn against my cheeks as I pace the room. When my pain is too heavy to stand any longer, I hit my knees and grab my belly.

I know he's not coming. And if he does, he'll have no choice but to cast me away when he finds out about my pregnancy. It's not like he can just kill them all and we can run off and live happily ever after. Isn't that what I used to read about? My momma was right. Books are absolute fantasy, meant to help someone escape their cold reality, and that's all.

Brilliant pink light ascends across the atmosphere, infecting my sadness with its beauty. But it also means it's almost time.

A knock at the door brings Andromeda inside, holding a black bag. "I'm here to get you ready for—" she stops short and takes in my crumpled, broken form. "This is going to take some work." She sets the bag down and helps me to a chair. "What's wrong with you?" She wrinkles her nose as she brushes my long locks back.

"They're forcing me to be bedded by a monster tonight." My voice is as hollow as my soul.

"Oh, that's funny. I thought tonight you had the honor of marrying into a superior race."

I grab her hand and squeeze until she squirms. "I am already superior, girl. And I'm also already married to a Koridon of the highest order." I toss her hand away, and the brush clanks to the floor. Her affair with the commander of these lands may be about ambition for her, but for me, this marriage is world-ending.

"Can I finish getting you ready, or are you planning to assault me some more?" She pulls out a charcoal pen and aims it toward my eye.

I grip white fingers into my thighs and sit back. "Finish. I would look ravishingly beautiful for my fucking funeral tonight."

The little servant gives me a smoky look around my eyes that mimics the dark coloration Koridons have naturally.

"Are you trying to get pregnant?" I ask her, wondering if she knows the risk.

She rubs me down with a sparkling liquid. "I wouldn't mind. It would give me position."

"I agree that the Koridons are capable of honorable love, but Drakon—"

"You don't know him," she says.

No, I guess I don't. I don't know him, or much about their damn species at all. But one thing's for sure: it won't end well for her. Especially because I won't hesitate to use her against him if I have to. I should treasure her life, but if it comes down to mine or one of the girls I care about, *she's done for.*

After I'm dressed in glittering lavender and my hair's braided in unique patterns, she packs up and moves toward the door.

"You know," I say as she reaches for the handle, "playing games with Drakon, dangerous sex games, will get you broken into a crumpled mass of flesh."

She turns around slowly and her brows pop up. "He won't hurt me. He's *my* slave."

I'm summoned and walk down to the banquet hall where my friends were branded with heavy steps. I think about my last ceremony and what it was like to pass through the invisible barrier into a beautiful, warm greenhouse full of hybrid plants, extraordinary flowers never before seen, unique and made better. Just like me. Tonight will be nothing like that, but at least there's no question of who I am this time.

An altar sits in the middle of the room flickering with candlelight, and the Koridons kneel around it. The ladies from my village, the future brides, sit in chairs behind them. This will be their first experience with this bizarre custom, so I have to be strong for them. Brekter meets my eyes from beside the altar and he's stunning, unfortunately, with his facial hair trimmed and his hair slicked back in an intricate braid. They part to allow me through, and Brekter kisses my hand. I wonder as I walk toward him if he envisions *Maria*.

"I found something for you," he says and nods toward one of the servants in the back. A beautiful sound strikes up, like a voice, a song, but with many instruments that meld together, and my heart flutters.

"It's music," I say, remembering mention of the piano and violin in books I've read, but I had never heard such sounds before. I let it rush through me, caressing my senses, but it quickly turns bittersweet. Another wonderful thing of my past tainted by my present.

With magnanimous faces, Drakon and his mate begin a round of applause. My fingers burn, begging to scratch their fake, entitled faces right off, and the song in the background rises. Brekter's timing may have ruined music for me forever. I loathe the sound even now.

My betrothed lays me down before his people in shadow, and again ice water floods my veins, my chest crushing with anxiety.

Drakon announces, "This is the official mating ceremony between Koridon and human. Before us will be the evidence of their eternal entwinement, body and essence." He waves a hand. "You may proceed."

Eternal entwinement? If he truly believes in this concept, then Kassien really is dead.

The enemy's hands slide up my thighs and remove my undergarments below the sparkling dress, and the cruel feeling of exposure touches my sex. Now is Brekter's moment to show them what a dominant alpha he is, what a creature of strength and reproduction over his new female he is. Where is his first mate, Lorai? Oh no. No, no, could she be here, watching? I haven't seen her, but that doesn't mean she didn't come here with him.

I tense as his fingers work in between my legs, preparing me, and the discomfort is amplified by anger that grips into my spine with its claws. I shake my head, and a terrible scream bursts through my lips. Brekter moves back in alarm as I take ragged breaths, trembling upon the altar. "Calypso," he says so calmly it frightens me. "You promised me."

I shake my head, trying to speak, trying to choke out the words that would explain the gutting feeling that rips through me, but nothing comes out. I did promise I would try, and as much as I don't want to be with Brekter, this isn't about that! I just can't be flayed open and exposed in front of all these beings. Not again. Not like this. I'm already pregnant—this ceremony is inhumane.

Fire sparks in Brekter's piercing quicksilvers, and I cringe as his hand violently takes my throat. "Little animal," he seethes, "you have humiliated me again." I'm lifted from the altar by his powerful grip and slammed back down. Sharp pain splits through my skull, as do my village mate's shrieks. Brekter's hot breath rasps into my face. "You *will* take my seed this night. Will being unconscious make this easier for you?" He slams his fist into my cheek and throws me onto my belly.

C.F. RABBIOSI

My fingers grasp toward the ones who watch, begging for them to stop this, blood dripping from my lips.

"Brekter, you don't understand," I whisper through the ache of sorrow in my throat. *You're ruining us forever.*

"You are nothing but a stupid animal. How dare you deny a god." He rips the dress up my back and hits the flesh of my ass. His handprint sears in and I cry out, so many areas of pain flaring from head to toe. "I loved you. I gave up everything for you!" He rips me down to all fours and transforms me into the animal he speaks of. "But you chose your weak husband over me. An insignificant attachment that couldn't possibly have compared to our love."

"What are you talking about?" I smear black across my arm, wiping my tearful eyes. "Kassien is anything but weak—" Then it hits me. He's not talking to *me* anymore.

"I was going to be gentle," says Brekter spreading my cheeks open, "but a slave should be fucked and broken by its master. So you shall be." I brace myself as his large crown moves against my backside.

"Stop, please, Brekter. I'm not her! Don't—"

Another hit into my back drops me to my stomach.

"How can you do this?" I crawl back up, choking on blood. "How can you allow him to do this?" I scream at their stone cold countenances, wondering why they are letting him beat me with his child's survival already a fragile thing. "You monsters!" I fly up, bursting with hate, and attack Brekter. My teeth sink into his neck and I knee him ferociously in the groin.

I taste his flesh in my teeth and he buckles from the onslaught. My nails tear into his face before I fly to the floor.

Fuck their ceremony.

Drakon's commanding voice finally rings out. "Enough! She has made a travesty of our sacred traditions, and you, Brekter, have only made it worse!"

146

Brekter recoils his fist from its strike toward me. "I know! Rage flows uncontrolled when it comes to her." He forces me against his chest. "But I will salvage this." He strokes my bloody hair back and desperately cups my face. "I love you." He blinks hard and shakes his head. "Forgive me." He kisses me.

"No, you vile creature, you'll never touch me again!" I bite at his face and he grimaces, holding me away.

"You cannot possibly allow this to continue." Gerakon stands up and addresses all of them who watch.

Drakon crosses his arms and tips his head to the side. "It most certainly will continue. She won't be allowed to get away with destroying the ceremony. And there will be far worse repercussions when it's over."

"I will not allow you to punish my mate, Drakon," says Brekter.

"Would a Koridon female be beaten into submission?" Gerakon interjects, coming head-on with the commander.

"Of course not," he replies, his sons appearing next to him. "Our females would never behave like little bitches to deserve it in the first place."

Gerakon peers over at Scarlet, who holds black-haired Alice in hysterics. "If we want to blend our people, we cannot behave like this."

"I agree, father," Ffaelty says, standing in front of me.

Brekter cradles me against him as I struggle. "Calypso, listen to me. I thought you were *her*. I thought you were Maria." He strokes my hair, and his tears trickle down my face. "Speaking of her has possessed me, and all the anger of a hundred years overtook me. Forgive me," he whispers so only I can hear. "Please, I will do anything."

The ache in my flesh turns my heart cold. I could ask him to bed me in private, to end this nightmare like I already tried, and then I'd forgive him. But I'd rather suffer than give him that. What he's done is indefensible. If I must be tormented, then so shall he.

"I will never forgive you." I spit blood into his face. That strange pulsing rises in my hands as the pain and fear tearing through my body becoming concentrated. I clutch his wrist and he buckles, the color leaching from his face. "Now do what you came for tonight, but know that this is the beginning of the end." I release him with a sense of reclaiming my power, my bruised body and soul no longer feeling any pain.

He blinks rapidly and steadies himself, a red-stained tear tracking down his cheek.. "It changes nothing." He drops me to my back and parts my knees. "I love you, Calypso, and I will *make* you feel it."

He ascends across me, and with his shaft in his hand, guides it in as my body naturally resists.

16

A huge crash shatters the air and Brekter rips away from me. He extends a protective arm around my back as everyone in the room jumps to their feet. A man in a black robe stalks into the banquet hall like a predator under the moonlight.

"Identify yourself," Drakon demands, and several Koridon females move forward, Arek and Kraetorr at their backs.

The intruder raises his arm and points a large weapon with moving parts that glide as though they were submerged in water at the approaching Koridons. They draw back immediately, and though it's reasonable to fear it, something about their reaction makes me look closer. A shimmering, moving mass of blackness attaches below the barrel, and without having any idea what it is, my heart still beats wildly at the sight of it.

"Release my wife," the large stranger says and pulls the hood off. His familiar voice matches his face in that moment, and I shove Brekter away to rush to him.

"Kassien!" I cry. He keeps the weapon pointed but grasps me into him with his other arm.

"And others you will be happy to see." His striking eyes pierce through my chest, and I hesitate before looking away. Behind him others rush in and remove their hoods. I collapse, but my mother catches me and I hug her tight, our tears spilling against each other's cheeks.

Finn, taller than I remember and nearly unrecognizable with anger and worry, steps beside me with arms crossed in front of his chest. He isn't the boy I used to see him as. Hardship has always made him seem older, his physique wracked with muscle and scars from dangerous hunts, but tonight he reminds me nothing of the mischievous young boy he was named after. The playful part of Huckleberry has gone away.

"Kassien!" yells Drakon. "I would ask how you are alive, but judging by that dark matter transcender, no explanation is necessary."

"Well hello again, Drakon. I have been looking forward to killing you. And no chance will it be by this thing." He moves the weapon's end to his lips. "Too quick, and I had days to plan your execution as I hung."

"What then?" Drakon asks, splaying his fingers to the side of his face. "Would you have expected me to spare you? One who kills our own to protect a human? You deserve worse."

"Calypso *is* one of us. And I will kill every one of you for her." He rushes Drakon and takes him by the throat. "Are you ready?" Drakon squeaks just before he slams into the ground. The smaller Koridon kicks wildly beneath him, but Kassien subdues him without breaking a sweat. He places his thumbs over Drakon's eyes and presses.

"Stop!" he yells out. "Desist immediately or I swear the Veragotan clan will hunt you down and every one of these humans you care about!"

"You think because I am outnumbered I will bow to you?"

he chuckles darkly. "I think you are intelligent enough to know I am capable of doing exactly as I say." He holds Drakon's eyes deeply into his sockets and turns toward me. I hear his whisper: *I just got you back...*

I shake my head, warning him to stop. My mother's here now, and all my village mates are hanging on by a thread. What if the murder of Drakondoes send a Koridon force from the skies after us? My expression softens as it sinks in. He's really here. Everything will be well now, because *he's here.*

"All right." Kassien releases the pressure, and Drakon lets out a relieved groan "You may keep your pathetic life for now. On the request of my love." He drops a fist into Drakon's nose. Then another blow shatters his cheek. He beats him rabidly, blood spurting through Drakon's teeth as he grunts.

A Koridon woman steps forward, one I've never seen before, and the atmosphere of the room somehow changes for the regal and beautiful being. She speaks in her tongue, but I recognize enough of it to interpret what she says: "Enough! Kassien, release him."

"Thank you, Eladia," Drakon chokes out, scrambling away.

"Drakon, I have come back to stop you," she says. "If what I have heard is true, I may let Kassien continue." Her voice as sharp and elegant as her features. She commands the room, and not a soul can look away from her.

Kassien steps away, his weapon trained on the commander who crawls to his feet. "Sovereign, you will have to kill us both then." Drakon turns his mangled face to Kassien.

"Yes, I am quite aware of the prince's involvement. But he didn't kidnap a village of women and keep them chained, either."

"It is a new world now, Eladia." With hands raised, he steps forward and Kassien aims the blaster at him. "You have been gone for years, searching for some place we can belong. But here, we belong." He stops to spit blood on the floor. "And we have found a way to continue on."

Eladia stands next to Kassien. "I have heard your plans. To enslave the human race and force them to bear your offspring. It is monstrous."

"No." Drakon glides his arm toward Scarlet, who is being shielded by Gerakon. "The women of earth are finding themselves content with their new lives." Glenda's pained expression toward Kraetorr speaks worlds. She's scared, and yet she wants him anyway. She doesn't want to go back to being locked inside the village with no future. "Perhaps we will all be more than content one day."

"And when one of them is impregnated with a male?" I ask. "What will happen to her then?"

"We will ensure survival of mother and child by all means necessary," says the commander. Gerakon cocks his head cynically.

"I'm not content," I say at Kassien's back. He's alive, and mixed emotions rush through me. I've been so angry, but seeing him now, along with my mother, it's the happiest I've felt in a long time. "I did *not* choose to be mated to Brekter."

Darkness surrounds my enemy lover as he moves toward Kassien. "And yet, she is mine now, *Prince*. You will not take her from me."

"Oh, I will," Kassien replies, "but only to free her. She will then choose who she loves." He turns his head slightly toward me. "If she still loves at all."

That isn't something I can answer anymore.

"She has been stolen from you," says Brekter, "in the only way it matters."

"She did not give her heart to you, fool. So she is not stolen."

"Not her heart," says Brekter. "I did not need her heart as I impregnated her womb."

The weapon shakes in Kassien's hand, and his eyes dart toward Gerakon. "She is pregnant?"

Gerakon nods one, begrudging time, then says no more.

Brekter runs his hands down the sleek blackness of his ceremonial wear. "Will you deny the true laws of our kind then, and take her from her rightful mate? Take my child?"

"What say you, Eladia?" Drakon asks. "Calypso is proof that interbreeding is possible. She herself is half-Koridon. Can you not see what this could mean for us? Beginning with Brekter and Calypso, life for us is saved."

The Sovereign's fascination is obvious as she considers the possibility.

Kassien pulls a cylindrical object from inside his cloak and points it at Brekter. "Never going to happen." He hits a button, and a blinding blue ray bursts from the tip. It strikes Brekter and his body pulls apart into a thousand suspended bloody pieces. Screams shatter my ears.

A brave, stupid female rushes Kassien and he blasts the other weapon. The shimmering dark substance fires out and splashes the air as though it hit a wall, and a black hole rips the world open. She's sucked into its haunting nothingness, and Arck gets caught in its pull. He grasps at the floor as he flies feet-first into it.

"Enough Kassien!" cries Eladia. "You may already be put to death for these crimes! Do not kill any more!" He keys a sequence of code into the weapon and the blackness recedes and slams back into the barrel. Arek falls to the ground, panting. "I will speak with both leaders on the matter of blending our species." She moves to Kassien's side and lifts her chin toward Brekter.

Brekter's bloody flesh, disseminated and frozen in time,

twists my gut, and I relive the horrifying expression on his face as his body pulled into pieces. *He's dead.* It's more than I could have hoped for, my freedom handed to me. And yet, something still tugs at me. *Why?* Why do I care? It angers me that I have any feeling for him at all!

Finn runs to his sister. "Are you all right?" my mother asks, touching my swelling jaw.

"Yes," I tell her with a nod. "I am truly all right now."

Kassien bows his head. "Are you entertaining the idea of allowing this kind of union?" he asks his queen. Something stirs inside me as I watch him. He's different somehow, but a glimmer of the perfection he planted inside me blossoms once more. He's a big brute like the rest of them, but he showed me who I am, and mere days together made me feel more alive than I ever have. I yearn for the love I thought I felt for him, and the place inside that greenhouse where we became one. Only he can erase Brekter's toxic infection within my system. *Make me good again!*

"I cannot make that call alone," says Eladia. "But we must consider it, if both human and Koridon can find happiness together."

"You said it was an unnatural forcing of the universe." His harsh voice cracks as sad eyes fall on me.

"Yes. But what are we willing to do to survive? The instinct to reproduce is the most natural and powerful force within biological creatures. There may not be much hope out there." She gestures toward the ceiling.

He keeps the weapons pointed. "But what if we've had our time already?"

Eladia moves to his ear. "That is not for me to say. Why give creatures such intelligence if we cannot use it to survive? What is fate anyway?" She nudges him. "Reassemble Brekter.

You cannot kill a Koridon just because he possesses the mate you want."

"You saw what he did to her," Kassien says with a warning flickering in his supernatural irises. Dominance emanates from his powerful build, and for a moment, I believe he'll blast everyone in this room to pieces. He raises a brow at the floating pieces of flesh. "Anyway, I quite like him this way."

"Do I need to remind you of my command? That if me or my instructions are compromised in any way, the storm that will be rained down upon you and this entire planet?"

He turns toward me and I freeze, wondering if he wants me to beg him not to. He let Drakon live because I willed it, so would he defy everything we believe in now if I conveyed my answer in a sly smile? He reluctantly aims the obliterator with the most subtle tremble. If he disobeys orders, he'll be punished with his life. If he doesn't... he'll be saying goodbye to me. The blinding light reappears, and the floating flesh squelches back together in an instant. Brekter falls to the floor, a quivering mass of nerves.

"He'll be in agony for quite a few days," says Kassien. "But in time will—"

Firm arms snake around my waist from behind and yank me against a steely chest. Kassien flips around and takes aim, and my mother stifles a gasp but doesn't move an inch from my side.

"Drakon!" Kassien roars. "Release her."

"Shoot one of those projectile weapons off and see your human sucked into freezing, suffocating space, or torn into a million pieces."

"What is it you want?" Eladia asks, her perfect calm unwavering. "Because you have taken it upon yourself to change the course of our history, and I just told you I am willing to consider it."

"There is no chance of me missing, Drakon." Kassien lightly fingers the trigger and swipes his tongue over his lip.

"Do you wish me to snap your bitch's neck, then?" Drakon gives me a fierce squeeze, but with a grimace, I refuse to whimper. "Place the weapons on the floor and step away."

He checks behind him and holds his ground. "Stay back, all of you! I still have an intense desire for blood right now." He growls at Brekter's shivering form. The shadowy figures of Drakon's sons and the females in the dark background stop dead.

"Don't do it, Kassien," I say. "Never give this sadistic pig power again." I think of the servant boy who was mutated into a vicious creature, the brandings into the skin of my friends, and the cruelness in his voice when he told Brekter to force himself on me as I lie bleeding.

"Fire on me, and I throw her into the blast," he says, his claws digging into my waist. "I am willing to chance my survival, sure that I will be upon you in that split second you hesitate from grief."

"You hung me on hooks and took my woman," he snarls. "I *will* kill you, whether it's now or tomorrow."

"You have sent one of your own through a rip in time," Eladia says, "and Brekter lies in ill repair. You will not harm another of your fellow Koridons, Kassien. Not even I will be able to save you."

I still want him to kill the bastard, against all logic. I fight past the pain from Brekter's fists and drop down, trying to break his grip. Drakon's steel arms hold firm, and the ache of wrenching downward flares up.

"Drakon, release her," Eladia demands, but he constricts my waist tighter.

"You won't hurt her." My mother moves in front of us, and

the weapons at her back send fear rippling through me. I shake my head furiously at Kassien and he lowers them.

"Woman," says Kassien. "Get out of the way!"

"Hush Kassien," she says. "I have something important that needs to be said."

"Persephone, what could you possibly—"

"Shh!" She turns around, and I sense the threatening face she gives him as I've seen it many times.

"Drakon, do you remember me?" She removes her cloak and lets her hair down to fall past her waist.

His grip wavers.

"Many years ago I lost my grandmother, my only living relative, and was being transported from the village in the east to a new one. A Koridon found me one of those nights as I slept and pulled me from my bed."

"You?" His voice falters. "And she is—"

Her long, auburn hair gleams and matches the fire in her eyes. "Now let go of your daughter and the heir that grows in her belly." Shock pulses through me and I retch upon her words. "My name's Persephone, if you didn't catch that. And it's time we talked."

His grip falls away and I break free, blinded by tears. "No," I say to her, touching a regretful hand to my stomach. "He can't be." Since I learned the truth about what happened to my mother out in the woods, I had envisioned my Koridon father as being someone from the east shores or somewhere remote, a bastard I'd never have to meet. I despise him and hate that I share his genes, but he has position, so I wipe away my tears and let it empower me.

"I knew it the moment I saw him tonight," Mother says, "and he knows I speak the truth."

Drakon's lips tighten into a thin line. His mate, along with several others, watch from behind him at the broken door.

"Give the flesh obliterator and dark matter transcender to Eladia," he says. "Then we will negotiate."

She nods at Kassien. "I see no other choice but to come to an agreement." Her form crackles as though it's immaterial, and I blink hard, trying to make sense of what I just saw. "And my time here is running out."

Drakon and the others move past us, giants towering with graceful movements, and we follow them to the banquet table. "I would ask that only myself and my mate discuss this matter with Kassien and the royal sovereign. The rest of you are excused to your quarters."

"No." Finn tightens his hold around Glenda's shoulders. "You won't discuss my sister's fate without me present."

Vaerynn steps in front of him and they're head to head. "You have no choice, human. Do as you are told or—"

"Or what?" He moves his forehead threateningly against hers. She shoves him, but even as the force knocks him back, he grabs her wrist. Flinging her around, he holds her back against him. "We stay," he whispers. His fingers trail down the middle of her chest and Vaerynn turns her face to the side, nearly touching his. Her skin flushes and she shakes her head, trying to clear her mind. He pushes her away and she stumbles. Looking up with humiliation from her hands and knees, she gets up and runs from the room.

Arek moves toward Finn and Glenda but Kraetorr jumps in front of him. "She stays." He takes Glenda into his arms. "She will be with me always from now on."

Finn's mouth falls open to protest, but the devotion in Kraetorr's embrace toward his sister quiets him suddenly.

Kraetorr and the brute Kjartonn are my brothers. It finally hits me. And Efaelty—she's my sibling also. All I can think of is being an only child and wishing I had a father and brothers and sisters. Never would I have suspected that creatures from another planet were my blood!

"Now we have an accord," says Finn, heading to the banquet table to take the first seat.

"The women and their," Kassien motions toward my mother, "*family* will be a part of this meeting if they wish. Too long have both our races suffered on this planet, so tonight we change everything." I take the seat next to Kassien, and my mother beside me. He may never be mine again, but by his side is the only place I feel safe right now. Under the table, his fingers brush against mine and I startle. He feels so right and so safe after all this time being in the enemy's grip, and I hold his hand, warmth washing over me.

"We weren't suffering before *you* came," says Finn and noisily scrapes his chair across the floor to be closer to the leaders at the head of the table. He plops down and throws a dirty boot up on the table top. "We've had to hide, scrape, and die in fear in our own world."

"They had come for help, Finn," I say. "We thought they came here to destroy us and take everything, but that's not how it happened."

"Oh really? And which one of these lying aliens told you that?" Finn asks with a scoff. I hide a grin at his audacity in a room *full* of lying aliens.

"My *sister* told me that," I reply to my old friend and once fiancé, feeling the heat rise in my cheeks. Efaelty limps into view and Kassien takes her in for a moment, happiness overwhelming his face that she lives.

"It's the truth," she says. "We had grown weak trying to live in space, and before that the depths of the ocean. We found this planet at the last moment, it seemed." A pang of jealousy hits me as I wonder if she and Kassien will be together again now that Brekter has a claim on me. Two of the females tend to his twitching body, preparing to take him to the med bay on their ship.

Eladia swipes her finger through the air and strange symbols materialize. She selects the floating buttons, and the transparent screen changes. "I will document our agreements this night and press for authentication in your favor if this is truly the path you wish to take," she says. "If you create a new species here, you will be left here as your own people, even as the rest of us move on."

Drakon's servant girl appears behind him, the chandelier casting an eerie glow, and he shudders, feeling her. His mate stiffens. "My eyes have been opened," the commander says. "I press that we make marriages between human and Koridon legal, even required, immediately."

"Required?" I say. "That's slavery. We should be free to marry who we choose. Including other humans."

"We do not have time for this to naturally play out," Drakon says, fist to the table.

Gerakon removes his hand from his temples. "We have been sending you word that our numbers were dwindling, our plants and creatures growing weak and sickly, *Entra Sovian*."

Eladia reflects a moment before speaking. "We have traveled so far to find an optimal planet that even at warp speeds it can take months to reach this place. For those of you unfamiliar with interstellar travel," she addresses us humans, "our ships travel faster than the speed of light by antigravity propulsion, powered by elements that do not occur naturally on Earth. This explains why even at the peak of your society you had not made it deep into space yet. Without the element, the contents inside a craft would be obliterated at such speeds. However, the universe is the size of infinity, and no amount of super speed is instant. It is why I am here now in alternate form with only my consciousness downloaded into this shadow body."

"You aren't here?" I blurt out.

She shakes her head, and her shadow form fades in and out. The connection to her mind grows unstable. I would worry that something could go wrong and I'd lose myself forever.

"But the weapons—" says Finn.

The rip in the world that sucked the female through wasn't a trick, and Brekter's floating pieces that reconstructed upon the press of a button put tremors through the world, but it *was* the real world.

"They were here already, says Eladia. "Kept in a hidden, indestructible box, and that is where they will be returned when I leave."

I can see that Finn's impressed: it's every science fiction novel he's ever read brought to life. As advanced as they are, as many other societies must be, I still never want to be like them. If they are what we are striving to become, I hope we never make it. They have weapons that do interesting and terrible things, as well as ships that can travel to different worlds, but they've lost the joy of *life*. Intelligence and always striving scientifically could leave us one day the gray-bodied, frightening-looking aliens described in books. They don't feel the rush of singing their hearts out, or the thrill of the kiss. They don't read their children stories before bed or laugh and play. *Advanced* is a relative term, a perspective, and that is all.

"I say if the humans want to exist in harmony, they surrender their women to us for breeding and that is the end," says Kjartonn, running his fingers through blond Alice's light tresses. She yanks away as Drakon adamantly agrees.

Kassien puts an arm around me and says, "We assume it is our right to exist. But we live on borrowed time, jumping from our world to others. I say we do this fairly and let fate decide if we are worthy to go on existing."

"That is not good enough for me," says Drakon. "You think of yourself and your ruined bride there, and not of the future of our great race."

He smiles toward the convulsing heap of Brekter. "I think of her, yes. But also of the ones she loves. We all want children, some of us have even had them, if only for a moment." His steady voice wavers with a note of sorrow. That and the look on Efaelty's face weave a story that he hasn't told me yet.

Vaerynn says, "It will not do just to make these girls mates. They must be conditioned to bear such a child and such an honor. They must overcome tests of strength, strong bodies, strong minds, better chances of bearing a healthy child."

"You have no idea of our strength, *woman*," says Finn. He pulls at the collar of his stained button-down shirt then intertwines his fingers in front of him. "For instance, Glenda was only six during the harshest winter we'd ever experienced. We were starving and she fell ill with one of her lung conditions. She could barely walk to the bathroom and yet, when Mother collapsed from starvation while the men were away hunting, she kept the fire going. Our mother gave every bit of food to Glenda, you see. A snow storm hit us while we were out there, but Glenda went out in it and found someone to help though the storm was blinding and she was so small, and so sick."

I remember that. She'd fallen several times, her clothes frozen to her body when she made it to Scarlet's door. They went and forced broth into Glenda's mother and she recovered.

"That's strength," says Finn, and Glenda lifts her chin proudly.

"I have seen their strength." Vaerynn admits. "Many of my

beliefs are being tested." Her long lashes blink up at Finn, and she grows strangely quiet.

"Do we then give them the choice to undergo the training as well?" asks Drakon. "There are many things that will have to be considered in order to make this work."

"Setting loose a rabid beast upon us, then burning our flesh horribly teaches nothing but cruelty," I say. "But if a woman chooses a Koridon male as her mate, the conditioning in Koridon strength and culture should be part of the vow."

Kassien's fingers intertwine with mine. He squeezes as he peers into my eyes. "You would take a brand into your skin and avow yourself to incredible pain?"

My chest crushes with the realization. "For you, I would." Distrust flows through my better senses, yet his presence and touch envelop me in a mesmerizing sea I want to drift away in forever.

The arguments continue hour after hour, everyone with a new, enlightening thought that just confuses things and makes it more difficult to come to an agreement. But this is what I know: the Koridons have our scent swimming through their blood and the softness of our skin tattooed upon their nerve endings and will never let us walk away. Even as Kraetorr stroked Glenda's back as she nodded off and Arek's gaze continued to land upon blond Alice who he proclaimed to be disgusted with, I knew our two species' paths were eternal.

We'd fight until our bones were broken, hate each other until we'd collapse from denying our love, but we were theirs and they were ours.

17

Eladia draws complex symbols into the air and they glow bright orange before fading away like a Koridon document written in permanence in some invisible interstellar file. "This is what I am proposing," she says. "The human females will go forth with their current betrothals to the Koridon males at this time. The training will be revised to strength and skill appropriate to the women's current condition and will only be used to strengthen the outcome of the challenging birthing process. If the women or Koridons wish to part ways, it will be only after the child reaches three years of age. The mating can then be terminated at which point both are allowed to be with whomever they choose. Currently-mated beings are no more, and all males, especially those of monarchal descent, must be mated immediately to ensure their genetically superior bloodlines. In return for these women's sacrifice, no human will be enslaved any longer, no human will be harmed, and all are free to roam the land from this moment forward." Eladia peers around the room. "Are these acceptable terms?"

I nod my head immediately, consumed with relief for my

mother and all of our villages who have lived in constant hiding. If this works, the Koridons will have new laws and will no longer be able to oppress our people. Only the few will suffer, *us*, and it's what I wanted the moment Kassien chose to take me as his mate. Without thinking, I look at him, and it's a grave mistake. My happiness floods away as the unnatural beauty of his face twists into a mask of despair.

"Will my Koridons unite once more under these new laws and cease the killing of one another?" the sovereign asks.

The Koridons nod collectively as Kassien stares straight ahead.

"And Calypso?" he seethes. "What of her?" His molten eyes flick up and the air around him grows hot.

Eladia purses her lips. "The child within her dictates she be with the father. But after three years, she will be free again."

"If I want to end it after the baby's born, what will happen to him?" I ask, thinking about the preciousness of a little three-year-old: their little hands and round tummies

Kassien jerks his head toward me at the revealing of the baby's sex.

"Three years with your child, and if you choose another at that point, he will be given over to the father and trusted elders to be raised from that day on."

My heart sinks. "Tearing a child from his mother at that age is cruel."

"The mother leaving the child is cruel," Vaerynn interjects.

No matter what now, Brekter has me forever unless I find the courage to walk away from both him and my son. I feel the squeeze of my mother's hand, and in that moment know I will *never* leave my child. "We can't agree to this," my mother says, sending murmurs, protests, and sighs of relief through the room.

"You will if you don't want all of your miserable people

hunted down and enslaved," says Kjartonn, who saunters up behind. His shadow reaches across the room and chills engulf me.

"Get away from her," Kassien growls. He jumps to his feet, and his massive form fights back Kjartonn's cold shadow. "As long as she is in danger, I will never stop killing. I'm *incapable*." His fist slams forward, stopping an inch from Kjartonn's face. "My life be damned."

The royal sovereign puts a hand up in warning, but I interrupt before she has to intervene further. I can't let everything we've just achieved be shattered to pieces.

"We will not agree to it unless something in your law protects us during the marriage." I lift my bruised arms and spit venom at the unconscious Brekter.

Eladia touches the discoloration softly. "I will write protection into the orders now. The binding will be dissolved if the woman is coerced into mating by violence or if she is brutalized by the one who is supposed to protect her." She creates more symbols in the air and Kassien reads them to us aloud.

I'm tired and broken but satisfied. Kassien called down the thunder and has saved us all.

Morning light seeps in through the curtains and Vaerynn, along with two other females prepare rooms for us in the mansion. No longer would we be chained to our beds at night. We'd have our own space, sharing with just one other girl, and I'll have my mother with me as well.

Brekter is scooped off the floor and taken to the ship's med bay. He'll never stop coming for me, and no law will keep his tormenting at bay. He likes my quivering, frightened flesh, and is aroused by my pain. I will pay every day for what Maria did to him all those years ago, and for how his heart beats for me. When I asked the sovereign to make the law, I knew it wouldn't benefit me. But it will help the others.

Blond Alice pulls the covers up to her tear-streaked face and turns over, sobs making her shudder in silence. Kjartonn shows the same cruelty his father does. *Our* father does. I replay the poisoned word. The others are harsh and violent natured, but their woman brings them to their knees. Especially with Kraetorr. But blond Alice's betrothed is driven by that crazed lust, under a black spell that leads to unnatural desire and violence to achieve sexual heights of a red maddened mind. I don't see her surviving this for long.

The beautiful warmth from my mother beside me comforts, and my tumbling thoughts subside enough for me to drift off.

A knock at the door startles me from my partial slumber and I sit up. Kassien peeks in through the cracked door and I quickly get out of bed, my blanket slipping to the floor. "I don't want to wake blond Alice," I say, closing the door. The hallway stands empty, though muffled voices float up from below.

Exhausted, there's nothing I could think to say that would matter. "What do you—" His haunting pools of quicksilver snatch my words away. He touches down the middle of my chest and I soak in his warmth.

"I could not save you from him, my Calypso."

I step back, the loss of his touch an unnatural pain. "You got what you wanted." I turn away, and strong hands snap me back.

"No." He holds me against the wall and presses his face into my neck. "I have not protected you." His voice pushes through me. "But I vow to kill him, even if it means my life for what I must do."

"I don't blame you for what's happened." Held against his

chest, I breathe him in, allowing his essence to fill me like I've dreamed of every night since I lost him. "I love you," I say hollowly. "And nothing has changed that."

"You were the only thing that kept me alive. I had to get back to you."

He seeks comfort at my lips, but I can't give it to him. I whisper against them, their near touch overwhelming my senses. "Goodbye, Kassien," I say, though all I want is to wrap my legs around him and melt into his skin. It's not sex or lust that makes me yearn to bathe in his light, it's the constant feeling of being treasured.

He holds me and I'm stuck tight, his pulse thundering against my chest. "Tonight a mating ceremony will take place."

"Will you be staying then?"

His eyes shine as he lifts them slowly to me. "Yes. But—" He presses his kiss against my hand then holds it to his cheek. In his smile is sadness, something hidden, but I'm so glad he'll be here. I feel safer with him and my mother than I have in so long. "I overheard Gerakon talking to Eladia," he deflects, "about a strange reaction Kraetorr experienced to protect one of the women."

"I think Drakon was so shocked when it happened that he let Glenda go to bed without getting the mark."

"He also tried to talk to her about something else that seemed urgent, but she faded away."

"Faded away?"

"The connection dissolved, and in quite a show of lights, she disappeared."

"What about the weapons?" I ask, wishing I could shoot a specific few of the Koridons real quick before the day ends.

"They are hidden once more."

Somewhere I hope Kassien has access to. I still don't trust Drakon or any of his lot, even with the new laws in place. "Any idea what else Gerakon wanted to tell her?" I ask, instinctively touching my stomach.

He shakes his head. "No. I cannot imagine." He kisses my palm and clutches it as though it were precious. "There is something I must tell you. I cannot leave your side. I will stay here with you, but the cost is high."

I tense in his arms. "What are they going to do to you? Please, don't stay if you can't bear it. I won't be able to live with myself."

"I took you from your world selfishly and nothing will stop me from protecting you in this new one. You may belong to Brekter by law, but I will be at his back ready to snap his neck if he ever touches you again." His fingertips tremble over my bruises.

"I found out who I really am because you took me. Though I suffer at Brekter's hands, I still think this is the best we could ask for in regards to our people." It hurts to say the words, knowing the villages may one day be safe but at a tremendous price for us few.

"I suspected your father may be Drakon or one of his spawn," he says.

The age difference between us glares, and I wonder how old my half-brothers are. Drakon has many offspring, but he must have had them a long time ago before their children stopped surviving here. And that many heirs is no doubt the reason he has become so powerful. "I don't want anything to do with that monster."

"You're so much more like your mother anyway. Except that she's *far* scarier."

I beam up at him. "She found you."

"She saved me. In my last moments. Tenak is gone, but if your mother had not come for me, I would have left my body as well."

I pause, feeling the sorrow of Tenak's loss. "I'm so glad we're all together. It isn't under the best circumstances, but I don't care. I'm so happy."

"Calypso..." His voice somehow rumbles into my core, a soft stroking that pulls at the desire I try to tamp down. "Three years, then you are mine eternally."

"Oh," I murmur, knowing what I have to say, though I don't wish to. But he has to know. "I could never leave my child, Kass."

"But he would be in the best of hands. Raised well. You will not consider it?"

"I want you, but I will never abandon my child. I'm sorry."

"No." He holds me once more, stroking the back of my head, desperate movements, as though it sinks in that we may never be. "Do not apologize. I never should have asked it. But my need for you is so strong I am blind to all else."

"And *you* will want a child, won't you?" I ask. He had an overwhelming desire to have my body, but the production of an heir was a huge part of it.

He takes a deep breath and moves toward the stairs. "Something has come up, in fact. It will be painful for you. But I fear it is my only choice."

"What are you saying?"

"Eladia has ordered..." He shakes his head and moves away. "I would leave, but I love you too much."

"Just talk to me," I say to his back, wishing I could go wherever he's going. "I don't understand." He descends out of sight, and I trust that whatever must happen now, I don't want to know before a good night's rest.

The sun comes up too quickly as I fade in and out of sleep. Vaerynn sneaks in and leaves three gowns on the vanity, and anxiety clenches my stomach. I get up slowly so as not to disturb Momma, and find the ceremony dress that's bigger than the other two. Holding the shiny black and gold material against me, I wonder who will be mated tonight in that awful show of power and domination. I should have asked the sovereign to do away with that barbaric ritual as well—after all, we're giving up most of ourselves to become Koridon mothers, so why can't they give up some things too?

"Caly?" my mother says. "What is that?" She sits up and gestures for me to hand the dress to her.

I toss her the one that will fit her. "We're to attend the gruesome mating ceremony of one of the girls tonight."

Blond Alice gasps and flies out of bed. Out of breath, she places her palms on the window and feels all around the glass.

"Will it be her?" my mother asks and throws the dress on the floor. "I won't watch this tonight."

"I don't know, and I don't blame you." I slip the dress over my head and fix my sky blue locks in front of me. "But she's supposed to be wed to a really nasty character, so I hope not."

"Isn't there a way she can marry one of the others?" Mother walks up behind the crying girl looking out upon the sea.

"Kjartonn has some sick obsession with her, and he's the commander's son. I don't know if there's anything that can be done."

"Oh, there is," blond Alice says and knocks on the glass. "It's so beautiful out there in the ocean, isn't it?" Her voice sounds soft and far away as she marvels at the vast waters rippling with pink rays of the sunset. "If I could walk into it just one more time."

"Alice," my mother says, turning the girl to face her. "Just do this. Pull out every reserve of bravery and... *ferociousness* that our women have burning inside. You will let him have you, but only because you're going to find his weakness. Only because you are going to find a way to destroy him from the inside out."

"I can't stop him from destroying me first," she says, blinking tears down her cheeks.

"Yes you can. They don't know how strong we are, little one. Show him. Show them all." Mother hugs her and their images blur through my stinging tears. She holds her, rubbing a hand softly along her back. "I was terrified when Drakon came to me in the night, but as awful as it was, it changed me forever. It gave me power to be loved by the enemy race. I was special. And the daughter that resulted was a reason for me to live when no other existed. Having a child is joy of the purest kind and worth every last pain on earth, dear girl."

Blond Alice bows her head. "I don't know if I can do this. I look into the future and only see darkness."

18

Once summoned, we follow the slave Andromeda down to the banquet hall along with Glenda, black-haired Alice, and Jane. The Koridons await us under candlelight, heads bowed to the floor, and in the middle, Arek crouches over Mary-Shelly's sprawled-out body.

Blond Alice stumbles, and Mother keeps her steady. She shakes with relief but a sob still escapes her as though she had *prepared* herself to get mating over with to Kjartonn. We kneel together along with the others and my pulse spikes at the sight of the entangled bodies, their skin dancing under the candle flicker.

Mary-Shelly's arms are lifted above her head by powerful hands, and red hair spreads out, contrasting with her snow white skin. Arek's face remains steady, a testament of his dedication to breed, despite his objection to laying with a human. His back ripples with muscle as he holds himself above her and her knees fall effortlessly apart for him. I do a quick check for Kassien, but don't find him. Gasps fill the air. I'm humiliated for my friend and look away, but a silent scream pulls me back to the scene, the echo of such emotion...

Arek meets blond Alice's eyes dead-on. He carefully guides his shaft through Mary-Shelly's open legs, and her body buckles as he moves inside. She gasps, her fingers digging into the ground to push against his force, but Arek remains fixed on the one he wants. The one he's always wanted.

His pace quickens as he holds blond Alice hostage. He makes love to his new mate without ever spiritually touching her. It's Alice only, and being in her eyes allows him to be in her body. Mary-Shelly's back grates against the floor as Arek works her, unnatural thickness thrusting in and out. She wraps her legs around him and lightly touches his ass, and Arek falters, distracted by her affection. She's trying to please him, but I fear what he'll do to her in the heat of the moment if she angers him.

He shakes his head and resumes the pistoning of his hips. Blond Alice squeezes my hand and they stare at each other, a slight moan slipping from her mouth. Arek groans and slams in one last time, and my breath catches as he knots Mary-Shelly. He grips her shoulders and holds her against him, her choked utterances muffling into his chest. Every muscle in her body tenses as his seed pulses. He digs in deeper as his climax continues to push through her and his skin beads with sweat.

Blond Alice collapses and lies on my lap, the spell between them broken. Now he will father a child with Mary-Shelly and she will be thrown to the mercy of Kjartonn. The Koridons stand and walk in a circle around them until Arek pulls away and is handed material to wipe his new mate down. He starts at her face and gently works his way down her chest, then places it over the nakedness between her legs. Taking her in his arms, he keeps her waist slightly elevated so his seed isn't lost, and carries her away.

I stroke Alice's hair and catch my breath, searching again for Kassien. "It's over," I purr. "We'll go to bed now."

"He was gentle with her," she sobs, not caring who hears. "I thought he would brutishly fuck her. I thought it would make me feel better."

Some of them do, I don't dare say to her. If I weren't part Koridon, there are times at which Brekter would have torn me to pieces. "I've noticed the connection between you and Arek. I'm sorry he couldn't be your mate."

"I hated him at first. More than the others even. But something comes to life inside me that I can't explain when he's near." She swallows with a shiver. "And I felt him more than ever just now. What's happening to me?"

"When Brekter makes me lie with him, I'm screaming inside the entire time. I understand." What I can't tell her is that I still end up responding to Brekter sexually, but that may be because he knows how to push a woman's body to places she doesn't want to go.

Kjartonn and Kraetorr move in front of us and blond Alice cringes. The servants clean the altar and everyone in the room takes their positions back into deep bows upon the floor. I put my arm around blond Alice. "No. Not another ceremony tonight?"

She jumps to her feet and backs against the wall, trying to speak, but only managing to shake her head.

"She really doesn't want to marry you, Kjartonn," I say, standing in front of her. "There must be another that can take your place. This isn't right. You can't possibly want someone who hates you."

Kjartonn tips his head and a slow, mad smile creeps along his lips. "She is mine. I have thought of nothing else since I felt that slick little crevice between her legs." He holds her by the waist and flicks his tongue on her neck. "I will have her and

175

when she is mine, I will abuse it until she can't move anymore."
He takes her by the back of the neck. "Perhaps a ceremony can
be done away with and I can take you now." His thickness
probes against her and he lifts her by one hand, her feet kicking
above the ground.

Kraetorr strikes a fist into his back and he lets her go with a
hiss. "You will wait until she can be yours properly," he says to
the lust-crazed Koridon. "Now let us take Calypso."

"Wait," she calls out, but they grasp my arms on each side.

"Where are you taking me? Let me go!" The room grows
deathly silent, and in that moment I realize that not only is
Kassien absent, but so is Scarlet. *Something has come up, in
fact. It will be painful for you. But I fear it is my only choice,*
Kassien had said, and I can feel the heat of his hand against my
cheek again.

They appear in the doorway and fire bursts inside my
chest. "No! You—" Anger blinds my judgment, and I snap my
wrists out of their hold. They jolt back as though a shock hit
them, and I run.

"She was to be spared the details of this night!" bellows
Kassien, and I slam into his arms. "Listen to me." He bends
down to take me prisoner in his eyes. "Under the new law, I
must be mated to a woman in order to remain here with this
outlying clan. I want nothing more than to leave! I want to take
you and run away forever so badly I can hardly breathe." *Of
course I could never allow that.* This isn't one of my novels, I
can't ride off into the sunset with my prince and leave my
mother and best friend to the wolves.

You're going to—" I bury my head in his chest and find
Scarlet's hand next to him. "I know you have to—" Nothing I
say can come anywhere near describing the gutting dread
welling up inside me. And it doesn't matter anyway. I was

there, I agreed to the new Koridon law as well. I hate that I can't justify the anger and betrayal I feel.

"Go back to your room, my love," he says and strokes my hair. "You know what is in my heart."

"No, I can't bear this! How could you agree to this union?" I say in defiance against what I already know.

"Because the woman *Scarlet* is special to you and with *me* she will be safe." I look over at Kjartonn, who cracks a wicked grin at blond Alice. She cocks her head at me, fear and urging splashing her face. Kassien leans into my ear. "And I promised I would do whatever I must to protect you from Brekter. So tonight, our families are joined."

"I'm sorry," Scarlet says, barely audibly. Her smoky colored eyes drip with tears, making her eyes sparkle the same vivid color of her gown, and I can't hate her. Of course Kassien is still expected to marry one of us and go along with this new world. And through the twisting and blurring of the candlelight around me, something inside knows that if it had to be anyone, I'm glad it's my best friend. And I'm glad it's him. So why does everything inside me burn? Fury from being trapped here, pregnant with the enemy's child and all the confusing things I've felt since meeting Kassien explodes, and my spirit melts. My legs fail and Kassien holds me up.

"Forgive me. And trust me," he says, holding the back of my head as I cry.

"I stand by them." I take a shuddered breath and make out my mother through the blur. "This prince is one of the only decent mates in the lot." She takes me in her eyes. "And there's nothing to be done about it now. She'll be safe with him."

"Of course," I bite out and shove Kassien away. Inside, I want Scarlet safe too. Happy even. And out of all of them, she would be so happy with—

"I cannot abide it!" Gerakon tears through the crowd, and Drakon takes hold of him.

"Control yourself," Drakon snarls into his face. "You have a duty, like all of us!"

"But there is something to be said about this union," he cries out, blinking rapidly. His connection to Scarlet has finally broken him. But it won't change this. Nothing will.

Drakon's sons stand threateningly against him, and he slumps in defeat. He shakes his head at Kassien, a desperate message silenced as they drag him away.

"Now take her out of here," says Kassien, moving threateningly against Drakon. "You swore she would be spared from this, but here she stands."

"Were you going to be married and keep it from me?" I ask him, hurt flooding my voice.

"Of course not," he replies. "I wanted to spare you the misery of knowing our exact moment together and tell you gently within a few weeks. I think only of you." He turns back to the commander. "Now get her out of here!"

The space between them sizzles and power radiates from Kassien's great form. Drakon's hardened demeanor softens and he backs up ever so slightly. "Well, of course she will be escorted out," he says, brushing off his cowardice. "It was not expected that she would be difficult."

Kassien smirks. "Now I know you lie." He runs his hands down my shoulders. "Go on to bed." He then turns abruptly, leaving me to my only wretched choice. "All of you! I will *privately* take this woman, Scarlet, as my *bride* I think the word is. And I am changing tradition. There will be no ceremony tonight."

"That is against our custom," says Drakon. "The agreement was made to prove you won't be a threat to us."

"And to cause as much pain between Calypso and I as possible," he says.

He shrugs and lifts a finger. "If you mate the human in private, we cannot bear witness, so how can it count as a mating without the celebration of your bodies before us?"

Kassien grips Drakon's shoulder. "I will do what I must to keep our contract... but it will be behind closed doors tonight. Anyone who challenges me will die slowly." Drakon buckles with the force, and Kraetorr reaches for something in his belt.

The older Koridon glowers up at him. "Very well. We shall see the result of the union in her belly then." He ducks away and touches Scarlet's stomach. My heart wrenches at the thought of her small body trying to carry Kassien's child. If it ends up being male, she may not survive it.

"I'm going to bed," I say, knowing I have no other choice. The world crushes down on me, but all I can do is go back to my room where my mother awaits. It's my one comfort. I turn to walk away but stop.

I hug Scarlet tight. "It will be all right. This is for the best." Leaving her without a word would have made this difficult night so much worse for her.

"I love you," she whispers. "I won't let him do it."

I squeeze her harder, wishing it were that simple because it eases my pain so much. The crowd, Koridons and humans mixed, seem to hold their breath as they shimmer in the dying candlelight.

"It won't help," I say, imagining Kassien's lips, soft against mine and entwined by some kind of magic in his rough embrace. I pull away, leaving her with a new thought.

19

KASSIEN

The valspridian armor I remove from my shoulders is heavy as I unlatch it and let it fall to the ground. The little light-haired woman jumps from its *clank* and I feel the smallest amount of remorse for scaring her. True, Drakon, that *fuck*, gave me Calypso's best friend to hurt them both, and to mess with my head, but I meant what I said to my love. I will care for this one that she adores like no one else, because she is precious and I would do anything for Calypso.

Scarlet paces the room then plops down on the bed. Her creamy thigh becomes uncovered and she quickly covers it. Then throws the dress off of it once more. She lies back and sighs.

I'm not sure how I'll get through this night.

Scarlet's chest moves up and down as I turn the brass key in its lock. Her scent floats into my nostrils and seeps into my blood, moving places of me to action as I approach her. I am an alpha predator, all masculine and brutish, and I can certainly impregnate such a lovely creature.

I touch her face and gently move my fingertips down her

neck, trailing them between her breasts, her robe opening slightly.

She opens the material and silvery moonlight floods along her breasts and creamy stomach, beckoning an already wild beast.

Calypso's voice whispers in the air between us and I shake my head, trying to scare away the demons with her face. She torments my resolve and ices my boiling loins.

I have to do this. Mating this woman is my only chance to protect Calypso, isn't it? By all laws and morality, she belongs to Brekter now. There's nothing I can do except move forward.

Save our race.

Save *Calypso*.

She isn't mine, but I still feel her, all over me and stabbing at the core of me where new unbelievable love has been born.

Scarlet slams the silky material back over her nakedness and sits up. "I don't think I can do this."

I dip my head, and a few loose tendrils fall over my heated gaze. "You do not have to do much of anything, though, do you woman?"

She bites her satin pink lip and rocks forward. "I mean, I don't want to have sex with you."

Sex. It used to be a physical reaction brought on by a decision to reproduce with my own Koridon females. Lust wasn't a part of mating, it was duty. But these women with their delicate beauty and intoxicating scents have reactivated sleeping instincts that were suppressed long ago. Oh, they're so pointless, weakening even, but so blissful I would fall to my knees and surrender to the right woman. "Have you been with a man or any such since the night your innocence was stolen from you?" I ask.

A chill ripples through her and I sit up, having the urge to take her hand. "I hurt for you," I say, remembering how she'd picked herself up from the ground the night I found Calypso and ran back to her village, blood staining the land.

"Caly already told me not to be afraid, that it's different with you. But I can't, *because* it's you."

A knock sounds at the door and I open it to find a servant with a bottle. "From Persephone," he says and hands it to me. *Old Vine Zinfandel circa de* 2022. She comes inside and sets two glasses down.

"Thank fucking *Pan*." Scarlet pours the red liquid up to the rim and gulps it down. "Have some," she says, nudging the glass toward me.

I lift it to my lips and carefully drink. It burns my tongue, but when I let off, she presses her fingers against the bottom and I drink it down.

"Wine," she says and wipes the ruby drops from her lips. "I used to sneak it during celebrations back home. Me and Caly both."

"It tastes like poison mixed with piss." I toss the glass on the table and pour another. "Listen," I say. "I will make this as painless as possible, but you will submit to me."

She twirls the stem of the glass in her fingertips. "I know. Just trying to knock myself out for it."

"The numbing effect is quite nice, I will say. Here, have some more."

The bottle lies on its side with little drops slowly making their way to the floor. She's talkative now, and I enjoy every word about how she grew up deep in the forest, her family and their traditions. I especially like the one she tells about stealing the eggs from their chickens and ducks to dye them colors from berries and hide them for the younglings. It's unlike me to find such an idiotic thing entertaining, and through my blurry thoughts I wonder if that's exactly the reason why I like it.

Scarlet laughs and lays her head on my chest. Her warmth is intrusive, but it's good to start contact. "Dad had the bird by its legs and was swinging it around and around. The screeching was awful." I listen to her laugh and enjoy the sound.

"Was there another here you would have preferred?" I blurt out.

She clears her throat, her chuckle stopping abruptly. "I don't know. I had this feeling with— with Gerakon."

The reason for his outburst earlier in the night. "His knowledge and thirst for science on this planet is incredible. He wants to know everything and fights to understand. He cares so much, that is why he betrayed me to be here."

"Betrayed you?"

"He left the compound with Brekter and Drakon, knowing my first and I were being left to die."

"How could he?"

"He once told me that we should find your villages. Take everything from you, all your writings, to help us in our planting, animal husbandry and general survival in this place."

"Why *didn't* you just take everything from us?"

"I am ruler here, and laws to protect you have been in place for two centuries."

She leans up on her elbow. "But Drakon has human slaves."

I wonder how much I should tell her. "Those were children born to slavery. Long ago, many humans were traded to us for certain protection." The human leaders were given Koridon cloaking technology for their villages in exchange for a hundred men and women as part of a deal after the war.

"So because we weren't supposed to know what our people had done, we've lived in absolute fear." Scarlet leans over to take her glass from the floor and sips the last of the shining liquid. "The women were never allowed to leave the safety of the force field because they could be taken or killed." She peers up at me, understanding what she must do tonight in order to end the oppression of her people. "You won't hurt me, will you?"

I know her kind has been trapped and forced upon by mine. I've felt as their scent possessed the sleeping beast inside to wake from his dormant slumber, that urge to slam inside her until milked to ultimate satisfaction no matter the ripping of her skin in my claws, or the cracking of her bones. The strange affliction hasn't penetrated my defenses yet with Scarlet, and even on that fateful night in the forest, I could hardly see her, being so drawn to Calypso. Maybe it truly is a spell the woman casts upon her chosen, even if she's unaware of her power.

"I will not hurt you, Scarlet." I grasp her hand and pull her to straddling me.

She drops the glass.

20

CALYPSO

K assien touches her light hair, then cups her face. Her legs tremble as he parts them, but he touches her softly until she grows wet for him. He's far larger than anything she's had inside her before, but as his head gently pushes through, her body vibrates and crackles with anticipation she's never felt. Lost in his gaze, her fear fades away, the bad thoughts disappear, and he moves deeper. She realizes she wants him to, and with pure pleasure igniting her lower body she feels special being the great Koridon prince's lover. His blissful utterances make beauty swirl within her, and pleasant shocks ripple across her exposed breasts as she shakes. He moves feverishly between her legs, desperately trying to be gentle, but uncontrollable sensation blasts through him. He roars, more beast than Koridon, and her fear returns. His world turns black and he can't hear her screaming. He can't hear anything.

"Stop!" I shoot out of bed and find myself at the door before the dream fades completely. I slick wet hair off my cheek and place my hand against the smooth wood. Weeks have passed since the night Kassien took Scarlet to bed in private. As I walked away from them, I knew Kassien changing the ceremony to behind closed doors would be so different from ours, so intimate and friendly compared to the mechanical version done before onlookers. I wish I could have been taken out and never had to know.

Dark, misty twilight turns into morning, and I make my way down to breakfast where we all gather to play nice with one another in the new world order. The huge banquet table is set for thirty of us, and I take my seat next to Drakon, my brothers, and Efaelty. Finn sits next to Glenda and the other humans, including my mother on the other side. The smell of strawberries and oats, fried eggs and toasted bread incites a little nudge from inside my belly. He's growing fast, and though I didn't want this, it's hard to deny the sweet feelings the tiny thing blooms in my heart.

Scarlet and Kassien join us and my breath catches. I force a smile, as I always do, even through the tears of Vaerynn's training sessions, and so does she. Truly, she did what she had to, and I hold nothing against her. However, something inside me is full of jealousy and pain for what she has. Kassien's child. I can't bring myself to fully be there for her any longer, and I hate myself for it. She's got it hard too, though. Torn between her best friend and the man she's been forced to marry, I can't imagine what she's going through. But I know she loves Kassien.

She touches her belly as she sits, and I cringe. The male that grows within her is four weeks old now. Kassien takes his place at the head of the table, and it hurts how I've become so insignificant to him. I have much to look forward to, a child and plenty of adventures of traveling and experiencing new things outside the village, but still, every time Kassien's near, the

memories of what he meant to me flood. They come bringing
chills and heat through my core, only to twist a dagger in
my gut.

Soft chatter ensues as we eat: Finn scolds Vaerynn about
how hard she pushes his sister, and Kjartonn broodingly tries to
make small talk with blond Alice though she won't even look at
him. A wicked grin seems to hang on his lips constantly, an
unsettling glimpse into his nature. Just like us, the Koridons
have potential for such goodness and yet great evil as well.

"Kassien," my mother voices, and the table grows silent.
"Glenda and Kraetorr are to be married soon, and I wanted to
discuss with you the possibility of changing the ceremony to fit
some of *our* traditions as well."

Drakon raises a hand and chews his food quickly.
"Absolutely not. The women are becoming Koridon as are their
children, and I cannot abide our ways being changed. In fact, I
have decided that everyone should also speak our language
now."

My mother laughs and Kassien says, "Drakon, this may be
your district, but I am prince over the region. Stay your tongue
while I think on this."

"May I speak?" asks Mother, and Kassien nods. "I wasn't
suggesting we do away with the mating ceremony," she coughs
into her hand at the thought, "but what if we made it more of a
celebration? Wine, music, dancing, and a feast to turn it into an
event."

I snicker, imagining the hulking Koridons trying to move
along with the music, alcohol tainting their already
questionable manners.

"I did enjoy the wine you sent up," says Kassien with a
smile so beautiful I can't bring myself to look away this time. "It
made me want to laugh and also say things I shouldn't. I
suppose it made me a lot more like a human."

"That's—okay, thank you, I think," she says. "I can help with the arrangements and perhaps it will make the girls feel more comfortable, maybe even have them look forward to their wedding."

"Still—" Kassien touches his beard. "It may not—"

"Our queens of the past had the same kind of celebration," I say, loving the idea and wanting to back my mother. "She had a spectacular party and then later on would be taken to the marriage bed, where the royal party would watch them lie together for the first time."

"It is settled then," says Kassien, giving me the first warm smile I'd seen in weeks. "Each woman giving herself to her new mate shall be treated like the queens of your past." His words are so warm they wrap around me and make me feel special again.

"Thank you, my lord," says Mother while Drakon lifts his brow and shakes his head.

The ocean is cold and choppy this morning as we crash into it and swim against the powerful undertow. We streamline like sharks into the angry waves, and though I lead by several lengths, not one girl struggles. Vaerynn swims just ahead, and with every muscle in my body on fire, I overtake her. The rush makes me push harder, and I ignore the rapid inhale and exhale of my oxygen-starved lungs. I swim farther and farther into the blue, but before long I run out of energy and turn back. Vaerynn whips past me halfway through, but I vibrate with happiness. I'm getting so strong. We all are.

Scarlet hits the shore a few minutes after me and retches into the sand. "Are you okay?" I rush over to hold her dripping hair back.

"I don't know. My stomach feels like it's tearing apart!" She cries out and vomits again.

"Vaerynn! Scarlet's in trouble!" I call out. She approaches and helps her to her feet. "Go back to your rooms and await instructions. I will take her to Gerakon."

They've watched as I've kept up with all the training through my pregnancy with no complications, but Scarlet is different and this pregnancy is dangerous for her. "I'll come too," I say, catching up to them. "My best friend shouldn't be alone right now."

"Do as you're told, Calypso, and go wait in your room," says Vaerynn, giving me a small shove. "She must deal with this alone."

I keep walking after them. "No she doesn't! She should have—"

Scarlet lets out a cry, and I stop dead from her agonized expression. Does she even want me with her, the woman her husband used to love?

The other girls pass me on their way back to the mansion, but I can't bring myself to take another step forward. The trees to the east call to me, thick and endless, a dark canopy I could wander through and no one could find me. For a while anyway.

Freedom intoxicates me as I run past the grounded Koridon ship and fly into the forest. A laugh bubbles up from my throat and I let it pour. Finally, I stop and find a mossy rock to lounge on and catch my breath in the chilly winter air. Alone and loving every minute of it, I listen to the symphony of insects and the sound of the trees blowing in the wind. My body becomes weightless with relaxation, and, not having slept well in days, I drift off.

Maybe minutes pass and my eyes flutter open to sunlight cracking through the leaves. My hand brushes against a plant and joy surges through my stomach when I recognize the plump blackberries growing there. The tart sweetness blasts over my tongue as I bite into the juicy berries and ease the hunger gained by my rough swim.

A branch cracks, and I freeze with a blackberry at my lips. Footfalls sound across the forest floor, and I duck behind the boulders. Peeking through the cracks, a filthy man comes into view in torn clothes. He dives behind the huge trunk of an old tree but is found immediately by two male Koridons.

"No!" he shrieks as they drag him away. "Don't take me back there!"

"*Exrot diverten int trivit,*" says one of the males, and I recognize the words *pain* and *house*. A memory stirs: Andromeda had mentioned a house of pain, asking manipulatively if Drakon would send her there. I allow them to create distance between us before emerging from my hiding place and moving in their direction.

The deeper I search for them, the more my peace dissolves. The forest no longer soothes my soul and everything begins to look the same. I don't know how I lost them. It's lunch time and they're going to be looking for me soon, but I have to know what they're doing to that man out here.

A horrifying scream sends the blood careening through my temples and I flip around in the direction the suffering came from. Cautiously, I move toward a glimmering in the distance I hadn't noticed before. As I draw closer, I find a dome-like structure just like the one from my mating ceremony with Kassien. Inside, several Koridons stand with their backs to me, appearing as dream-like, foggy images through the strange force field. I creep forward, every move racked with fear that they'll discover me, but they can't see me, their eyes trained forward on something before them.

A woman's cries rise up and I move around until she's in view. Naked and bleeding, she holds her knees to her chest and pleads, "Don't do it again, I beg you!" Long black hair cascades down her shoulders and she whimpers as a man is thrown on top of her—the same one running through the trees earlier.

Many of the males who sat for breakfast with me a few hours ago must be present, but they're so distorted through the energy field, I can't make them out. Hearty, muffled laughs fill the room as knives clank to the ground beside them. The woman, eyes wild, lunges for the weapon, but the man only shakes his head and stands trembling before her.

"*Zre tolgat*," says one of the males, and the woman slides the blade into the other human's belly. He hits his knees as cheers ring out all around them. The huge males swarm in on her.

"No, please! I did you what you wanted!" she cries as one throws her onto her stomach. My heart lunges into my throat as he slathers his oversized cock with something creamy then jams it into her ass. "Not again," she whispers on the edge of tears and grips the floor, the color leaching from her face. The others cheer him on as he pumps in and out, her body jolting forward with the impact. She grits her teeth as the male gives one final thrust and, shaking, grips her roughly into him. I watch, fascinated, as he knots deep within her.

Another male slides down beneath her and shoves his mouth between her legs. He licks and sucks on her sex, and yet another smack her backside and says, "*Ovikam, ovikam!*" She rolls her hips slightly against the tongue that works her on command, and I grow oddly aroused.

The first male pulls out, pearly liquid splattering to the ground, and the one using his mouth forces her up to her knees. He fists his cock in front of her face, twisting from the root all the way up to the tip.

Smack. His huge girth hits her cheek and she groans, touching the reddening spot. His crown breaches her lips, and everything grows silent within the force field. I cover my gasp as he pushes himself into her mouth, her jaw unnaturally wide and her teeth digging into his flesh. *It can't fit*, I think over and over as the whites of her eyes turn red and she grunts, trying to breathe.

My fingers splay out toward the moving energy, and tiny shocks force them back again. They wouldn't dare hurt Drakon's pregnant daughter, and surely I can throw a big enough fit that they give up on torturing the woman in there? But what will this do to me if I pass through it? I step back and look for the entrance, but every wall appears solid and delivers a near painful shock when I touch it. Damn. I can't risk my child's life by passing through this force field. The one at home creates an opposite effect, an invisibility for whatever's inside it, but this is different. "Hey!" I yell out, preparing for every head to turn my way. "Stop this or I'll get Kassien!"

A horrible *crack* bites through the focused quiet as the unnaturally large cock disengages the woman's jaw bones. Her face is ashen as she silently shrieks, her throat completely blocked. My chest crushes in with terror, and I run.

Every step away from that poor woman hurts because of what she's enduring at their cruel hands, but it also relieves as I leave it behind. The image of him shoving himself down her throat until she suffocates makes the world around me haze, and I trip over a branch.

"Calypso!" Kassien's familiar voice drifts on the breeze, and in a shaking panic I run toward it. His huge form comes toward me in the distance, and I careen into his arms.

"You found me," I say and press my face into his chest.

"You went missing, and I followed your scent here." He hesitantly touches the back of my head, and I die knowing he can't stand to be close to me anymore. But it doesn't matter.

"You have to come with me immediately," I say and pull back.

"Let me take you home." He grabs my hand and I yank it away.

"No! They're going to kill someone!"

"You should not have come out here." He takes my arm, and this time, there's no getting away.

"You know about it, don't you?" His gaze says *yes*, and I groan with disgust. "You have to stop them, Kassien. They're killing her."

He scoops me into his arms and takes off, a burst of wind blowing my hair back. "You cannot understand, but the place of pain is necessary."

Anger stops me from forming a single word. He's really defending this? I struggle until I slip from his arms. "You need to go back for her!" He regains his hold and continues with even more speed. "You're just like them."

He sets me down and kneels to my level. "Worse, probably. Never forget what I am, Calypso. It might save you one day."

"That place is disgusting." Anger quakes in my voice.

"That place is an illusion," he says.

"An illusion?"

"It is a technology that allows for the aggressive parts of... *us*... to be worked."

"But— What I saw wasn't just violence. It was sexually destroying someone. Why would anyone want to do that?"

"It is not real."

I'm relieved but still unsettled. I don't want my son—or any of them, for that matter—to be so ghastly inside. The horrific images of the woman lying in agony with a broken jaw, hoping to die before they come for her again, disappear. He says she's not real, but she sure looked real.

"You're not like them," I say, running my fingers over the

soft hue of cobalt hair. He's a breath away and grasps my arm so fiercely, it takes me back to a time where such a hold would have me thrown to the ground and my slit threatened to be worked through mercilessly. I wonder if he knows that it hurts, or that I *like it*. I've dreamed of his weight pressing me into the ground, his frenzied touch painful as he forces himself to control it.

"I am just like them," he says. "At this moment I wish to betray everything I believe."

The urge to kiss him burns on my lips, to make him feel me again like he did once, so tempting. I hurt for him to erase what Brekter's hands have branded into my arms and what his hateful utterances have imprinted into my soul. Maybe being loved by the one I feel special to will somehow undo the damage.

His eyes close and he shivers. "You need to step back," he says, his arms wrapping my waist, his knees firmly planted into the ground. "Because... I may not be strong enough."

Those words. They wash over me and sate a thirst that has been drowning me in darkness. I want him. I want him so selfishly even as my best friend suffers with his child growing within. Kassien was mine first, and all of this has been forced upon us. I might hate myself, but what if I could make him mine right now? Is one moment worth a lifetime? What if this binds him to me to claim in the future when the time is right?

He looks up at me, the same longing devouring him, and I know it's in his nature to take what he wants. Violently. I touch the hem of my dress and lift it slightly, every nerve in my body on fire, blood pounding.

His hand snaps around my thigh, holding the material in place. "It is too late now. You cannot run," he says in a low growl. His voice rumbles down my spine, and my leg aches in his grip.

"I could. Do you want to chase me?"

Long tendrils sweep over the supernatural beauty of his face as the breeze picks up. "I would be upon you before you could blink, and only *hungrier*."

"Then run I shall." I land a kiss on him, and though it hurts to rip away, I use the shock to shove him off me.

I turn around smiling and take my first step to jaunt off deeper into the woods, but I stop. My feet won't move an inch. Scarlet's in the med bay, scared and in pain; how could I even think about romping through the woods with her husband? My grin fades, and I turn back around slowly.

"I understand," he says, but his stance remains ready to attack.

I wanted to be selfish and give myself over to him completely, but I can't. "Is Scarlet okay?" I ask as leaves crunch below our feet. We didn't cross the physical line, and I'm grateful for that considering how pregnant I am. Still, the intimacy rekindled between us has me exhilarated.

"She is for now."

Dread grips me. "The pregnancy is already hard for her, isn't it?"

"Gerakon is doing tests and trying to find ways to help her through."

"Don't let anything happen to her, Kassien, or I swear you'll wake up dead one day."

He chuckles, and it raises my spirits, like the sound of rain after a long summer. "I will do whatever I must to protect her."

"You care about her, don't you?" *Say no, please say no.*

"Yes."

"Kass?" I touch my protruding belly. "If this had been your child, would you have kept me?" Dra endavetas ve dantenne, he used to say. But only part of this promise will ever be true. He will always protect me, but can no longer hold me. I can hear the rushing of blood in my ears as his silence goes on for what feels like forever.

"I am tempted," he finally says, "to kill Brekter and everyone who opposes me to have you in my arms again. Every day."

"He's still in med bay, you know. It would be so easy."

He lifts me into his arms again. "Ask me to do it and I will."

The words find their way to the tip of my tongue, but I bite it, knowing I can't risk everything we've achieved for my people. And what would happen to Kassien if he broke their laws? Well, *more* of their laws. But god, I want to. The thought of Brekter's body seeking pleasure and taking everything from mine makes me want to die. "I hate him, and I don't know what I'll do when he heals."

"I can get a hold of the flesh obliterator once more, I believe." He beams down at me and I want to kiss his beautifully wicked grin.

"There's no one for me but you." I lay my head against him. I want to believe that somehow he'll be mine again, but what would that mean for Scarlet? Lying with a Koridon such as Kassien with all his strength, kindness and royalty is one thing, but now she carries his child. What if she has fallen in love with him? What if they've slept together many times since their private mating ceremony?

21

M usic from the banquet hall drifts up to the room at the end of the corridor as I braid Glenda's light hair.

"Are you nervous about your marriage to Kraetorr?" I ask, then take the braid out and let the hair drop around her shoulders. She should look like *herself* for the wedding, not the Koridon idea of what is attractive. My mother has been working for weeks to make sure this ceremony would be a meeting in the middle between our different races, so sexy fall-in-the-face hair it is.She shakes her locks out and puckers her lips in front of the vanity mirror. "Calypso, no. I *want* him. I know it's not rational 'cus we barely know each other, and well, he's an alien from a planet that died, but I dream about him being mine. Like, what it will feel like to let him finally have my—" She waves her hands around awkwardly toward her lap. "Me. To have me. I've never even kissed a boy before, so I don't know why I want sex with him so badly."

"I get it completely. These males do something to us, too." Our chemicals mix and collide, creating something explosive.

"I can do this," she whispers in the mirror, then her round

baby blues flick up at my reflection. "I can do this, right? I mean, he's so big."

My expression remains neutral, but I am afraid for her. When she's near, his skin glistens, his pupils dilate and his breathing becomes erratic. He's already one of the biggest males I've seen, but when he *grew* in size to protect her, he was hellishly frightening. "You'll be fine. I hate that such an intimate moment is supposed to be shared out in the open with everyone in some weird bonding ritual, but we've arranged for certain," I clear my throat, "*lotions* to be used so you won't be too uncomfortable."

"Oh, I'm not afraid of his huge penis," she says. "He can't be bigger than a baby, and our vaginas take *that* beating just fine." She chuckles. "He wishes."

A boisterous laugh slips out, and I cover my mouth. She's absolutely right, they are huge, but *oh* so delicious. We've all snuck a romance novel back at the village, and it's no secret that the hero of the story was always well endowed. "When I first saw the size of Kassien I was intimidated, for sure. But now..." I sink my teeth into my lower lip. "I crave it. It even excites me to think about it—"

"So how big is it exactly?" She puts her hands about six inches apart, and her mouth forms an O.

I shake my head, and she makes a space of twelve inches. I nod and then make a circle with my hands, showing her the girth.

"Oh stars, I'm dead." She laughs nervously and tosses her head back. "I also wonder how we're going to fit together. I guess Arek just opened Mary-Shelly's legs and dived in."

"Oh yes. He'll find a way. He's male, after all."

I finish with the sparkle on Glenda's skin which hides her paleness and rub rouge onto her lips. "I think that will do."

She takes herself in at the full-length mirror, and I as I

stand behind her, watching her timid expression transform into confidence, I can't believe the beautiful woman she has become.

I rush to the bottom of the stairs and raise my hands, quieting the spirited crowd. "Announcing the lovely Glenda!" Glenda holds the violet sparkling gown above her ankles as she makes her way down. Announcing her arrival isn't one of our traditions, but that's how Victorian ladies were introduced to a party, and being that we don't really know who we are, we're making history as we go.

Kraetorr pushes through the mix of his kind and ours as Glenda makes it to the bottom stair and he takes her small hand. "You are beautiful," he says, and I smile at his candor.

She touches the engraved silver armor over his chest, and his spine straightens. "We are doing this movement, where I step here and there with you stepping here and there, to *music*, your music, so I decided not to wear the ceremonial robe."

"Do you mean to say that we will *dance*?" Glenda asks, leaning in with a smile from ear to ear.

"Yes. But also I thought my *drikken* may fall out."

A moment of silence befalls us before she and I burst into laughter. Thinking about the big brute dancing around was already funny—

Mother puts her arm around my waist and I hug her tight, noticing the hanging lights over her shoulder that set the floor gleaming with aquamarine light. "It's perfect, Momma. The party's just amazing." *Goodnight sweetheart well it's time to go...* plays in the background, along with instruments I've never heard.

"Do you like the music, Caly?" Momma asks. "Isn't it strange? I found the records buried in the attic of this place." She steps back, and I realize I've never seen her like this before. Her long auburn hair pulls back into an ornate braid, and a silky gown hugs her curves, flowing down to the heels she wears.

"You're stunning!" I say, forgetting the music. "There isn't some other ceremony going on tonight I don't know about, is there?"

"Of course not." She smacks my shoulder playfully. I spot Drakon standing in the center with his arms crossed over his chest, looking perfect in black and gold dress clothes. Arek and Kjartonn stand beside him, looking much the same. Mary-Shelly stands over by Vaerynn, sipping on a glass of spirits, her abdomen still flat as the day she was born. She steals glances toward her mate as he speaks boisterously with his father.

Finn cuts through the crowd, not a hint of emotion threatening his features, and stands beside me. He sighs as he takes his little sister in, and the newfound beauty she glows with. He boils with the realization that the glow is partly because of love.

"Nice to see you dressed up," Glenda says, noting he looks exactly the same as always.

His glare is stone cold. "This isn't right, Glenda. He's not even the same species as you. This is shit."

Her satin lips shut abruptly, and Kraetorr moves in front of her.

"You're right," I say, "but Glenda wants this. So you have to respect her decision."

He cracks his knuckles. "She wants this. What a joke."

"Wine!" says Mother as a servant moves toward us with a serving tray. We grab a glass of the red liquid, happy for the distraction, but Kraetorr remains locked on Finn.

"Finn, my brother," says Glenda and weaves her arm in his. "I'll be all right. Please, just be here today. Well, be here until the mating starts. *Then* please go."

He pulls away. "If you hurt her," he says to Kraetorr, "I'll tear your throat out."

"If I hurt her," he growls, "I will tear my own throat out."

"Well." Finn steps up to him. "That's something I'd look forward to."

"Why don't we dance?" I take Finn's hand and lead him out to a clear spot on the black and white checkered floor.

"I don't want to fucking dance," he says, removing my arms from around his neck.

"Well, we're going to anyway. Come on, we used to play all the time like this." I place his hands on my waist and drape my arms back around his shoulders. "Dance with me."

He reluctantly moves his feet, stiff and awkward as I lay my head against his chest. *Earth angel, earth angel, please be mine. My darling dear, love you for all time...* a beautiful song plays in the background as we sway.

"This place, these *things*," his voice booms. "How can you even be pregnant by one?"

Kassien enters the room with a very pale Scarlet beside him. "I asked the same question once." I say. "The universe creates beings like us on all kinds of water planets within good range of a sun. We're similar enough, and our parts fit well enough. So it's possible."

"Apparently," he snickers. "Doesn't mean it's right."

Glenda drags Kraetorr over and tries to find a comfortable position for a dancing, but when her arms only reach his pecs and he's too tall to hold her around the waist, he sweeps her into his arms and "steps around," as he called it, with her cheek against his.

Finn shakes his head. "I just don't get it."

"Shall we eat?" Kassien shouts toward my mother. "Is it ready?"

The banquet table steams with grilled meats, vegetables, and fresh breads while fruit pies and pastries tempt us to sneak bites before dessert has been announced. I nod at Momma, alight with happiness at what she's done. For the first time it really feels like we're all a family. Or... at least one people, working toward a common goal. Even as Kassien helps Scarlet get food on her plate and encourages her to eat, nothing seems capable of ruining this moment.

"So what god do you believe in?" Finn asks over the quiet of enjoying such a feast. I perk up at the question, very curious myself. From what I've read of different spiritual books and religions over time, and different cultures, most people on our planet are pulled toward a higher power, and how he manifests himself to the people is always different. Egyptians and the sun god, *Ra*, the Greeks and the many gods they felt close to, and Christians who have a relationship with their god as well. After most the people died on this planet, there wasn't a set religion left, and over the years we recovered many writings that exposed us to so many at once. To me, they all had a beautiful truth about them, and no *one* was correct.

Kassien finishes chewing and puts a hand up to silence Drakon, who readily begins to answer. "There is something that has always been there. *Always* is a hard concept to grasp, because we biological lifeforms are born and are then meant to die. But there is a conscious power that has always been there. Don't bother trying to imagine it, let alone understand it, for such things are beyond our reach. This being isn't carbon based with living cells like we are. It is made of elements such as helium, hydrogen and iron among others. He found that pieces of himself created *stars*. The tiny stars made from the elements of his form grew and multiplied, growing hotter and hotter, *little suns*, but separated from him, they did have an end. Eventually the stars died, and the creator found this interesting."

"Sounds like the myths we've read," says Finn, flicking a piece of steak off his fork.

"Please continue," I say, remembering the textbooks that described how stars formed in the blackness of space, and the way these molecules did indeed multiply and burn hotter than fire.

Kassien takes another bite, then lifts his fork up. "When a star dies it explodes, and its particles enter the atmosphere. Joined by gravitational forces, they begin to create planets and moons."

"But how did *we* get here?" asks Scarlet. "I know about evolution and chance, but still I feel special. There's just no way I'm here, with all of you, by chance right now. There's no way."

"Kassien runs a finger up her wrist and goosebumps flush up her arm. "You are what this universe creates. Your essence, we might call it, something hidden in your DNA that can't be mapped. And you reoccur over and over in an endless expansion of time, and in endless different places."

"You're saying our DNA, which is a fuck bunch of different genetic codes that occur only because of our exact ancestral line, happens to reoccur?" Finn shakes his head. "That's a number that doesn't exist."

"No," says Kassien. "You have figured out DNA, yes? But that special thing that makes you *you* is something else. Your genetics will differ, you may look different or have different talents, but it is still *you*. This is not dependent on a complex set of familial genes."

I'm mystified. "So, we never truly die. We would always

exist in a way, because even if I don't reoccur again for five billion years, it would be instantaneous in my perspective."

Kassien gives a pleased nod. "This is what we have come to find in all our travels and meetings with other planetary life."

"Where is the creator now?" asks my mother.

Kassien shrugs. "Doing whatever star beings do, I suppose."

After a round of questions about other *planetary lifeforms* from my mother and Finn's many arguments, the hour of Glenda's mating ceremony approaches. Cold prickles my fingers numb and my chest flutters, thinking about what's to come. Servants place the last of the lit candles around the altar. The record player makes a tearing sound as the needle is pulled away.

"Was it well enough?" Kassien asks Glenda. "Dancing and drinks, a feast and existential conversation?"

She gulps down a knot in her throat and nods curtly. "I'm ready."

22

"What do I do?" I overhear Kraetorr ask Kassien in their language as everyone gets into a bowing position.

Kassien says, "You have a mate. You know how this will go."

"It is not the same with Lorvel," he says. "I feel this woman in my core, she grips it with both hands and has not let go since the first day."

I open my palm to reveal a bottle of clear oil. "Use a lot of this." I widen my eyes at his crotch, and he takes the lubricant from me quickly. "And be careful with her, she will break. You can't ever lose yourself, not for a second. Have you ever had sex with a human before?"

"No. I stay away from women. I follow the law." A wicked smile spreads his lips. "But Glenda is my betrothed, and I touched inside her, under the table during our night meal."

My brows pop up as he pulls his armor off, moving toward her. "I want my drikken in there now."

Kassien steps in front of him and takes hold of his

shoulders. "She is yours, brother. Take care of her heart and her body, for these are now yours to protect."

He nods, regained control present in his focus. "Stay close, Kassien?"

The prince agrees and does not bow but sits behind them to keep watch.

Blond Alice sits with her legs crossed alongside my momma and the others, while Finn is nowhere to be found. I'm glad he got out of here—this is disturbing to watch even when it isn't your sister being mated. I bow with my forehead on the back of my hands, and the last glimpse of Kraetorr rushing over her sends a tremor sliding down my spine.

Glenda lets out a sensual sigh, and without meaning too, my attention moves up to the scene laid out upon the altar. Her fingers search his chest hungrily. She doesn't care that everyone watches, because every waking desire after her emotionally-charged dreams is finally going to be caressed, stroked and released. Her ceremony was postponed a month due to the change in celebration plans, but as she welcomes him between her legs, she's ready to breed.

Kraetorr takes aim toward her sex and I suck in through my teeth, willing him to remember the oil. He pulls backward again and slathers himself roughly, then carefully pushes the tip in between her legs. She works her hips to ease him further and he grunts, veins in his muscles surfacing with effort. He works it in, inch by inch, and grabs the back of her neck with an animal sound escaping his throat.

She arches and wraps her legs around him. Kraetorr grips the middle of her back, bringing her toward him as she undulates. He braces her, his eyelids fluttering slightly as she moves, letting her set the pace and rub along his shining cock. The training has made her strong, and she's so clever to have taken control.

The muscles bunch along his arms and back. His breath bated, he's the embodiment of calm before the storm. His eyes are black with a ring of silver as he watches her breasts bounce. He turns his head quickly, the excitement overtaking him.

Glenda touches his cheek, and he twitches. "I want you to knot me." She flicks her tongue softly along his lower lip. "I'm your woman now, and you feel so good that I want all of you."

Kraetorr places her hands around the back of his neck and grasps her hips. He wrenches her along his shaft and she whimpers but quickly composes herself. "Yes, do it!" she cries, taking another harsh jolt as he slams her against him.

His breath rapidly increases, and with a desperate utterance, he slams her backward into the ground. I jump to my feet amongst the gasps, and Kassien rushes to place a hand on the Koridon's dripping skin. "Kraetorr!" he says, studying Glenda beneath him. She pulls in a deep breath, and the whites of her eyes flash wildly. "You have hurt her. Back away, now!" I drop next to Glenda. She's ghostly pale, her mouth opening and closing with no sound.

Kraetorr growls and buries himself inside her to the hilt. My mind screams with alarm— *Kraetorr's gone.*

Kassien pulls him backward and Glenda cries out, her pelvis being yanked with him. The knot firmly in place, Kraetorr roars and grabs her by the throat. Kassien takes his face in his hands and pleads with him while I helplessly watch her fade. Blood trickles to the ground and, like a rabid beast, Kraetorr yanks her attached body up and runs, slamming her back into the wall. A horrible *crack* permeates the screams and cries piercing the room.

Finn tears inside. "Stop! Let her go!" He lands a solid blow into the side of Kraetorr's face, and when the huge beast is unphased, cocks his fist back and hits him in the back of the head over and over. He grasps a knife from his belt and wields it at Kraetorr's neck.

Kassien shoves Finn back and braces Kraetorr as he spills the last of his seed, and I hold Glenda's hand, trying to force the tears back to comfort her. An expression of terror freezes on her face, the pain panicking her voice away. "It's gonna be okay, we'll get you two apart and you'll go into the med bay on their ship—"

She shudders and her head lolls to the side. "Kassien!" I cry out as he struggles to keep Kraetorr still. A gurgling bubbles up in Glenda's throat. "Knock him out!"

"It will not stop him!" he says. "They are knotted until the swelling releases."

"She'll be dead by then!"

Vaerynn bursts through the crowd holding the nanohealer and I take my first non-crushing breath. She hits a button and a red light scans her from the head down. "Oh," Vaerynn exclaims, taking in the readings. "I will repair her skull damage first, but she bleeds internally as well."

Finn says, "Do it, hurry," and helps me hold his sister up by fingers braced into her ribs Kraetorr shakes and smashes his fist through the wall beside Glenda. She doesn't respond.

Liquid metal glides out from the healing tool and spreads in midair until it settles along Glenda's head. "The healing particles will move through her scalp and repair damage," Vaerynn explains to Finn. "But her brain is swelling, and the repair may inhibit the fluid from exiting and put a lot of damaging pressure on the neural tissue."

"I can relieve the pressure," says my mother. "I studied it in our medical books and did it once to a girl who got a concussion in our village." I'm more thankful than ever that our people are well studied in medical science, as well as everything our texts could teach. Living in captivity would have been unbearable having to do the same job every day, and now I realize how valuable we are.

"Find a long, thin tube of some kind and something to drill. Something small!" Efaelty nods and rushes away, followed by Gerakon.

The tiny particles gather in small liquid pools as they complete their work, then drift down Glenda's chest. She sags in our arms as Kraetorr bursts away from her. We lay her down and I gasp at the bruising that blooms on her abdomen.

"No!" he howls, grabbing his head with both hands. "What have I done?"

Kassien moves in front of him. "She is injured badly. You must stay back."

He pushes through him, only to be subdued by Kassien then shoved away. "Just let me go to her! Please, whatever I have done, I need her to know I love her!"

"If he comes near her, I'll fucking kill him!" Finn warns.

Glenda lets out a sob, and I jerk my head in surprise. "It hurts," she manages. Her body convulses as she tries to sit up.

"Don't move," I say. "You're being healed." The nanos disappear beneath her chest, leaving tiny blood beads behind on her skin.

"Let me see her," pleads Kraetorr. The beast shakes with tears spilling down his face.

Kassien shoots me a frustrated glance, and even though Finn severely shakes his head at me, I tell Kassien to let him come. The craze has passed, and I hurt for the happiness they displayed when they danced and the change in Kraetorr's heart because of her. The *hope* his gentleness with Glenda had given us. Finn balls his fists, so angry no words are possible, and I know that he was right.

Kraetorr collapses beside his crumpled woman and his large hand swallows hers. "My love, my poor love," he says.

"You will be healed, and I will never go near you again, I promise."

She whimpers, forcing a small smile. "This is all—new," she fights to breathe. "You didn't know."

"We did know." Finn snatches the dagger from his side. "We've always known what you monsters do to women." He holds it level to Kraetorr's eyes, but they stay locked on Glenda.

She sucks in a sharp breath and her chest flutters.

"What is happening?" Kraetorr asks, Glenda's hand draining of color in his.

Vaerynn scans her again, blue light showering her head and neck, then it turns red as it hits her chest. She chokes, and blood bubbles over her bottom lip. "Head's fine, but her heart is failing." The scanning light flashes red as it travels the length of her abdomen. "And so are the *filerns*. The kidneys."

My mother shoots me a look that tells me she's thinking *shock*. Glenda shivers, and her teeth chatter. "Glenda, stay here," I say, jerking her face toward me. "Talk to me!"

Her lashes flutter and her light grows dim. Her song rises in my memory, that night where all the Koridons fell under her spell at the power of her voice. Then the song fades away.

"Please," Kraetorr's eyes shine as he holds her limp hand. "I will never find her again."

Finn snaps the knife at Kraetorr, but like lightning, he dodges and snatches the weapon away. Rage seeps from his pores as his body ripples with growing muscle.

"Don't hurt him!" I scream. "Kraetorr, don't hurt her brother!" The grief-stricken Koridon attacks Finn.

Kassien and Arek rush in front of him. "Kraetorr, stand down!" Kassien crouches, ready to fight, one leg out straight, his hand pointed. Arek wrestles Finn to the ground.

Kraetorr shakes his head frantically. "This— What we are doing, it is wrong." He looks at Glenda, a cracked porcelain doll lying in a pool of blood. "We will all pay for it." He plunges the dagger into his throat and blood sprays from the shredded vessels. Kassien hits the weapon away and everyone in the crowd stands back. The broken Koridon hits his knees before Glenda, his crimson drops of life warming her chilled flesh, and takes her into his arms.

Kraetorr nuzzles into her hair one last time and cradles her as he falls.

The panicked cries and gasps cease, and the saddest silence I've ever known falls upon us.

23

D rakon steps forward with a stern brow. "Clean this up."
His eyes fall on my mother. "What a disaster."

Finn stands over his sister's body with a haunted gaze. I
want to go to him, but I'm too afraid. He turns to Drakon.
"We're leaving. Today." He storms over and takes my hand.
"This is my fiancé, I'm sure you didn't know, and she's fucking
coming with me."

Drakon crosses his arms. "The breeders will not be leaving
anywhere."

Finn signals toward Kassien. "Tell him. This is over and I
need you to back me."

"I will always want what is best for you and your people. I,"
he places his hands on his chest, "hurt, for what has happened
to our family." He focuses on the intimacy between Finn and
me for the smallest moment. "But this is still a small price to
pay for your freedom."

"My *sister* is a small price to pay?" I squeeze his hand,
knowing what Kassien means but feeling Finn's pain.

"That is not how I meant it," Kassien says softly.

Sybil nervously raises a hand. "Scarlet *can't* leave, she'll die without their care." My best friend is nowhere in sight, having been removed when it grew dangerous.

"She's already dead," says Finn. He snaps away from my side. "You did hear that fucker's last words, right? *You will all pay*." He extends a hand to me. "Calypso, let's go."

Kassien puts an arm in front of me. "You will not take her." The severity in his voice jars Finn.

I don't know what I'd do if he let me go. Finn is right in so many ways—we should be free to leave after this. This was murder. I'm torn, because Kraetorr was my brother, and these are my people too. I still want a life together.

"Caly," Finn motions me to come to him, "and all of you who actually want to live. Let's go." Mary-Shelly stands up from her chair at the banquet table and moves toward Arek with determination. But then she stops. Her mate watches in distress as blond Alice runs into Finn's arms. Palms open at her sides, she waits for Arek to notice her, sad yet longing for him, begging him to see that she wants him still, even through the terror and the blood.

"Come on!" Finn shouts. "This breaks the deal." He storms over to his sister's body. "*This* breaks the fucking deal!"

Blond Alice kicks the door open, sending a sliver of moonlight across the floor. Mary-Shelly walks slowly past Arek to join them, her head hung low.

"Finn," I say. "The world can't stay the way it is. I loved Glenda, and I'm sorry." I shake my head and feel the full force of his heart drop. "We're all still learning. And Glenda knew this could happen. She wanted him, Finn. She told me her heart had decided."

"Fuck that." Finn joins black-haired Alice, Mary-Shelly, and Jane. "They won't just kill every single one of you slowly by raping you, or painfully when their spawn rips you up from the inside out. But you will destroy *them* as well."

"All right, we have tried it your way," says Drakon, strutting toward the cowering girls. "Now we do what I want to do. Chain them up. Chain them *all*."

Kassien grabs him by the shoulder, and Drakon rips away. "Kassien, we have dethroned you before, we can do it again." He signals toward Arek and Vaerynn, and the other Koridons follow. They form a half circle around Finn and the girls.

"Don't let them hurt Finn," I cry out, wishing Kassien had the weapons to decimate them again.

"They won't," he snarls and snaps his hand around Drakon's neck. The Koridons break their guard on the women to draw close to the new threat. Kassien jerks Drakon into the air. "I could kill your defiant leader with the flick of my wrist." He slowly turns his head toward them. "You will not chain these humans."

A scream pierces the night and I run to the door, my legs tingling from the terror. Blond Alice's hands drag the ground as she disappears into the trees. "Kassien! Something's got Alice!"

"Kjartonn!" Arek's cries shatter the darkness as he disappears after her.

"Kjartonn took Alice!" shouts Mary-Shelly.

"Get her back, please!" I touch Kassien's shoulder. Drakon stops struggling and lifts a snide brow, daring Kassien to choose. "I am going to subdue your son and lock him up for taking the woman." He drops him. "I may not have permission to end you, but you will be going in a cage with him when I return. Run, Drakon." He turns to leave, and I release the breath I've been holding. Kjartonn will torture and destroy blond Alice, and I don't trust anyone to get her back except him. Fear immediately replaces my relief as the predators around me gear up to follow their orders.

"Kill the boy and get the women in chains," says Drakon. "We will take no more chances. The ones who have not taken hold of seed will be mated by all males from now on to increase the chances of conception."

"No!" Finn rushes him, the girls' horrified cries in the background. Drakon cracks a fist into his head and sends him careening to the ground. The females grab Mary-Shelly, black-haired Alice, Jane, and Sybil, their desperate cries cut off abruptly as they're slapped to the ground.

Drakon reaches for Finn, splayed out on the floor, and I slam into him. "You touch him and I'll find a way to make you die." I grab Drakon's wrist and use the pain from our collision to fuel the strength behind my grip.

The female Koridons dig into my back as they rip me away, and Drakon pulls with us in my vicious grasp. One of them smashes her fist into my forearm and my fingers pop open.

He circles Finn. "You all have been entertained for longer than you deserve." He kicks into Finn's side and he groans but doesn't go down. He kicks back, landing a foot into the commander's groin.

"You underestimate us," Finn says, landing a sharp elbow into Drakon's back as he doubles over.

"You always have," I back Finn up. "Even if you abuse us, torture and chain us, we will find a way to beat you!"

"When Kassien gets back," Drakon pulls Finn up by the throat, his feet dangling, "don't stop until you have vanquished him," he says to his crew. "*Erdat enclaveasor.*"

Game over.

Finn's neck makes a popping sound and my emotions surge. Desperation shreds me to pieces. Kassien is so outnumbered. I imagine all of my beloved village mates broken and bleeding like Glenda. I see Finn face down in the dark sea, floating forever. I scream and something inside me explodes, sending all the females flying off as though they'd been struck by lightning.

I pick myself up from the ground, a strange weakness affecting my limbs, and blink Vaerynn into focus. She cracks Drakon in the head and Finn falls in a heap to the floor. Drakon drops next to him, a stream of red trickling over his brow.

Vaerynn brings Finn to sitting and his eyes shutter open. "Are you hurt?" she asks.

He cocks his head to the side. "Aaahh." He rubs his reddening throat. "He gave me a good pop. That was nice." He reaches around her long braid and latches onto the back of her neck. She lets him draw her near.

"Thank you," Finn says softly, his coldness bending into a heated glow. Her oval eyes sparkle, reflecting Finn's deep emeralds as she takes his domination, and their mouths come so close they could touch at the slightest shiver.

"The agreement still stands!" Vaerynn yells, ripping away from Finn. She moves like a god of war as she commands. "These women will not be chained, they are free beings. They will still uphold their betrothals as well despite the tragedy today." The commander stirs, and she smashes a foot into his temple. He stops moving. "And take Drakon to the holding quarters." She comes face to face with Efaelty. Vaerynn lifts her chin and dares the female to move against her orders, the daughter of the commander, a vision of equal splendor.

Efaelty grips Vaerynn's hand. "I am with you."

I stand beside my sister and take her hand in mine as well. We create a stronghold together, and the Koridons that remain follow us without question and drag Drakon out.

Vaerynn dips her head in respect at Efaelty and I before moving toward the door. "And the boy is not to be touched!" she yells as Finn mourns over Glenda's body.

I come up behind her outside. "Can you see them?" I ask as she squints into the darkness.

She shakes her head. "I will go after them."

"Kassien and Arek surely must have taken him down by now. He can't beat both of them."

Vaerynn's forehead scrunches with worry lines. She launches herself towards the trees.

"He'll come back, won't he?" Scarlet says from behind. She limps through the sand, and the sight of her so weak and sickly, yet still my lover's mate, is a contradiction that enrages and confuses. A floodgate bursts, washing away the last of my strength.

"I have to go help Finn with Glenda." I can't look at her as I turn on my heel and race back through the door.

Inside the mansion is silent, the girls having gone up to their rooms, and only Finn and a female sit beside the bodies. Kraetorr appears so blue compared to Glenda. The scaling effect of his skin is incredibly pronounced as well, now that his heart has stopped forever. They truly look like a different species in death: a demon and an angel.

"He was perfect just as he was," says the sharp-featured female at Kraetorr's feet. "He is dead because of what she turned him into." She rises and stalks away. "And what a travesty to die such a pathetic creature!"

Finn's mouth twists into a sneer, and I see the female's painful death playing out behind his eyes.

"And we've just met Kraetorr's rightful mate," I say, breaking Finn's murderous trance. "Come on old friend. Let's prepare a grave for her."

We wander into the back, two spirits drifting, nothing seeming real, not even ourselves amongst a forest of dark trees touching the inky sky. I struggle to find hope to hang onto. As long as they refuse to kill Drakon, he'll push to take us in violence. These creatures are wicked by nature, bestial, and Finn is right. We have the ability to destroy each other with the giving of our hearts and the offering of our bodies. And I worry about my child. I hope he can be raised differently.

"How 'bout here?" I ask and force my fingers into the earth. It's cold and damp, and the thought of putting Glenda deep within it makes me yank away.

Finn, utterly defeated, doesn't answer or even move as he stares through the spot I've picked and into nothingness. I collapse onto my back. The leaves and dirt fly as Finn falls beside me. I count the stars, marveling at how each one of those suns could have an earth-like planet nearby. Or several. Millions of brilliant stars splash the sky, and I wonder if any of them will belong to me one day, to my planet, when I reoccur out there somewhere.

The minutes tick by as we lay with our desperate thoughts and silent cries, slipping farther away from reality and deeper into dreams from exhaustion.

A back door flings opens and Jane's voice rings out. "They have her!" I wake up shaking and dash inside to find Arek, bruised and bleeding, clenching blond Alice to his chest.

"Help her," he says to Gerakon who rushes in behind them. He lays her on the floor and blood pools underneath her.

Kassien bursts through the door. "We found her like this. Kjartonn is still out there."

"Did he—" Tears cloud my vision as Kassien nods, confirming that Kjartonn did just as he'd promised.

Vaerynn and Gerakon work together, scanning her body for breaks and tears, and move quickly to introduce the nano-healers into her wounds. "Alice?" I say, ignoring Vaerynn's warning glance. I shake my head slowly and bite back the ache in my throat that begs to give way to sobbing. "I'm sorry. I'm so sorry." My tears fall on her chest and leave a trail down her dried blood.

"He threw me on the ground." Alice's wavering words cut through my horror. "A sharp pain went through the back of my head." She sniffs. "I remember blackness and pressure, almost to the point of pain. I kept moving in and out of dreams, my face shoved in the dirt. I kept hitting against him so hard." He wasn't even careful with her. She winces as she bends a bloodied knee.

The floor shakes as Arek drops beside her. "I am going to tear him apart." He carefully runs his fingers down her cheek, afraid he'll hurt her. "You will live, but he will forever be taken from the world." He leans over and touches his cheek to hers.

She squeezes her eyes shut and shakes Vaerynn's scanning light away from her forearm. Reaching up to Arek with a small cry of pain, she touches his face, wanting to say something to him but knowing she doesn't need to.

Kassien reflects their pain as he speaks to me quietly. "Kjartonn knew exactly where he was going to take her when he had the chance. He lost us both out there, and Arek only found her when he smelled the blood."

"This isn't working, Kassien," I say. "We're not safe here." Glenda's covered body catches my attention, and the *crack* when she broke against the wall echoes through the memory. We dreamed once in each other's arms and were willing to sacrifice ourselves before an unknown altar. But the dream's been shattered, and the shards have left fatal wounds.

"Drakon is locked up as you commanded," one of the females tells Vaerynn. "What do we do now?"

Vaerynn hands over the scanners and shakes her head sadly. "I do not know." She throws a questioning look at Finn, but he doesn't seem to know anymore either.

24

KASSIEN

"What am I to do with you?" I stand with my hands behind my back and look down at a seething Drakon. I've let him rot inside the seclusion chamber of his own ship for a month before coming to speak with him, and that gives me such joy. The sovereign made it clear that Drakon's family is incredibly powerful and harming him will bring on a war that could destroy everything we've built here. It isn't much, but the children that grow within two bellies is everything that keeps me from taking the risk. I sigh heavily, thinking of Scarlet and the strong heartbeat of the little life I can hear when laying my ear to her stomach.

Drakon rises slowly then lands a fist into the force field, making it sizzle and glow a pretty blue. "You cannot keep me in here forever. Or have you forgotten that I have a right to rule just as you do?" A low growl rumbles from his throat.

"You *will* stay in there forever and as long as you are entertaining the thought of binding our women to be used as sex slaves."

"And my children?"

I put an inquisitive finger to my chin. "Well, one tore his own throat out, and your other son will be thoroughly tortured to death when I find him."

Drakon blows an indignant breath. "Over a little bitch that has as much right to live as the hogs in the forest?"

I square up in front of his invisible cage and let him feel my size. My *ferocity*. "You still do not see them. You are incapable of knowing their beauty."

He steps back casually and straightens his worn, leather collar. "You have two of them, don't you? One that will surely die and the other pregnant with another man's spawn. Such beauty."

The blood boils in my veins, but my face remains calm. *Love*, the word Calypso taught me, beats within my ribcage in new ways, and though I cared for the son I lost beyond anything, these women have taught me to love completely. And I already love my child. My *baby*. I have always been taught that caring about anything but the battle was a weakness, and though I believe it still, I won't go back.

"Goodbye, old man." I turn and walk away, the sound of Drakon's cries a captivating blend of angst and despair. I'll keep him alive, but he won't ever leave that room.

I stop around the corner from Brekter's room and peek in.

His hair has grown in three inches and the muscle stimulators have kept his build intact while he heals. I deactivate the forcefield and step inside the doorway. "Your pieces are healing back together well," I say, taking a seat next to him. He sits up with some effort. "You only look mildly disproportionate." I smile a thousand watts to hide my disappointment.

He rests an elbow on his knee to keep himself from shaking, and I shove him to watch as he knocks off balance so easily. He groans and scoots himself back against the wall. "Why have you come?"

"To ensure our new order is followed once you join the pack again."

His jaw tenses. "And what of Calypso?"

"You won't be going near her again."

His nostrils flare. "You cannot stop me from being with my child."

"Watch me." Remembering the limp in Calypso's gait and the marks on her face, I have to force down the aching in my fists to break his skull in two.

His mouth curves up on one side and he runs a hand down his chest. "Have you ever felt her clench and pulse around your cock?"

"Brekter, when your body was in thousands of tiny pieces, how did it feel?" I shoot him a look that promises there will be no reassembling the next time I zap him into oblivion. I smile inwardly, thinking about the location of the obliterator, given to me after sending word to Eladia about the disaster that had befallen us. And now it lies hidden again, just within reach of the one I would see protected the most.

He grimaces and pushes himself to the end of the bed. "You may have her heart, but I own her body. She fights me and gives in. Every time. I feel the begging beneath her skin."

I snap my hand around his neck and lift him from the bed. The tendons in his throat snap in my fingers, and his gasps fuel my flames. "She will never be yours, and even though I am forbidden to kill you upon pain of death, I will. I will kill you if you even utter her name. They can hang me by my own entrails and I will welcome it." I throw him into a crumpled ball in the corner.

His crazed laugh fills my ears. "And what you do not seem

to understand is that I welcome it also! She has destroyed me. You cannot see it, but she has destroyed you as well."

I'm sure the sovereign will understand. I whip out the knife at my side and slash his cheek, enjoying the drip of crimson before I move the blade to his throat.

"Kassien," comes a voice from behind, and I spin around. "She has awaken," says Gerakon.

I sigh and engage the force field on the way out. Brekter will have to live yet another day, regretfully.

"Is she faring all right?" I ask, rushing to Scarlet with Gerakon struggling to keep up.

"The child is strong. Too strong perhaps." His voice trails off with a note of pain that unsettles my stomach.

I stop in front of her door, my finger poised before the entrance button." Only a few months remain before my child is viable enough to survive outside the womb, but every day Scarlet grows paler and thinner. A Koridon child can't survive the flora of this planet without having a human mother, and now it tortures the vessel that nurtures it.

"I am running tests, but—"

I squeeze my eyes shut, then trigger the door open. Scarlet smiles, her arms shaking as she sits up. I rush to her side, telling her to stay lying down, and catch a pillow before it falls. "I'm okay, I'm fine," she tells me, but her voice is as weak as her heartbeat.

"Are you having any—"

She retches, and I jump up to get a rag. "I'm so sorry," she whimpers. "I'm trying not to lose your baby, Kassien," she says breathlessly. "I promise, I will never give up."

Gerakon cleans the mess, and I carefully take her into my arms. "No, no of course you would never." I stroke her hair as she quivers. "I will stay with you from now on, as much as possible, by your side." I throw a desperate look at Gerakon, but what he's reflecting unsettles me.

Gerakon asks her to lay down and scans her extended belly. "The child is quite large for only the second trimester. Ten pounds. That would be much even for a Koridon female." She shifts her spine with a little grunt, struggling to breathe, and Gerakon jumps to finish another test. "I apologize, Scarlet. Just one more thing to check and we will assist you into a more comfortable position." His fingertips trail her side, the briefest touch that sparks furiously nonetheless.

He coats the large needle in a numbing agent and slides it through her abdomen. I stroke her head, still fearing her discomfort, but she doesn't budge. A vivid hologram of the small child projects from the top of the needle, and I lose myself in the perfect image of my boy. His small hands open and close slightly as he floats, the umbilical cord connected to his smooth little belly.

Scarlet clutches my wrist and forces a smile. "You love him already, don't you?" She wipes away a tear. "I do too."

Gerakon removes the device and turns his back. "Your blood nutrients are normal, but your kidney tests show a rise in toxins, and your blood pressure rises also as your heart fights to beat adequate blood to you and the child." He keys something into the air log and orange symbols glow as he translates the information. "If her body fails, we must remove the pregnancy."

My heart trembles beneath the cage enclosing it, and I shake off the disturbing emotion. "When will he be able to survive outside the womb?"

"Granted he has the capability to survive in this world with his mother's human immune system, he needs lung development enough for a breathing chamber to oxygenate him. Two months. I would not chance any sooner."

"And if her condition deteriorates before then?" I almost don't ask in front of her, but it's not in my nature to be gentle, and she needs to be a part of the decision.

"If her organs collapse, we may be able to heal them with the nanobots, but that will not sustain her for long as the child will continue to tax her body."

Many things plague me as I hold Scarlet's clammy hand. She is dear to Calypso, and though the child is dear to me, Scarlet matters as well. The child may still suffer from the ill effects of this world with alien biology. Though we believe the mother will grow and pass on the necessary microorganisms as was in the case of Calypso, there could still be unforeseen complicating factors.

"I don't want to die," says Scarlet. "But I promise I'll try to save him, Kassien. Will you let me die?" Her desperate grip locks around my wrist.

I sigh inwardly and hate myself for the lie. "No."

"I know you love Caly, but you and I have something too. Between us." She gulps hard and licks her lips. "I think about the night we—we mated and this life within me was created. I wasn't able to be good for you, I was so nervous and unsure, but I think about how it could have been. I think about how it still can be. *With us.*"

Laying with the girl was a duty, nothing more, my desire driven only by the need to have a son, someone who could be a testament to my life once I'm gone. Still a spark exists when I remember the act: her tight, slick walls, the trembling of her body as I held her and knotted deep inside. Mating of any woman by my sexually dormant species cannot exist without an element of passion. To mate a woman, any of them, regardless of age or body type is a true gift, with their unique features and vivid coloration, their softness and perfectly wanting crevices. The way their faces light up when they laugh, the way their voices waver with excitement when they tell a story. I never knew beauty until Calypso, and now she has brought it out in every woman I meet. It would have been impossible to mate Scarlet without loving her on some level, for any Koridon with newly opened eyes would be lost inside her laugh.

"We can be happy. I'm right, aren't I?" That lovely smile peeks through Scarlet's misery, and it's more beautiful than can be possible.

25

CALYPSO

Dawn's soft glow glistens upon the crashing waves below our room. Arek kisses blond Alice's cheek and carefully gets out of her bed. She stirs as he sneaks away.

"Don't go." Her whisper floats through the dark. "He doesn't haunt me when you're near. I would never sleep if you didn't lie with me at night."

"I must go," he says gently. "There are so few of us now, and with the servants having been released, we must hunt this morning. But Kjartonn is nowhere to be found." Alice cringes upon his name. "Vaerynn and Finn are standing guard at all times. Especially when I have to be away."

"I understand," she says quickly. "We're not thriving, are we?"

"We will be all right." He lifts her chin. "Now that a new order has been enacted we will soon be placed together. If you will have me."

"I can't—" She pulls the covers up, and his touch falls away. "Please understand, I don't think I'll ever be able to—"

"Of course I would never." He pulls her face toward his. "I

will never feel you in that way after what you have suffered. I
—" His mouth brushes her bottom lip, and a shudder rocks
through him. He breathes her in, the roundness of her breasts
visible beneath the thin bed shirt.

"But, maybe someday." She presses her lips against his and
he devours her kiss, an unbearable thirst quenched.

The bed squeaks as I turn over, my large belly stretching,
and a tiny foot digs into my lungs. "Sorry to wake you, little
one," I say out loud to my quickly growing baby, who I can't for
the life of me figure out a name for. I wish Brekter didn't taint
every thought of the little one, and because I can't see him, or
hold him, I can't find who he is. He was created out of the worst
circumstances, but it wasn't his fault, and I still feel the love of a
mother welling up within my being even though a wall keeps
going up that I must break down.

Arek pulls away and nods toward me as he leaves, and
blond Alice rolls on her side toward the wall. Mary-Shelly may
have turned away from her, devastated that Arek loves her, but
I never will. I sit up and press my fingers against my belly
where a little nudge pushes against the inside of my abdominal
wall. Again and again I feel him kick, and a smile creeps up my
cheeks. I wonder if Scarlet can feel this yet, or if she's too sick to
enjoy it.

"Arek is really wonderful." I tilt my head toward Alice,
though I don't expect a response. "Somehow, through the
tiniest chance of fate, you two have found each other. The odds
of that, the chance that this happened is just profound, don't
you think?"

She sniffs and faces me. "So is it fate then, or just chance?"

"What you're feeling is more than luck, Alice. Don't ever
doubt how special we are." I groan and pull myself up to get
dressed.

"You were possessed by a Koridon against your will as well.

How did you manage to live again?" She hugs her pillow, preparing for another day of being forced from her bed to join the rest of us by Vaerynn. "You know I can't trust Arek, no matter how true his heart. He's a beast, he's one of them, and we aren't meant to belong to them."

"Being part Koridon, it's easier for me. I am one of them, but even still, belonging to the beast who hurt me... It's unbearable."

"Any chance he won't recover?" she asks, the twisting of her expression showing the memory of his sudden mutilation into floating pieces. That image of Brekter is one I still see every day. The gore. The smell.

"Kassien tells me he will be among us again soon." I slip on a silky gown and stare at myself in the mirror. My stomach's heavy, but I feel strong, energy pulsing through my blood. "I may be having his child, but he won't be allowed to touch me again. Not with Kassien being here now."

"Are you angry at Scarlet? Like Mary-Shelly is angry at me?"

I pause with my hand around the door knob. "No. She didn't ask for any of this. None of us did."

"I just feel like with Kassien, she could have denied him. Don't you think?"

I scrunch my brow and try to force away the painful images of my best friend and my love engaged in pulse-pounding coupling. "Maybe." With Drakon still around, not complying with the agreement could have brought trouble upon both of them. But, I guess that trouble was worth more than me.

Alice sighs lazily. "So are you off to breakfast and Nazi physical training now?"

"No," I say thoughtfully. "I'm going to see my friend."

Spring's dew drips from the trees in crystalline drops around me as I make my way to Drakon's huge grounded ship. The forcefield immediately disintegrates as I touch it to pass through, as Kassien ensured in case I ever needed to get to the med bay in an emergency.

The ship looks exactly like the one Kassien kept me in, and though I'm eyeballed by several Koridons on the way through, I find Scarlet easily. She lays staring at the ceiling through the sparkle of the barrier.

"Hey." I step through slowly and give her a hesitant smile. "How are you?"

She touches her belly and says bleakly, "There's not much time left." Her eerie words strike me hard, and I can't hide the concern in my face before she sees it.

She drops her thin, shaking arm back to her side and I note the nutrients running through an intravenous line into it. She appears so tiny compared to the obscenely stretched stomach that forces her over to her side. "Do they know when the baby can be taken out?"

"Oh, I'm sure they'll pull it once I'm dead."

"No." The awkwardness and discomfort fades and I rush to her side. "I promise you I won't allow that. Kassien would never allow—"

"He has to!" She coughs weakly. "He has to allow it because the child is all that matters to them." A confusing feeling of relief floods upon knowing that Kassien values his child more than his wife, and I instantly feel guilty for it. What kind of person am I, that I still think of love while my best friend lies in her death bed?

"I don't care," I say, taking her hand. "Whatever I have to do, that baby comes out this day."

She removes her hand, though every bit of the effort taxes her. "Soon you'll have him back."

"That doesn't matter to me anymore, Scarlet!" My cheeks burn and I tamp down the frustration that rises. "I want us to have our children together, I want to share this with you."

"It's okay. You'll have Kassien to share it with. Maybe you two can raise him together."

A whirlwind of anger and sadness twists within me. *Why are you giving up? Why are you so hateful of me when I've always loved you no matter what?* So many thoughts pound into my mind, but I would never utter a single word of it.

"That night in the forest, when we were taken from the village by Alexander and his men..." Scarlet pulls me from my tumultuous thoughts. "He came for you. He saved *you*. It's always been you. And here I am, the mother of his child yet nothing but a dying wretch. I can't even get up to touch his hair or laugh with him. I can't brush out my own hair or look pretty for him." Her sunken in, bloodshot eyes gloss over. "Being with him felt like a betrayal to you, but that's not really fair, is it? I guess I did think for a moment about having a family with the prince of the Koridons. About being happy. I grieve those wonderful thoughts." She breaks down, and I lean over to hug her as she cries.

"You were never betraying me, I understand." I'm unsure if I ever did feel betrayed by her, but I truly mean it now. "You're going to live, and you will have those wonderful thoughts, Scarlet. You will have your dream, so don't you give up." My tone is severe as I grip her bony shoulders. "Do not allow yourself to slip away." I have to go to Gerakon who time and again has shown passion for her. Even if he must be coerced by his love for Scarlet to save her, *he must*. But then Kassien will suffer too. This situation is merciless.

"Go on," Scarlet whispers. "I'm tired." She turns away to hide her tears.

"I'll go, but don't worry anymore. We're going to figure this out." Gerakon should be in the lab, so I immediately go to find him. We need to discuss the options for Scarlet. I'll have to talk to Kassien too. Is there a right answer? If tomorrow I found myself dying because of my baby, what would I do? Would I be willing to die so that he might live?

"Calypso. My... *love*."

The blood freezes in my veins, and I find myself stopped in front of a room. I should run from that voice, that loathed sound, but instead I slowly peer inside. "Brekter. You're looking well." *Unfortunately*. He gets up and stands with his elbow cocked against the wall, his movements holding an underlying weakness he tries to hide.

"You have gotten so big," he smirks.

"I guess your hair follicles weren't restored with hair, were they?" I ask. "When all your pieces...parts snapped back together?"

He smooths back the short raven locks of only a couple months' growth and stands tall. "Are you ready to take your place at my side? Where you belong?"

"This child doesn't make me yours."

"No. That trembling pussy I tear up does."

"You're disgusting."

"You like it."

I walk away with fury overtaking my senses. *I fucking hate him.* "Come near me ever again, and I'll kill you!"

"My death already awaits!" he yells. I stop dead, knowing I'll regret this, but I don't care.

I rush back to his quarters. "Tell me more. I like where you're going with this." I force the hot tears of anger back and level out my expression to show him nothing.

He comes forward, so close I question the forcefield between us. Fear trickles down my spine as his fingers outstretch toward my face. "Since the moment I breathed you in, you infected my system, and I knew our only path would be through fire. Burning, screaming. I knew our destiny would lead to being thrust straight into the ground."

"For once, I agree with you." He kindles passion from torture and bends pain into pleasure, and to be near him hurts because of what he's turned me into.

"It's worth the agony," he whispers. "You fight me at every turn, but I always get you. You are mine."

I shake my head sadly and step back. "You like the fight and thrive on my pain. Brekter, this isn't love, and I'll never be her. I'll never be your first."

"I have no desire for her. Not since you."

"You desire me only as a way to feed the thing inside you that still wants to hurt *her*." He was so new to the world when she scarred his soul. He hadn't even mated one of his own kind yet when she taught him passion and dealt him ultimate pain.

"Stay with me," he whispers. His hand drags down the barrier and I feel it somehow, descending along my chest.

"Goodbye," I say weakly.

"Wait!" he growls. "Come back to me!" But his cries fade away as I leave the ship.

26

Ocean foam pours over the large rocks along the shore as morning tide comes in. The gale tosses my icy blue locks around my face, and the scent of a fresh new day by the sea fills my nostrils. I'll find Gerakon soon, but after seeing Brekter again, I'm too shaken to fight for her. Scarlet doesn't have the time, and yet I need just that. A moment in time, alone, just my feet sinking into the cool sand.

Another set of footsteps crunch into the wet ground, and my pulse spikes.

"Calypso." Kassien puts a hand up for me to wait. My pulse continues to soar. "May I walk with you?"

"Of course." I say goodbye to my quiet moment and man up. "I need to talk to you anyway. Scarlet is going to die, Kassien."

"We are doing everything we can to avoid her demise."

"Not everything."

He stops and puts his arms behind his back. "You would have me sacrifice the child?"

"I don't *want* that, but Scarlet was forced to conceive. She didn't ask for this, and preserving your species isn't a good enough reason to watch my best friend die."

"When our newborn was lost, I turned away from my mate and my true hatred for this planet, for *life*, grew."

"Your newborn?" He hinted once that he'd had a child. It explains why he pushed so hard for me, so driven by that need to replace the one he lost.

"No," he says, knowing my thoughts. "Though despair overtook me as another conception was unlikely, meeting you took all the pain away. I needed you with every ounce of my being and could think of nothing else. Not until I was hanging by those hooks did reality revisit me, and my focus returned."

The reality that love wasn't important, but creating life was all that mattered. I understand— he could do that with any human. Now he's finding that as his mate lies dying, it won't be that easy.

He touches the side of my neck, a light brush that springs chills to life down my arms. "I still feel it when you are near. A deep, overpowering craving..."

Familiar, sickening disappointment eats at my stomach as I think about what could have been if only Brekter hadn't impregnated me. That *one factor* takes my life from wonderful to completely hopeless.

I shrug sadly. "It's the same for me."

"Everything I'd been denying myself came flooding back when I touched you, and all that joy at once possessed me. I killed for you without a thought and tore my own brethren apart."

Then why don't you kill Brekter? And kill that hideous Drakon? If not for them, Scarlet may have had a girl with Gerakon, and Kassien and I could raise my child together. I look down at my feet. If he'd still have me. But maybe raising another's son would be unacceptable or dissatisfying.

"But when I heard the child's heartbeat within Scarlet's belly, and felt him moving..." He places a hand on my stomach and his warmth fills me with happiness. "Everything hit me again: love, hope, just how it felt when I was with you."

I'm devastated for him, because he's losing that precious little life slowly and nothing is going to stop it. "Kill Brekter," I say just above the sloshing of the waves. "Be with *me*, where you belong, and let Scarlet have her life back before it's too late for both of them."

He brings me into his chest but keeps a hand planted against my stomach. I will him to connect to *my* child, to feel that same breathless loyalty for him that he has for his own. He is still a Koridon child. He is the future.

"You would see Brekter dead?" he asks, his tone rocking me with how quickly it turned cold.

"Of course."

He squeezes me and his breath warms my ear. "You have been with him several times since. He claims you are more than willing."

Shame flushes my cheeks and I yank back, only to be held tight by his massive arms. It tortures me that I'm sexually aroused by my tormenter, a man I'm supposed to hate, and it's humiliating that Brekter told him about it. I've never wanted to sink into the earth like I do now. "How dare you say this to me, after the night you stormed the mansion and saw what he was doing to me during the ceremony!"

His eyes flash with dangerous jealousy.

"I have been used for the pleasure of others more times than I've—" The words sting on my tongue and I fight with my thoughts. *More times than I've been taken in love.* "I hate him and he knows it, so he makes me feel things I can't control."

His embrace tightens and he heats up against me. "I am heavily distracted these days, but when he told me that you bend until you break beneath him, my world turned red. In one small moment I decided to rip his head off, the consequences meaning *nothing*."

"I wish you had." He's so strong my lungs fight to expand, and I wish he would squeeze harder.

"The red mist returns," he says with a whisper of madness. "You make me want to kill everyone here and drag you across the world where we can live forever in hiding."

"Ohh," I utter softly, scared yet exhilarated at the same time. I've seen this unharnessed side of him, and he's frightening. My adrenaline skyrockets as the request drips from my consciousness, so close to leaving my lips: *Yes. Please yes. Take me away...*

Voices drift on the breeze, snapping me back to a place where sanity reigns. Vaerynn and Finn appear by the bridge, distressed words passing between them. Kassien breaks from his trance, alarm rising as he takes them in. Vaerynn tips her face up to meet his, so close, and I marvel at their moment, the fiery atmosphere in their background saying everything they can't.

"It was the hardest thing I've ever done." Kassien peers into the sky where a bird flies overhead. "Pushing the reassemble button on the obliterator."

"Why did you?"

"Because I've killed for you, and there will be consequences one day. To take the lives of more Koridons will see me killed in return by the sovereigns. Then how can I watch over my only love, *Calypso*?"

"You love me?"

"Since the moment I carried you broken in my arms." The

tension in my being releases. "You are mine. Even if another has rights to you."

"Rights to me," I repeat. "This is a broken world, where my abuser is allowed to own me."

"And we are fighting to create a new one."

I roll my lips together and a hint of salt touches my tongue. The tide kicks up and I startle as it makes a powerful crack against the shore.

"I want to protect you," he says, "but I cannot always be there. Under your bed, the floor boards have been loosened, and beneath you will find a most feared weapon."

My brows pop up. "You don't mean?" He got the flesh obliterator back?

He nods wickedly. "In case you or Alice find yourselves in danger. It was the best place I could think to hide it."

"I can't believe you got it back! How?"

"Let us walk," he says, shooting one last glance toward Finn and Vaerynn. "I contacted Eladia and told her of what happened that night of the ceremony."

"And just like that, she granted you access?"

"She is my aunt, after all."

What news! I breathe easier knowing we have such fire power on our side, and right there in my room! When I hid behind Kassien the night he returned, I saw exactly how he used it on Brekter.

"How has the pregnancy been for you?" Kassien puts his arm around me as we walk, the sand scratching the soles of my feet, and my legs grow heavy as I sink into the ground.

"Gerakon says this is new for him, but according to the imaging, it may be safe to come out in as early as a week." The cold sea foam reaches our feet, and the tiny bubbles crackle as it recedes again. "He's going to pull him straight out of my stomach to avoid complications of trying to deliver a fourteen pound baby naturally. You guys are bloody huge." I hold the bottom of my massive belly and step away from the creeping water. "And I'm quite ready to have my child now."

"I never thought about how *you* felt carrying your enemy's child. How can you care for such a thing?"

"This baby comes from my enemy, yes, but he's still a part of *me*. And my mother." He's also a part of my *father* by default, but I choose not to dwell on it. "Children are scarce in our villages too, by choice. There aren't enough resources, and the cloak we used to disguise ourselves kept us trapped, really."

As we walk back, I think about the kiss I gave Kassien by the lake when we so nearly stripped each other bare and mated before proper ceremony. He had never felt another's lips before, and I knew it was dangerous to tempt him. But I trusted him. Even when he changes, becoming the threatening beast that seems to live in all of them, I still can't fear him.

"Kass, consider what I've asked of you, please. You can't let Scarlet die. Your baby will be strong enough to survive with all your advanced medical equipment because they're part human and belong here now."

"Yes, half-human. That is cause for worry in itself."

I nod my head, understanding. While a Koridon child may be strong enough to survive coming out this early, the human in him may not.

Days go by, and every new sunrise amazes me as my body holds out against the onslaught of the Koridon male growing inside me. My lower abdomen aches, and I throw the covers off to use the bathroom for the fourth time tonight. The child's head bears down against my pelvic floor and I sometimes worry that it's trying to push it way out, ready to come into the world, but my body stays closed, oblivious.

As I sit and relieve my bladder, I think of the little heartbeat thrumming away in its six chambers, the lub-dub-thud sounds the strange hybrid organ makes. I remember how Gerakon's hands shook, holding the stethoscope as he explained that Koridon anatomy consists of two hearts among other striking differences.

I asked him to save Scarlet, but his words to me were purely logical, *the life of the child is all that matters*...although his avoiding eyes spoke of things he could never take back. I have to believe that when the time comes, he won't let her die.

A soft murmur snaps my head up as I step down the hallway. I crack the door open an inch and realize it's going to be awkward getting back to my bed with Arek visiting Alice. And I really want my bed. She puts her arms around his shoulders, his bare back stretched out, his massive body hanging off her bed. I sit down in the hall on the ornately carpeted floor and run my fingers over the paisleys. Maybe I'll just wait another minute. My morning fog dissipates and I remember—Arek's on a hunting trip.

A choking sound brings me to my feet, too quickly, and my abdomen lights up with pain. I hit the door open, ignoring it, my senses on high alert. Before I can make out the figure in the dark, I'm yanked inside and hit the wall. I crawl to my feet and try to scream but choke on the plea.

A sharp elbow shatters my chest and the cry dies in my throat. I watch helplessly as Kjartonn ties Alice's mouth shut. Cracking pain alerts me to true damage of my sternum when I move, but all I can focus on are the whites of blond Alice's watering eyes and the sound of desperation slipping past her gag.

Kjartonn, covered in a layer of dirt and hair wild, takes her down to her knees. He rips the underwear off her backside and jerks them from her ankles. Where's Vaerynn? Oh god, Finn. What has happened to them that Kjartonn has gotten through? He turns his cruel gaze on me and a wicked smile curls his lips. His hand lands hard into the fleshy globe of her ass, and tears squeeze down her face.

I crawl toward my bed. Pain seizes my reach as I feel along the floor for the loose boards, and I grunt as my large belly pulls me down. I toss myself to the side, feeling the baby squirm from the pressure. I croak out a cry for help and force myself to my hands and knees through the stabbing pain in my chest, but it's too late. He grips his cock and plays the tip against her backside. Her face suddenly twists into my own, and I see *my* silvery hair pulled until the scalp is raised, *my* lips praying for it to end. His large hands hold her hips firm, and when he turns to me, it's Brekter that has taken his face.

He grips the top of her head and jerks her up to his mouth. "The very closeness of you," he says, "...the feel of your kiss when you thought I was *him*, it stunned me and enraged me. You want to be his?"

She whimpers in reply.

"Never," he growls. "I would rather you were dead. And I know just how you will die."

I frantically search for the opening in the floor, but I'm shaking so badly. I take a deep breath and force my nerves back. Kassien gave me the weapon to prevent this. I can't fail her. Slowly I search again, and a floor board moves against my pinky.

Kjartonn turns toward me with a curious squint. "However," he caresses her hair back as she cries, "I'd like to do this slowly. And perhaps for many days after you have gone cold. So I will take you away from here, somewhere where no one will ever find us."

C.F. RABBIOSI

I reach in and grasp the object securely in my hand. I envision the weapon by the feel of it in my mind's eye. Still trembling, I accidently hit something and it powers on, casting a blue light underneath the bed. Kjartonn drops her, and I aim the light straight into his fucking head. My excitement overrides the pain.

I press a button along the right side of the handle, exactly where I remember Kassien activating it, and nothing happens. "Leave now," I say hoarsely but with enough strength in my spirit to make up for it. "Get out of here and I won't shred you to pieces." I press another button, and it still doesn't fire.

He tips his head, his grip on Alice tightening, and I wonder if he can tell that I'm bluffing. Even if I can get this thing to fire, what if it takes her out too?

"Stupid girl, you have no idea how to use that." He grins with the tiniest tremble, but blond Alice comes to life. *Do it*, she dares me silently.

I press into the side once more and hold it down as hard as I can. A ray of light shoots from the device and Kjartonn lunges forward, tearing it away from my grip in an instant.

He swipes it from the ground, and in my attempt to save Alice, I have given him the ultimate power to take over everything. Icy dread pulses through me as I realize that everyone here is going to die.

27

K jartonn chuckles darkly. "Goodbye to you first, Kassien's most treasured possession." He aims the obliterator at me, and I back up against the wall. "I guess there is no need for us to run any longer," he muses toward Alice. The gun activates, and the sensation of hot needles flushes down my neck.

I can't die now. I want to hold my baby, I want to *live*, even if Brekter's always at my back. It's worth it. Everything is just to be here—

Alice smashes her weight into Kjartonn, and though he hardly moves, it's enough. He misses, and I force myself forward with that strange urge to grasp him, skin to skin. My hand wraps around his ankle as he fights with Alice. Everything suddenly snaps into focus and I tap into that place that holds something...some *power* I've never understood. I squeeze into him and summon every horror I've ever felt, every sadness that's crushed my spirit, and it all takes form, swirling in my core. My fingers tingle, and the swirling ball of power moves toward them. My palm lights up and a rush transfers through. I send pain to him. I send despair. And above all, I send *fear*. He buckles, his face a twisted mask of horror.

Alice captures the obliterator easily, and as Kjartonn twitches, his body a squiggling mass of angst, she aims—

Fires.

And doesn't fucking miss. He disseminates, his flesh ripping apart, and sparkling rubies drip from his suspended pieces all around us. With the taste of blood on her smile, Alice lays the weapon on her soft pillow and we watch him bleed to death.

Exhilaration gives way to blackness and I hit the floor. Alice rushes to my side and wipes my face. "I'll get help. We'll get you fixed."

I grab her wrist as she gets up, and she flinches in my grip. "No." I struggle to say against the constriction of my chest and let her go, afraid I might zap her with my strange gift. "The nano-healing device, it's hidden in the floor." I felt it in my panic as I pulled the obliterator out.

She kneels over the hole in the floor and takes it from its hiding spot. She stares at it a moment. "Do you know how to use this? We should go get Vaerynn. Or Gerakon!"

"No," I say and rip my nightshirt up. We've seen this done many times. I take the tool and hold it over my aching sternum. Most the pain I transferred to Kjartonn, so I'm able to move easier. "We must do this ourselves." The child moves and kicks softly, exacerbating the painful area. But he's all right.

The red scanning light streams over my chest and sparkles in Alice's eyes. "What did you do to him?"

I shake my head, the strange tingling resurfacing in my hands. "It's happened before, a couple times, but I could never fully harness it. I felt this overwhelming urge to touch him, then it's as if I somehow *transferred* all my suffering to him. Maybe because he lacks most emotion anyway, as most

Koridons do, all that human feeling flooded his system and paralyzed him. Can you imagine being numb, and then being struck with all that?"

She blinks hard. "Is this some kind of gift because of the splicing of our two species?"

The thought excites me and I touch my belly, just to get zapped by the scanners, and pull it away. "It has to be! Something about the Koridons' heightened senses mixed with human's intuition and empathy, maybe." One ability heightens the other, and I can send pain in the form of energy into someone. I read once that emotional pain cuts deeper than physical pain, and Koridons don't stop when inflicted with pain. They welcome it. "When I was young this happened, do you remember that? I was being beaten by the older boys because of my appearance." I never understood that day until now.

"No, but look, I don't see why we can't get help. They need to know what's happened here."

Tiny healing particles float out and attach to my skin. The aching dulls, becoming pressure, and I take a large breath like ecstasy for the first time since Kjartonn hit me. Relief floods and I sit up despite Alice's fussing for me to stay still. I take the nasty weapon and study it, a haunting fascination alive in my thoughts. "Because this day's going a whole other direction. We're going to write our own story from now on."

Alice helps me up, a vein in her forehead bulging, and we head down. We walk down the stairs, arm in arm, my free hand filled with a weapon of instant death—or very painful life, if reassembled—and Alice holds the healing tool.

Vaerynn moves into our path, completely unaware that Kjartonn attacked us. But she and Finn are untouched, and right now, we aren't going to tell her a thing. She notices my fire power and steps aside, her arms raised in bemusement.

"Let's walk away," Finn says, his hand lightly touching the small of her back. Her forehead wrinkles with worry, and Finn's fingers dig in.

Twigs snap under foot, the sound amplified in my paranoia as I constantly look over my shoulder on our way to the ship. The entrance shimmers before us and I take Alice by the shoulder. "Stay behind me, I'm gonna blast any bastard that shows himself."

"Let's hope they *all* do," she snickers, and I appreciate that the one time she jokes is when we're about to get ourselves killed.

"Move fast!" I put my hand through the barrier and it falls away, letting us pass.

We move swiftly through the control room and down the hall to the prisoner hold. Drakon lies on the floor, his hands folded on his chest.

"Knock knock," I say, and he flies to his feet. The obliterator hides behind my back.

"What are you doing here?" His eyes dart around, trying to make sense of our unaccompanied presence.

"I'm tired of you," I say simply. "Many of our problems will be solved once you're dead."

"You cannot kill me." He stamps his foot, making the ship shudder, and he truly believes he is still in charge.

"Really? What's stopping me?" I ask.

"I am the reason for your existence." He avoids the word *father*, and his airy tone gets under my skin. I think of how he planned to chain us all up and let his huge Koridon horde have their pleasure between our legs whenever they liked. "And also, it is a physical impossibility," he nearly laughs. "If you even think to—"

I draw the weapon and his arrogant chuckle shatters.

"Put that down," he sputters and backs up into his waste

receptacle. "You don't even know how to use that, I demand you—"

I put my hand through the glimmering barrier and it recognizes my DNA, letting me slide right through. I hit the trigger sensor, and with a flash of light, Drakon flies into pieces, *obliterates* before my spreading smile. Juices pour from the floating flesh in slow motion, and I move my finger to the trigger that will reassemble him. What fate am I securing for myself by killing one of the most powerful Koridon leaders? There are clans all over the world, and several more on distant planets. What will they do to me once they realize what I've done?

Guess I'll find out.

A laugh rolls off Alice's tongue, a sound I've never heard before, and I lower the weapon. It's almost over. With Drakon and both his sons dead, we're safe. No more enslaved women forced against their will. "Sorry *Dad*," I say, trying to fight blond Alice's contagious glee that threatens to bend into hysterical laughter. "I'm in charge now and everything's going to be—"

A horrible choking sound splits my joyful moment, and I spin around to find Andromeda against blond Alice's back. A steel tip protrudes through her side, crimson bleeding into her ivory nightdress. I turn the blaster on the servant and she grabs the healing device from Alice's failing grip as she stumbles.

"Put him back together!" Andromeda screams and stalks forward. "I saw it done at your wedding, now fix him!"

"Never." I point the obliterator at her head and play with the trigger sensor. "If he gets out of here, he could imprison us again! As long as he lives, we are all in danger." The smell of exsanguinated flesh surrounds us, and I wonder how long he can stay this way before it's too late. "Don't make me kill you."

She stomps on Alice laying at her feet, inciting a terrible cry. "I'll let you heal her once Master Drakon is saved.

Otherwise..." She snatches the blade out of Alice's stomach and sits her up to use as a shield. Andromeda stabs her violently through the shoulder. "Or she dies too."

"Fine! Trade." I slide the weapon across the floor, and she snatches it up.

"How do I work it?" She dashes over to the force field and takes aim toward her Koridon lover. I dive for the healing device she left behind and activate the scanning rays over Alice's abdomen.

"Press the two sensors that look like a triangle at the same time!" I say. She examines it then aims. If she pulls this off, and he lives, I am so dead. Maybe during his long recovery I can try killing him again—

Light bursts from the gun and I pray it's too late to save him...

T he light ray hits the shimmery barrier of the cage and ricochets back toward Andromeda. Her face twists in terror before her body rips apart.

Alice squeezes my hand and sheds a relieved tear. I drag her down the hall, away from the dripping servant girl, and slam into something.

"What have you done, you psychotic women?" Gerakon steps over us and puts his hands to his head. "You killed Drakon." He picks up the obliterator from Andromeda's seeping fluids and deactivates the barrier. "You better hope this works, though I doubt it will save you." The nanos flow into Alice and I get up slowly, keeping the healer firmly behind my back. Gerakon sends the ray of light into his leader, and the tiny pieces slam together with a horrible squelching. He runs at me and rips the healer away.

"No!" I lunge for it so he can't retrieve the microscopic machines from Alice's body, but he shoves me down. "Gerakon, she'll die!"

He types in a code that instructs the nanos to retreat from

Alice's damaged tissue, and she shakes her head desperately, begging him to save her.

"Isn't there another nanohealer? Why can't you just go grab—"

"It is in use!" he yells, and I immediately recognize the pain in his voice. It's being used on *Scarlet*. He side steps Andromeda's floating flesh. "Who's this other one?"

"His bitch lover." I spot the dagger in the corner that Andromeda stabbed Alice with and edge toward it. I'm not going to let her die. I'd rather kill another of these bastards than lose another of my friends.

Drakon's body reforms; bones snap into place, raising his sunken spine into position, and Gerakon lays him down.

I take the blade from a puddle of blood.

Wiping his forehead, Gerakon begins the scan and red light floods over Drakon's body.

I creep up behind him and lift the dagger high, aiming in between his shoulder blades. I don't want to hurt him, but I need that healer back, now. Alice's tortured whimpers as she fights to breathe strengthen my resolve. Heart pounding, I summon all my strength before I strike...

The red light over Drakon's body pulses wildly and I drop my arm.

Gerakon sighs heavily and sits back. "You killed a very important leader, Calypso."

"Guess *I'm* your leader now." I snatch the healing tool and reactivate it for Alice. The scan already completed, the machine gets right back to work on her.

His head snaps up, mouth gaping.

"Isn't that the rule of war?" I ask, slipping Andromeda's dagger into my boot. "Of course, Kassien stands undisputed prince. I'll let him rule beside me."

"We didn't want a war!" He jumps to his feet and towers

over me. "We wanted to survive, and the bigger, better species always does."

"We'll see." I nod toward Drakon's cyanotic corpse.

Kassien appears at the end of the hall and fear rushes through me. He entrusted me with his weapon, and I've used it to put myself and probably many others in grave danger. But this new world they're trying to create isn't good enough. I stand tall as he runs toward us.

"She's killed Drakon and his mistress." Gerakon hands the obliterator to Kassien.

"I had to," I say. "As long as Drakon lived, the humans I love were in danger. I won't apologize."

He raises an amused brow.

"You must give her over to the Sovereign Eladia for her crime. If not, you will pay as well."

"Of course I would never," Kassien says. "Do you understand what you have done?" He drops to his knees to hold me by my shoulders.

"Yes," His people forbid *him* from killing any of these blighters, not me. "Now I would have you return that weapon to me so I can continue my rampage. Please."

He runs fingers down the length of his tied beard, and in his face I see the realization that there's no going back now.

Gerakon tips his head in disbelief as Kassien hands me the obliterator. "I am behind you, Calypso," he says, tightening the strap around his bare chest and tapping the hilt of his knife. "Whatever you have done, I will protect you."

"And for whatever I'm about to do?" I ask, licking the blood of Koridons from my lips.

He leans his head against mine. "Always."

I look in the direction of Brekter's room as Gerakon protests, but Kassien sends him back to Scarlet. "I believe you have very important work to attend to," he says to the doctor.

Gerakon does as he's told, his hands shaking as he returns to my best friend's side.

"You truly, *truly* please me, my prince," I say, putting my arms around his waist.

He snaps me against him. "Let me do it." He touches the weapon and I recoil.

"No. It has to be me." Covered in blood, I feel wild and *warrior*, and I need Brekter to see me like this. As I was truly meant to be. And I need to see his face as he dies.

"You will be in danger. I cannot allow it." Kassien's fingers dig into my arm. My lips part, but he shuts them when he puts a hand to my belly. "For your child's sake, go rest now, and let me finish what you have started."

As if on cue, little knees nudge my side and the deep pressure sitting on my pelvic floor resurfaces. "I want to be alone with him one last time, Kassien. Look what I've done already. I've killed the commander and also his dangerous son. You must learn to trust me now."

"Kjartonn is dead?"

"He snuck into our room this morning and..." I'll explain the strange phenomenon brewing inside that hurt him enough for Alice to shoot him some other day, but it's another reason I feel confident confronting my tormentor alone. Brekter and I share something very dark and very private, and Kassien cannot be a part of it.

He drops to his knees and lays his head upon my stomach. Somehow, with everything a mess and Alice still struggling to survive, everything is perfect. Love radiates from his touch and my spirit pulses against his warmth. "Let me finish this," I say softly. "I need you to deal with Gerakon and anyone else that tries to stop me. Surely more will come."

"Only if I can remain near. *Right outside the entrance* near."

"Deal." I pull away before he changes his mind and head toward Brekter.

He stands at the barrier, fear splashing his features as I approach, his form trembling from weakness. He's not the same alpha that could easily hold me down and bend me to his will. "Hello, my love," he says, a heady excitement in his voice.

I step directly in front of him and tap the metallic surface of the flesh obliterator. He knows exactly what that sound is. "You know why I've come."

A dark laugh rumbles from his throat. "I always expected to die for you."

I put the barrel into his cheek, a single finger allowed through the barrier. "Not *for* me. *Because* of me."

"The very darkest part of me connects to the very darkest part of you. We have something more powerful than love." A low growl of pure predator makes a strange thrill dance through my veins, a familiar and unwanted effect.

"I'll never love you," I say shakily, "and you couldn't force me to as much as you tried."

"Yes," he lulls. "Sweet human, explain to me what *love* is before I die."

Kassien, just around the corner, looks unamused, but I feel compelled to answer him. "Well, you would say it's nothing but biology. That chemicals make us fall in love and create a bond that in turn leads to reproduction."

"Facts."

"Yes. But the interpretation is wrong. There's an intangible element that can't be seen. It's the piece of the puzzle that *causes* that burst of chemicals. It's an element of fate and an entwining of the soul, that's why it doesn't happen with just anyone."

His eyes close and he droops as though at any moment he

will give out under his own weight. "But why then may someone love another, yet that love is not returned?"

"Maybe you don't really love me."

Gerakon rounds the corner and whispers something to Kassien. His gaze shoots to me and his skin pales. "Finish this now," he demands as Gerakon pulls him away. "Blast him and come quick!"

Something's happened to Scarlet. "Let me send you to her," I say, and my forefinger and thumb brush the triggers. "The one you're supposed to be with is waiting for you."

Swift hands tear the blaster from my grip, and I'm ripped inside the room. I swallow my scream as Brekter's palm slaps over my mouth and he presses me against the wall. Fighting his hold, my nails scratch off skin and my knees thrust into him, but it's no use.

"I believe you, you know." He secures my wrists above my head and his tongue flicks against the pulse on my neck. "If there was no fate, then I never would have felt you in my arms again. Yet here you are."

My muffled, *let me go,* sounds from underneath his hand. "You know, we could have had a life together, you, me and..." He touches the roundness of my belly. "And our child. What a life was promised." He frees my mouth and slams my head back, sending pain through the back of my skull. "Scream and I'll snap your neck. Then we both die. Well, we all die, and trust me when I tell you," his bottom lip caresses my cheek, "I want that very much." I twist my head to find the obliterator lying on the ground behind him. He seemed so weak that Kassien and I both misjudged him.

"What do you want then?" I struggle to keep my voice just above a whisper. "Kassien will be back any second."

"We'll make this quick." He spins me around and yanks the dress up my back. "One. Last. Time." His knuckles hit my backside as he fumbles with himself. He bends his knees and crams his oversized crown against me.

"We don't do this to each other." Desperation clings to my whisper. "We don't hurt the ones we love."

"I love you beyond my control, Calypso. Threat of death bears down on me, and all I want is to die inside you." His mouth searches my shoulder then brushes up the side of my neck. "Please come with me."

I jolt down and a hand breaks free, my fingertips just touching the hilt of the blade I hid in my boot. He slams me back against the wall. "Ask me again why I could never love you!" I cry. My chest burns as a ball of energy sparks to life, and I know the more he hurts me the more I'll make him suffer with the secret power that wells up inside.

"Oh, you *have* loved me, harder than anyone." He touches against my lips, a hungry plea, and his kiss starves against the corpse he's created. He holds the back of my head and utters a frustrated cry that shakes me to the core. "Please. Love me once more, and I will lay down my life without a fight." He holds me against him, and the agony within bleeds onto my skin. "Please. Fight me no more. Just once, pretend I am *him*."

"I can't," I say.

He slams his head into the wall and roars in my face. I squeeze my eyes shut and mentally prepare myself for when he rips my clothes off and takes what he wants. *I'll use it*—every sickening thrust, every horrifying pain, and I'll blast it all into him.

He takes a shuddering breath, his mouth stretched in anguish as he fights back tears. He growls with exasperation and rips himself away.

I pull the dagger and rush him. He grabs my wrist, sending the knife tip up. My bones crack in his grip and he stifles my cry. His face twists into a demonic sneer, and it's now or never. I will the energy to grow, and my heart dances in anticipation.

He releases me and drops to his knees. I freeze, opening and shutting my fists in confusion. I didn't have time to shock him.

"Quickly." He rips his shirt open and exposes his chest. "Take me from this world and far away from you."

I touch the gruffness of his cheek, and he leans into it. "Maybe we *were* destined, Brekter. But you hurt me. You abused me. And no soul bond could *ever* be created in such darkness."

"Teach me," he pleads tearfully. "Maybe I could—" His expression twists with realization. "I will change for you, and we can start again. The Koridon reign of force and violence over your people is no more. I can now forsake our previous ways and be the *man* you deserve. Choose me," he takes my hand desperately, "and I'll spend the rest of my life making you glad you did."

My heart quivers upon seeing such a beast transform into something so gentle, so broken. "Brekter, it's too late."

"Calypso." His voice rumbles through me, caressing my nerves and my eyes close. "Just give me a chance." His lips press into my wrist. "I love you and I'll prove it. Please, Calypso, please? I want you. I want our *baby*."

I remember Scarlet's twisted face as Brekter stabbed the burning brand into her skin, and the coldness of his eyes, the glee in his smile. I feel the ache in the back of my head from when he slammed me to the ground during the mating ritual. He then still prepared to take me sexually, even as I so despairingly asked him to stop. I touch my stomach and mourn for our child, *one that will never know his father*.

I thrust the blade through his heart, and his spine straightens unnaturally as the pain bites in. Black blood streams down his chin, and he wrenches the blade out. He opens his arms toward me as though asking for me to join him once more, and I jump backward. But as tears fill his eyes, he slides the steel through the other side of his ribcage.

Two hearts. Both broken and bleeding, a body killed, a love destroyed.

"Calypso!" Kassien storms inside and cracks Brekter's neck. As he falls, the blackness holding me captive dies with him. Somewhere through the mist, Kassien's voice becomes clear. "Scarlet is declining. Come!"

29

S carlet lies twitching on the table. A rhythmic beat sounds from her heart monitor, weak and irregular.

Gerakon scans her body, and the red light flashes over her heart. "This is dire." He quickly works over her, strange machines moving like fluid along with him as they manipulate her with tubes and other devices.

It's happened. They had less time than they thought, and now she's going to die as the giant, strong Koridon within compromises her circulatory system.

I feel Kassien's eyes upon my torn dress and know he will have questions for me later. He didn't expect me to end up inside the barrier, alone with Brekter. I told him I could handle it and to trust me, and I almost got myself killed.

I take Scarlet's hand and her eyes pop open. "Hold on," I say. "The nano-healers are already inside."

"You have to pull the child," says Kassien, his color draining.

My mother, along with Efaelty and Vaerynn, bursts in the room. Vaerynn says, "What has happened out there? A massacre has occurred." She stops when she sees Scarlet's graying skin and struggling breath. My mother moves to her side. "How can we help?" Vaerynn asks.

"Check the settings on the fluid," Gerakon tells her. "And you two lift her up so her lungs can expand." My mother and I each support a shoulder, and Efaelty stabilizes her huge belly. The monitor plays a stronger, more monotonous heartbeat.

"They're taking him out, Scarlet! You hold on to life, don't give up." She nods vigorously, and for some reason I'm struck with the memory of us lying by the fire during a full moon celebration back at the village. Her laughter, her beautiful light. *Please*, I beg silently. Let me see her like that again.

Gerakon turns to Kassien. "I cannot imagine the infant living if removed. However, they both stand to die as it is now."

"I know. Do everything you can," says Kassien, the saddest I've ever heard him sound.

An alarm rings out and all of us turn back to Scarlet. The scanner reveals red pulsing in her lower region. "What's happening?" asks Mama.

Gerakon reads the images that appear from the healing device. "The heart has been healed, but its initial failing has caused a mass organ decline. The liver and kidneys are losing function." He keys something in and an image of her womb appears above her, the child tucked inside. His arms move and he rolls, his back and bottom making her skin ripple. "The nanos are working quickly, but it is not enough."

The precious little person moves about happily in the hologram, and we all grow silent. Seeing his small body and frailness bursting with such life brings tears spilling down my cheeks. Kassien steps backward, a hand to his chest. I have an overwhelming desire for his baby to live and have to turn away from the image. I can't bear to think how Kassien must hurt as that beautiful life is about to be torn away from him.

"Prepare the incubator and power up the machines." Gerakon brushes through the air, keying in symbols, and from the ceiling a liquid metal arm descends. The metal transforms into a sharp tool and Scarlet trembles in fear. "The incubator has already been programmed, but I will add the final details when we have the child in hand." He keys another code into the air, and a sparkling blue substance travels down the tube into the three-pronged access system to Scarlet's veins.

She screams out, her arm filling up with fluid, and my mother rips out the tubes. "That chemical ate through her veins!" she cries and ties material around the swollen tissues.

"Why would it do that?" I ask.

"I cannot say!" Gerakon keys in another code but a buzzer sounds in response. "The anesthesia must not be compatible with her." He squints, reading the glowing orange that appears on his mid-air screen. "I did not anticipate this! The chemicals broke down the proteins in her veins. They are destroyed and she is bleeding out! We need—"

Blond Alice. The thought of her rips through me. "The other healing tool!" I burst from the room toward the hall where we left her. How could I have forgotten about her? A sharp pain stabs through my belly, but I don't stop until I see Arek cradling blond Alice in his arms.

"Is she?" I can't finish the sentence as I take in her pale, unmoving form.

Arek puts a finger to his lips. "She sleeps."

"She survived?" *Thank you, universe,* I say under my breath. "Where's the healer?" I scan the area but the tool is nowhere to be found.

"When I arrived there was nothing but her." Arek strokes her golden locks. "I failed to protect her again."

I run with great effort, holding my aching belly, and stand in front of Brekter's quarters.

Oh my god. the room stands empty, blood streaked across the floor.

Another stabbing pain strikes through my abdomen, and I limp back to med bay as quickly as possible, every step getting heavier.

"It was gone." I flick my eyes toward Kassien and give him such a look of fear that he understands exactly what else was gone as well. Someone must have taken Brekter and the healing tool.

"I set the nanobots upon her arm to stop the bleeding, but we need more," says Gerakon, furiously working to establish a new access line into her other side.

"Are there only two of those healing tools?" asks my mother.

"You cannot comprehend the amount of resources and power that goes into the creation of a *Kren~sanfendic.*" Gerakon touches the air and a symbol glows. "I have to do this now. Hold her down." He works so quickly his hands blur. "Persephone! Kassien said you are skilled in stitching flesh."

"Yes! I'll go get my kit." She leaves, and my anxiety grows.

The liquid metal scalpel slices Scarlet's skin in a perfect line and depth according to the hologram guide. She gasps as Efaelty and Vaerynn hold her down, and her screaming curdles my blood. Black dots swarm my vision, and I brace myself against the wall. The agony on Scarlet's terrified face fades to black. Bones pop as she's held down and pressure grips my lower body. Sitting down, I catch my breath and blink several times.

Gerakon reaches into the incision as Scarlet's body is racked with shudders, and he scoops the living bundle from her womb. "Persephone!" he yells.

I force myself to stand up and tamp down the fear that my own labor has begun. If I'm having contractions, it'll still be hours before the baby must be extracted, so I'll be all right. I have to be, Scarlet needs me right now.

"I'm here." My mother scoots in and quickly threads her needle. She makes quick work of the separated flesh.

Kassien stands before the baby in Gerakon's arm, and his hulking form wilts in defeat. "I—" He moves away, halting his hesitant reach that seeks the softness of the new little child. "I want him so much. How can I love something I have never met?"

Pressure bears down on me, but I force it aside to place a comforting hand on his back.

"How can I have dreamt of the preciousness of his skin and the sweetness of his cry just to have it taken away?" His voice wavers and he turns abruptly.

Gerakon places the wriggling child in a floating incubator and the walls around him shimmer and change to a light violet. His mouth still tries to cry, but the sound ceases to come out. Oxygen and heat fill the chamber, and several robotic arms dive inside to hook up feeding tubes, fluids, and to monitor his vital signs.

"Will he live?" asks Kassien. Gerakon touches the sensors of the floating incubator and focuses harder on reading the results and setting the controls. His little body has a pink flush, but slowly the color leaches away.

Scarlet's teeth chatter, and agonal breaths wheeze into her lungs. "Finished." My mother puts her hands up, needle and thread dangling, and steps back. Scarlet's arm stops swelling as the nanos do their work, but the blood seepage beneath her skin leaves a black and blue discoloration. She twitches violently and tries to speak. "I— I don't want to die—"

"You aren't going to," I say, holding her clammy hand. "The baby's out and the healers are doing their magic inside you." Just her being awake and able talk must be a good sign.

"Is that why it doesn't hurt anymore?" she asks, staring blankly into the ceiling. My mother shakes her head slowly, and I realize that with those thick hand-done stitches to her uterus and abdominal muscle, she should still be hurting tremendously. Maybe she's in shock, or her adrenaline is numbing her after being cut open so barbarically when the anesthesia failed.

The nanobots pull from her skin and flow through the pores of her belly.

"The microscopic systems mimic specialized tissue and replace cells," says Gerakon. "They then reproduce inside the damaged organs." He says the words, but no emotion shines through.

I keep waiting for the alarms to settle, but her pulse continues to decline and her temperature dips. "Do you remember last Hallow's Eve?" comes her weak voice, and I nod vigorously. "I was the white queen." We must have read *The Lion, the Witch and the Wardrobe* three times that year.

"We sewed your dress with old curtain material that wasn't at all white anymore," I say. I had dressed up as Dracula's wife in one of my mom's old black gowns and a cape we made.

"I loved it," she says with a hint of that familiar fire. "The first night rain of the season came and we danced and danced. You never got cold, and I didn't care that I was."

Another pain, like burning pressure, seizes my lower abdomen and I bite back fear. The contractions are only minutes apart, and they shouldn't be.. The first part of labor lasts hours, so these may be false pains. But what if I'm forced to deliver vaginally if I wait too long? Is that even possible? My mother peers at me with concern, and I force myself to stop gritting my teeth.

Efaelty hands me a wet rag. "We always danced in the

rain," I say to Scarlet, wiping her teary cheeks. "Everyone ran inside, but we stayed until the last ember died."

"And then you shoved me in a mud puddle."

A chuckle escapes me, followed by another deep, aching pain to my abdomen "I didn't think you'd slip like that." It's strange, but as my best friend struggles to live and my own fate still hangs in the balance, there's nothing I'd rather talk about.

Gerakon vigorously presses air symbols near the baby and my smile drops. Kassien paces, the blood pulsing visibly against his skin. Gerakon feels Kassien's glare. "It keeps adjusting for different oxygen levels, but the child's condition still declines. Readings for his heart, lungs and other organs are holding at the low end of acceptable." He throws his hand through his hair. "The cause should be clear by now." The child grows still, and his chest sucks in, exposing the ridges of his ribs. "I have negative pressure working the air into his lungs, but his blood-oxygen levels refuse to rise."

Scarlet's teeth chatter again, and her skin appears eerily similar to the baby's: blanched with a tinge of gray. Mama places a hand on my shoulder. "It's said that our hospitals in the past used to save premature babies. They used to put tubes down the infant's throat and have a machine breathe for them." Her hand lifts abruptly as I work to calm my strained breaths. "Calypso, are you..?"

Damn it.

"Child, if you're in labor, you need to tell me." She moves to my side and leans down, my avoiding eyes growing wide.

"I'm fine. You know it can take hours before the second stage even begins."

"But this isn't a normal situation. Especially after what you've been through today. Come, let's—"

"No!" The alarms above Scarlet quicken, and I turn back to find her still and unnaturally quiet. Gerakon rushes over and checks the healing device. "Her heart has failed." He presses into the middle of her chest with two fingers. "I am going to manually perfuse her." His fingers dive in and out with lightning speed.

The alarms go silent but still flash, and my own heart skips a beat. "Mom?" My throat aches, bringing the burn of crying to my eyes.

She touches the shimmering walls of the baby's chamber and her reflection speaks to me. "While he's pumping the blood through her body, the organs are getting blood. We just have to wait to see if they'll start functioning again," Gerakon nods as she pauses, "on their own."

Scarlet's body moves lifelessly as Gerakon presses her sternum. She reminds me of an old rag doll, even the color of her skin. Momma rushes over to hug me and I still see the flashing red behind my closed lids.

The healing bots have fled Scarlet's body and hover above her bare stomach. Gerakon stops to grab the device, and the alarms sound again.

I pull away from my mother. "Well, tell the nanos to go back in!" They shouldn't be allowed to give up!

Loose hair falls around his face. "She has gone." He places a hand on her chest, his horrified gaze searching, then rips away.

"She can't be." A strange feeling of relief that the suspense is over hits me, followed by a wave of utter sorrow. Deafening screams shatter my thoughts: *You should have taken the baby out earlier! Why did you wait? Now they'll both die. what was the point of this?*

"Gerakon!" Kassien says, snapping me out of my head. "The child is still in need of you!" More alarms sound around the baby's chamber, and Efaelty reaches inside to touch his little white chest.

The crazed Koridon backs against the wall, his breath heaving, and has no clue what Kassien begs of him in this moment of madness.

"*Oh!*" I don't mean to cry out, but a tearing sensation brings me to my knees. Kassien pulls me into his arms and the echo of his voice cries out for Efaelty and Vaerynn. Momma rushes to my side as Kassien carries me out.

Gerakon's frantic yell stops us in the doorway. "Persephone, wait!" He grabs her shoulder. "Stay, please." He points toward the incubator. "I cannot—" he shakes his head, his breath hinging. I'm—"

She places her hand upon his. "I have to go with my daughter."

"We will take care of her," Vaerynn says, signaling for Kassien to take me out. "We know our equipment well. You have nothing to fear."

I want her with me, but she *is* the only one who can help Gerakon right now. I suck it up and tell her stay.

I lock up in his arms as the infant's head seems to rip down into my cervix.

30

KASSIEN

I can't bear this.

Calypso, the beauty, the broken maiden who always fights me, now hangs limp with that monstrous belly pulling her out of my arms. We rush to the room beside my dead mate's, and Efaelty clears the bedding from the medical table. I set her down.

"Not on her back," says my former mate and helps me position her to the side. Calypso stirs and grimaces. "Can you hear me?" After an agonizing moment of hesitation, she nods.

Gerakon has never broken down before, not even over his precious dying plants and animals he tried to save from our world. So why now? He always supported the idea of invading the human villages, not for their breeding capabilities but for their hidden books and knowledge. And there he stands, well, *barely*, a broken being before a meaningless girl. The thought of Scarlet's lifeless body sends a deep pain through me, even though I've seen many, *many* horrible deaths in my years. Though I didn't love her, she was very dear to me, the mother of my beloved son.

"What's happening to her?" I ask, forcing my feet to stay planted even as my baby calls for me with his last breath. Gazing upon him was the final push into pure love. I'd felt the smooth movements of his back and bottom when he rolled inside Scarlet's belly and strong foot bumps against my cheek, but seeing him—his frailness, his transparent skin, and those big glossy eyes, almost black as they searched for me and *found me* — I would have taken his place in an instant. My own mortality had no meaning in that moment.

Vaerynn runs in with the machines that tried to keep Scarlet alive and quickly syncs Calypso into their care. Readings begin to populate in the base, and Vaerynn nods vigorously. "She's fine internally, but her cervix is very thin and the child's head sits low inside. He's coming."

"I will get Gerakon," I say, torn to be here with her but also to be with my little son.

"No." Vaerynn puts a hand on my shoulder. "Your child is struggling. He needs Gerakon, and he needs you." I sigh inwardly and look upon my love. She has another's child in her belly, and yet I love her more now than I ever thought possible. She asked me to be with her, to raise her child as my own, and it hurt me at first to even consider it. But I wonder now, after seeing my own, would another's offspring strike the same chord in my heart? I think I would try, for her. Unless she doesn't want me anymore for letting her best friend die. She begged me not to let it get this far.

Calypso cries out, clutching the side of her bed.

"She may have to push." Efaelty studies the holographic image of her womb, and I lean in. The child has moved down, opening her birth canal like a boulder forcing its way through a narrow tunnel.

"No, I can't!" she growls. "Just pull him!"

"His size is twice that of an average human child," says Vaerynn, spreading Calypso's legs wide and suspending them on stirrups. "With her genetics, can it be done?"

She moans, her eyes screwed shut, and when she opens them again, they shine with misery.

"She wouldn't need the anesthesia," says Vaerynn. "No risk of it disintegrating her veins, like with the other woman."

Calypso groans and tries to sit up. "Fine let's do this." She touches my chest. "But not with you here. Please, I can't bear for you to watch this."

"We can handle this." Efaelty looks up, confidence emanating from her being. She moves the symbols around in the air to set up the controls for Calypso's natural childbirth. "Go to him."

I kiss Calypso's dewy forehead and linger there, taking in this last moment, for I cannot say where we will be in the next. "Thank you, my Efaelty." I take her hand and squeeze with grateful pressure. Just a few months ago, I left her side to be with Calypso, whose life now lies within her hands.

And I walk away trusting her completely. As I always have.

I step toward the room where my child's mother lies rotting, and my insides rip apart wondering if my son now lies in the same state. Forcing myself to move forward, I find the incubator. My son lies in the same, unnatural looking condition, struggling for air and twitching, and I'm overtaken with relief. Persephone has a hand on Gerakon's shoulder and speaks quietly, a stern yet gentle sound, and he nods with determination. That woman is a fine testament of human strength and intelligence, and with her coaxing, Gerakon shakes away the hysteria. He flies from here to there, adding medicines and tissue enhancers to the incubator's controls.

Persephone slides material over Scarlet's face.

She was someone's child. And I killed her.

"How is she?" Calypso's mother whispers.

I give a simple nod then turn away and address Gerakon. "What is his condition?" My voice booms, shocking him with my presence, but he doesn't hesitate in his task.

"He teeters on the edge, not giving up. But he does not improve."

"What is the key? What does he need?" Surely my brilliant geneticist and true student of the combining of our two worlds can figure this out.

"I have been studying in great detail the human fetus amongst the texts Persephone brought," he says, "and we know that a Koridon infant's immune system cannot survive a world that they were not biologically developed in with its innumerable bacteria and other organisms. Now, this premature baby is of both species, so I thought I could anticipate his needs, and yet I am failing."

"No," I growl. "You will succeed. You will save him."

"In humans," he says, "the premature newborn often dies from underdeveloped lungs. For a premature Koridon, his protective skin layer develops last, so he will often pass from an excess loss of heat and fluids."

"His lungs are receiving adequate oxygen," says Persephone, "and his skin is being enhanced to protect from fluid loss.

"Go to your daughter," I order her. I am torn with guilt for leaving Calypso and can at least send her mother to her.

"I will," she replies, "but she is strong and in good hands. I am needed here. For you."

Gerakon rushes to the floating device and inputs more calculations. The machine arms work fast. "We are giving nutrient X2, but I wonder if in fact it is hurting him. Scarlet received it during the pregnancy, but Calypso was born healthy without it. She developed the need for it later."

Persephone nods. "Calypso was born at thirty-five weeks and was bigger than most babies born to us. But she was healthy. We knew that children like her die young. Without the X2, which was unknown to us of course, everyone expected her to die in a few years."

"And she would have," says Gerakon. "Perhaps that gene doesn't activate until later, and right now, it does harm to the newborn." He touches the air, lighting up several symbols. "Let us try."

Hope fills me, and I fear the feeling. We're dealing with a new species, and so much is unknown. We're all children of the universe, in need of the same things for the most part. Oxygen, water, nourishment. What is the balance here? We're a disaster on this planet, but our technology is good, and Gerakon is a highly intelligent being. Several minutes pass.

Alarms chirp, and my body is engulfed with chills.

"Give him a moment to stabilize," says Persephone, who watches his oxygen levels plummet without a hint of emotion, and I try to draw from her strength.

But I'm dying.

Cracking stone makes up my outside, but on the inside, visions play of my first child: lively, supple, the magic of his firm grasp around my finger. Even he appeared so much healthier than my poor new baby, and I still lost him. It's always about survival of our kind, that's all that we have cared about for years, but *hang all that*. All I want is him.

"Kassien, you should hold him one last time," Persephone's voice cuts through my reverie.

"He could still—" I swallow hard, and the reality of her words crush me into oblivion. Gerakon doesn't dare look at me as he continues to work, but I realize it's a show. He's done all he can, but my baby was never destined to live, born many months before he was ready. I long to burst out of my skin and tear this whole place down around me.

Instead, I walk slowly to my small boy and place a hand on his still chest.

31

CALYPSO

A nauseating *crack* resounds within my pelvis as the baby relentlessly pushes through. My lower body screams with shattering pain, and my mouth freezes open, unable to utter a single sound.

"The infant is stuck!" I hear the echoing of a voice as black dots swarm my vision. "We have to extract now!"

"Should we run the anesthesia?" another voice resounds.

"We either risk it or cut her open right now..."

"Run it," I say hoarsely. They don't hesitate and I'm relieved, not having the strength to argue. "Goodnight," I whisper, strength building once more at the prospect of finally being free of this torture.

"Did you do it?" The blinding pain dulls, and I close one eye to peep at them with the other. "Are my veins rotting away?"

"It is done," says Efaelty. The liquid-like arms descend over my belly without a sound, and I flinch, or my mind sends the signal to flinch, but I stay perfectly still.

"I'm going to be awake?"

"Of course," says Vaerynn.

What a horrifying relief. I don't want to be asleep to possibly never wake up, I want to be within every frightening moment even if it's up until my last.

Before I can fully realize my fear of being cut open, a feeling of light pressure slides across my pelvic region and Efaelty dips her hands inside to pull out the large bundle that I've come to love in the last few months. My stomach recoils and Efaelty takes the fluid-covered infant to wash off in a basin. "Is he all right?" I ask as Vaerynn sets the micro healers to do their flawless work on my incision.

"The child is," she rubs his chest and a robust cry bursts through the room, "well!"

I sob with joy. Just like that? After what Scarlet went through I praise the heavens and tell her, *I made it. I wish you could be here now, my friend. We made it!* I can move again, and I realize Vaerynn's at my side, inputting new controls to cease the nerve paralyzing agent. "Can I hold him?" I ask. All the reading I did on how to care for an infant has fled me, but the one thing I do remember is that he needs to feel my skin. And my heart longs to feel his.

"Vaerynn," comes Gerakon's voice, and she quickly goes to him. His brows furrow and his composure wavers. *Oh no.* Poor, poor Kassien.

"Rise," says Efaelty, and my bed moves into a sitting position. The wiggly crying baby passes into my arms, and I get lost in his perfect features. He turns his head toward me, his mouth open wide. Its utter cuteness puts a happy tickle in my soul.

"He wants to nurse." My mother appears in the doorway, and that's when the tears flow endlessly. "He's so beautiful," she says, wiping her eyes to embrace us.

"I can't believe my joy right now! Just to hold him, it's the best thing I've ever felt," I caress his soft, light hair. I didn't expect this! Yes, I was fascinated by him, loved the way he felt against my palm when he moved around in his liquid home, but *this*. I could live here forever.

"Here." Momma positions him in my arms against my breast. "Pinch the nipple and put the whole thing in his mouth. The whole thing. Shove it right in."

I would laugh, but I'm entirely too focused on the moment. She lifts a thin blanket over us. I awkwardly do what she says, sure I'm going to fail, but his full lips latch tight and his crying turns into relieved whimpers. His cheek flutters, happily suckling. "Let him eat all he wants, and encourage him to," says Momma. "He'll likely fall asleep, that's okay."

Vaerynn and Efaelty whisper together in the corner, and Gerakon departs. Efaelty's face pales, and she brings a hand to her chest. Her troubled gaze falls on the bundle within my arms. I can't ask. I can't have Kassien's torment confirmed, not now.

"Calypso," says Vaerynn, "I must tell you something."

~Kassien~

Gerakon's hand warms my shoulder as I mourn. My insides have collapsed and I'm nothing but a hollow shell. The strongest being in the world and I'm too weak to even fall to the floor. "My child." The words are heavy and break as my chest is racked with pain. "I could not save you, precious one, but know that I would lay down my life for you this moment." His skin stays warm under my hand, and I don't know if I can ever move it away for fear of him growing cold. "If only I could." I know now that we were meant to die, just as Calypso once said. Our world had come to its last, and hanging on as long as we did, *fighting*, was a fine effort. It's over now. What is left for me to live for?

Calypso and her people find joy in everything. They use their voices to sing, to laugh, to pretend they're someone else, and their imaginations to pretend they're in faraway places. I was bred to be huge, to be skilled in fighting, and to survive, but for what?

This is the one thing I wanted.

"I should have told you," Gerakon says, and the fear shaking his voice makes me turn, my hand slipping away from my baby forever.

"Told me what?" I stand, his haunting visage prickling the hairs at the back of my neck.

"They wanted me to lie to you so you'd follow in line. So you'd mate Scarlet and leave Calypso to Brekter." He steps back, and only then do I realize I've rushed into his face.

Anger ripples through me, and the need to snap his neck is only outweighed by my desire to hear his truth out loud. "Calypso's child?"

"Is yours."

I slam my fist through the air, stopping a half inch from his face. He doesn't so much as blink. "Why would you do this?"

"Drakon told me to lie. He wanted Calypso to be Brekter's to torture you. He knows she is your weakness."

"*Knew* she is my weakness," I correct with a sneer, enjoying even more the way Calypso splattered him all over the wall.

"I betrayed you once more, brother. I understand if you must take my life." He kneels and bows his head. "Your son has been born healthy, strong," he offers.

I gaze upon the sad little body of my son, still being artificially heated and oxygenated, trapped within a body that will never grow, never run, and with a heart that will never love. I should be overjoyed by the news of another, yet how can

I betray this child that I've loved every moment of his existence? Am I just to move on now without a care? "I—"

"Kassien?"

From behind me comes a voice, a sound that vibrates through my surface and holds my aching soul so tight the pain ceases.

Calypso's face shines with tears and uncertainty as she edges toward me. I swallow every pain, every fear, and take her into my arms. I can't form a single word, and neither can she. "This is our life now," she says. "Be with me. Live this beautiful life with me." I set her down and she sucks in through her teeth, her balance faltering. She takes my hand.

As we move from the room, Gerakon bounds to his feet and looks strangely toward the incubator.

———

Efaelty and Vaerynn bow their heads and leave us to be alone. Calypso takes her child in her arms and rocks him lovingly, coming toward me, but I take an involuntary step backward.

Her satin brows scrunch together. "Kassien?"

"My—" I choke on the word and force myself to stay calm. I don't understand what's happening to me. "My child just—"

"Oh, of course. I'm sorry." She takes him away, and her mother gives her a reassuring nod.

"Hold him, Kassien," Efaelty says from the doorway. "You must love this one the way you did the other."

I know, you damn female, but I can't! Calypso holds him out to me and I want to take him, to get to know this new child, but a wall has formed. Only minutes ago, I thought him to be my enemy's, and it's suffocating even to look upon him, so I turn away and storm out.

The cry is what stops me at the end of the corridor. I place a palm against the wall and listen to the sound. His demanding cry beckons me back, forcing me to push my own turmoil down and be the father he deserves. I can at least hold him so he knows who I am.

The women stand to attention when I step through the entrance of the med room. "Give him to me," I say, feeling stone encase my heart.

Calypso brings him to me, and though he's bigger and more active than the other, I still fear hurting him. He rests in my arms, but I still can't look him in the face. He's precious silk against my skin, and sweet utterances make their way to my ears and soften my resolve. I don't mean to, but I meet his eyes, so wide and bright, and I'm captivated.

I bring him close and break, weeping into his chest.

32

CALYPSO

The waves crash onto the shore and white foam streams up to the tips of my toes. I lay back in the warm sand and stretch my arms above my head. White clouds shift and blend above me, and I think of all the Koridons out there in space. They haven't come for me yet for killing their high-ranking brethren, but Kassien says they will. He lifts Kaden into the air and spins him in circles, nearly stepping on Jane as she scurries out of the way.

"Calypso," he says over our son's giddy laughter. "You will be all wet for the ceremony." I sit up and bid farewell to the deep blue to take my seat. In the last year, my mother cultivated a garden that produced some good vegetables and all these sweet smelling lilies that decorate the chairs and aisle. She looks beautiful sitting in the other row, her auburn hair twisted into ornate braids and tied up, her striking royal blue gown shining in the sunlight.

"Is it time yet?" I ask Kassien as he sits next to me. Blond Alice's baby crawls across the ground to play with Kaden, and I bask in a life I never thought possible. Arek grabs her as she walks by and playfully pulls her into his lap, telling her that's her newly assigned seat.

I take a moment to think of Mary-Shelly, who disappeared the day I had my son.

"There she is!" says Julianne, one of the human servants that lives free now. Vaerynn holds a bouquet of fresh cut flowers and two more ex-servants play a wedding march on their violins. The Koridon female is a vision: golden shadow sparkling on her face and wrapped in a white lacy gown just like the one I envisioned Bella wearing in one of my favorite old vampire books. She approaches the anxiously awaiting Finn, and though he's all human, he has her locked down as hard as any Koridon male—as evidenced by the very human wedding taking place instead of the horrid tradition of Vaerynn's kind.

She places her arms around his neck. Her protruding belly presses into his and he kisses her as Gerakon reads from his notes in a hilariously monotone voice. "Dearly beloved, we are gathered here today..."

Kassien gives Gerakon a teasing smirk and he stumbles over the next line. They have certainly become close again after what Gerakon did for him. Infusing his own blood for a period of weeks, never sleeping, never leaving the med room, he nearly wasted away from starvation and exhaustion.

Efaelty walks down the aisle with that panther grace I've always admired and hands Kassien his little boy. Kassien's face lights up as Scardrek happily grabs him around the neck, wearing a pristine black tux that my mother made. Something catches my eye on the shore by the cliffs. A familiar desire tugs at me as I see him and my heart races. I go numb with fear but when I blink, the figure's gone. "Don't you look handsome," I whisper, pulling my attention back and kiss Scardrek's cheek. "Momma!" he says too loudly and giggles. He reminds me so much of his mother.

Everything is new, everything is unknown, but we're all on the same page, working together for the world we have always dreamed of. As I watch my eldest son run along the shore with his smaller brother, being careful not to pass him, I don't know what the future will throw at us, but as my amazing mate puts an arm around my shoulders and holds me tight, I'm not afraid.

I'm ready for whatever I must face.

END BOOK 2

Thank you for reading :) If you could take a minute to leave a review, that would be amazing!

My books: https://www.amazon.com/C-F-Rabbiosi/e/B06XFZP4Z9

Also, enjoy another of my dark stories by claiming for free here:

Snatch Me: An abduction fantasy tale https://claims.prolificworks.com/free/qjeAcIBx

Faith's Dark Captives

Come join my readers' group on Facebook! We'll talk about books and the darker side of sensuality. Lots of giveaways and fun promised.

My Newsletter:

https://www.subscribepage.com/05t8n3

Be the first to find out about new releases and free dark romances.

***All Photos licensed by Shutterstock

Deliciously Dark Reads
by Next Chapter Publishing

Atrocity
ISBN: 978-4-86750-397-3

Published by
Next Chapter
1-60-20 Minami-Otsuka
170-0005 Toshima-Ku, Tokyo
+818035793528

4th June 2021

Lightning Source UK Ltd.
Milton Keynes UK
UKHW010725170621
385673UK00001B/272